D0337497

WITH W

His hands were on her shoulders. "I've been humbled Shan T'u by your art and poetry, and by your beauty and innocence and courage. I had thought of you as a child, but no child could heat my blood as you do."

"No, please . . . I cannot love you. Yes, I was tempted, but now I must accept my destiny."

De Rais drew her body closer. His voice was thunder and his look was lightning. "Shan T'u, I also knew what my destiny proclaimed. And you, too, are meant to defy your destiny." His hands tightened and his voice became strained. "Can you tell me you don't want me? Can you tell me *this* means nothing?"

Without warning, his mouth sought hers and forced her lips apart. "No," she protested, but there was no denial left. His lips were on her tender throat, moving down, leaving fiery souvenirs of his passion. He released her, drawing apart the folds of his kimono, removing the damp silk from her shoulders.

Shan T'u could not reason. She turned her head and saw him rise to his feet like a vengeful giant. His tawny body glimmered in the torchlight and he was, for that instant, unutterably beautiful and absolutely barbarian. And for that instant, her very spirit left her body and yearned toward him.

Dear Reader,

We, the editors of Tapestry Romances, are committed to bringing you two outstanding original romantic historical novels each and every month.

From Kentucky in the 1850s to the court of Louis XIII, from the deck of a pirate ship within sight of Gibraltar to a mining camp high in the Sierra Nevadas, our heroines experience life and love, romance and adventure.

Our aim is to give you the kind of historical romances that you want to read. We would enjoy hearing your thoughts about this book and all future Tapestry Romances. Please write to us at the address below.

The Editors
Tapestry Romances
POCKET BOOKS
1230 Avenue of the Americas
Box TAP
New York, N.Y. 10020

Most Tapestry Books are available at special quantity discounts for bulk purchases for sales promotions, premiums or fund raising. Special books or book excerpts can also be created to fit specific needs.

For details write the office of the Vice President of Special Markets, Pocket Books, 1230 Avenue of the Americas, New York, New York 10020.

Jade Moon

Erica Mitchell

A TAPESTRY BOOK
PUBLISHED BY POCKET BOOKS NEW YORK

This novel is a work of historical fiction. Names, characters, places and incidents relating to non-historical figures are either the product of the author's imagination or are used fictitiously. Any resemblance of such non-historical incidents, places or figures to actual events or locales or persons, living or dead, is entirely coincidental.

An *Original* publication of TAPESTRY BOOKS

A Tapestry Book published by
POCKET BOOKS, a division of Simon & Schuster, Inc.
1230 Avenue of the Americas, New York, N.Y. 10020

Copyright © 1984 by Erica Mitchell

All rights reserved, including the right to reproduce this book or portions thereof in any form whatsoever. For information address Tapestry Books, 1230 Avenue of the Americas, New York, N.Y. 10020

ISBN: 0-671-49894-0

First Tapestry Books printing January, 1984

10 9 8 7 6 5 4 3 2 1

POCKET and colophon are registered trademarks of Simon & Schuster, Inc.

TAPESTRY is a trademark of Simon & Schuster, Inc.

Printed in the U.S.A.

Chapter One

SHAN T'U SPRANG FROM SLEEP, AND HER HEART BEAT like the wings of a caged bird. *My love*—she cried silently.

She sat up in her lacquered bed and listened to the gentle summer wind in the chimes. Somewhere in the palace a stringed instrument played. Was her father awake? Prince Chang Hu, whose name meant "tiger," was a violent, impatient warlord with many ambitions. He sometimes kept servants and musicians awake through the night.

Shan T'u slipped out of bed, careful not to wake her servants. Her silk robe whispered around her tiny feet as she moved to the window and looked out. Her loose black hair spilled over her shoulders as she gazed out beyond the gardens of her father's palace.

She saw the bathhouse, and the building that housed the magically cooled summer rooms. She saw the stables and heard the faraway nicker of her father's prized Persian horses. She saw the great gate, and beyond the gate, the empty meadows.

Why had she awaken? Why did her heart hurt so deeply, as if betrayed by a lover? She had no lover.

I was dreaming, she realized. But the pain was too real and stung too sharply for a dream. She had often daydreamed of a dashing warrior who would ride from the mountains and kidnap her away, who would ravish her and force her to live on roots in the hills. Her delicate mouth curved into a smile. Father would have her whipped for those dreams. She was the obedient, properly trained princess of a province ruled by Prince Chang.

No! She balled her hand into a tight fist and tried to stem the sudden flood of tears. Maybe *that's* what had awakened her: the approach of the day when she would be sent from her home forever, far across the hills and the mountains, to India. To marry a fat, greasy potentate with foul breath who would rape her and beat her, and keep her naked in a cage.

Shan T'u, you're impossible. She shook her head, nearly smiling despite her misery. Of course she knew no such thing about the prince she was destined to wed. The arrangements had been made by her father. The potentate's queen had died and he wanted another woman of royal blood. He had told this to Kublai Khan himself, and word was leaked from Khan's court to Prince Chang, who had a marriageable daughter—a daughter whose feet had never been bound and who was therefore unattractive to Chinese nobility. But perfect for a grieving Indian prince!

Thus Chang would gain Khan's favor, and also woo a possible foreign ally *against* the Mongol emperor.

And gain me a fat old husband, Shan T'u thought bitterly. She turned from the window, the moonlight outlining her back in silver. She looked into her bronze mirror and saw her eyes shining with fear and defiance. She saw only a shadow of her exquisite oval face, with its high cheekbones and splash of humor in the classically lovely mouth. A highborn princess, with an antic temperament! Beneath her robe, she sensed the swell of her young breasts. They ached with need. Her tapered fingers hovered at her throat, and her skin burned, as if her blood were the liquor dispensed at feasts.

She shut her eyes. The Imperial Instructress had told her to stifle these dangerous aches. And the Lady Feng, wife of a noble lord, had giggled, "You will quench *that* fire when you marry." And the Instructress had told her, "Forget such flames. Be humble, yielding, and reverential to your lord, and your flesh will be at peace."

Shan T'u made a rueful face. All very well, but Lady Feng liked to indulge in intrigues, and the Imperial Instructress had lived many seasons with a cold hearth. What did they know of the fire in Shan T'u's body, the fire that would not be drowned in a hundred baths, not under fountains of ice-cooled water.

That noise—!

Shan T'u spun, half expecting to see the huge, reeking forms of Mongol warriors. But there was nobody.

Yet *something* had awakened her tonight!

Her eyes turned inexorably toward the window.

3

Something out *there,* something beyond the gates of the palace. Her pulse seemed to pause as she returned to the window and strained to see.

There was the vista of dark grass, and the dim bulky shapes of buffalo dozing. There were the willows whose graceful limbs sprayed like fountains, the bridge and grove where she secretly met with old Master Po. There was the black lake, reflecting the white fire of moonlight. As she watched, a wind sprang up and moaned through the trees. Waterfowl clapped into flight, and suddenly, in the sky, there was a shower of blinding white stars racing toward the southwest.

Shan T'u's blood thundered in her veins. She gripped the sill of the window and thought she heard a shaking in the earth. Was her father's army on the march?

Or had the red snake come? The serpent that the fortune-teller had told Prince Chang would swallow his baby daughter because she would not be able to run. A prophecy that so shook the superstitious prince that he forbade her feet to be bound, and doomed her to ridicule—and an Indian prince.

The wind stopped and moonlight showed only the grass and the willows. There was no dashing warrior on horseback. Even Master Po, who had given her so much that was forbidden, could not give her *that.* Her imagination had awakened her to frustrate her with a drunkard's vision.

Disappointment flooded her. No armies clattered through this calm summer night. No warriors would clash by the gates, sever limbs with blood-soaked swords, pummel down the walls and sweep her onto the lathered back of a great war-horse. Not tonight.

Oh, soon enough she would taken from here—in a cart, drawn by a camel. And after months of heat and flies and disease, she would be delivered to the man her father had decreed for her.

Shan T'u punched the woven mattress in fury. She didn't want to live in India, or be the wife of a potentate. She wanted . . .

She wanted places and moments she did not dare to name. She knew that her longings were forbidden, and led her seductively to the borders of chaos. But knowing this didn't make her heart ache less. It devastated her that she had been awakened tonight by a stupid dream.

Shan T'u lay back in bed, her hair flowering on the rolled pillow. Unconsciously, her small body arched, yearning. Her eyes filled. *Come to me,* she pleaded to her phantom.

The tall man on horseback sniffed at the hot summer wind and smelled other horses. Under the cowl of his coarse robe, the man's eyes gleamed brightly. He was not from this land. His eyes were light and he wore a clipped beard that framed an angular, good-humored face. Yet there was danger in the face as well.

His horse was laden with the man's worldly goods, and the man knew he could not outrun attackers. He was not greatly afraid, though he knew the legendary savagery of the Khan's armies. But the man had been in China for many months, and before that Persia and Arabia, and he was no longer a stranger. He knew well by now the polish, courtesy, and respect of these people. Except for formal battles, the man had not witnessed quarrels, blows, combats, or bloodshed, so much a daily occurrence in his homeland. He had seen wagons and property left without locks and guards. Poor, gullible fools!

The man sat upright in the saddle, though illness sapped his great strength. Now he could hear approaching horsemen, a dim thunder, growing louder. The man's teeth gleamed for a moment as he smiled in anticipation. Perhaps this time he was close to the stronghold of a Chinese prince, a man of great wealth and influence.

The man kept his horse at a slow walk. He topped a small rise, and at the same time, the moon slid gracefully, like the prow of a ship, from behind great clouds. The meadow was bathed in cold white light and the man cried out softly as he saw the gates and the turreted buildings. *"Oui, Mon Dieu!"* he murmured. There was no doubt; this was not simply the house of a well-to-do farmer. This was the palace of a prince.

The thunder rolled over the man's head and he turned his gaze to the six warriors who urged their mounts up the hill. The bearded stranger had faced other knights in other lands and sensed that these were skilled and honorable fighters. They were also the knights of a rich lord. Huge men, they wore iron plate armor—gilded, if the stranger rightly interpreted the blazing glints under the full moon. As the warriors rode closer, the bearded stranger saw that the armor boasted chain mail of a type he had seen in Persia.

Imported armor! *Très bien,* the man thought.

The warriors reined up in a clatter of hooves and metal. In less than a second, six mulberry bows were poised, six steel-tipped arrows aimed at the hooded man's throat.

"Good evening," the bearded man said in stilted Chinese. "I am Friar William De Rais. I have ridden a long way and I need shelter for the night."

There was a murmur of surprise from the warriors, but the bows never faltered. De Rais's sharp eyes noticed the sheathed swords worn by the soldiers, swords with shagreen-wrapped hilts decorated in what might be gold or silver, or possibly rhinoceros horn.

Magnifique, De Rais thought.

"Where do you come from?" one warrior asked.

"I am Burgundian—from France, on the continent of Europe, in the holy kingdom of Christ," De Rais replied sonorously. "I have been to Arabia and Persia, and through many provinces of China. And I am *very* tired. Will your lord deny me the hospitality of his castle for tonight?"

More murmurs. Clearly, the warriors were impressed and surprised. These southern Chinese may have seen Persians and Turks who journeyed freely under the rule of Khan. But a European—that would be an exotic sight.

"Hand over your weapons," the chief warrior demanded.

De Rais affected a simple smile. "My friends, I carry only the word of our Lord as a weapon. My mission is to bring the Mongol infidels to Christ."

Now there was animated conversation among the warriors, who, De Rais knew, were Chinese and not Mongol. The Mongols would have sent an arrow through his throat first and asked questions afterward.

"Ride ahead of us," the warrior said finally.

"Mon plaisir," De Rais said charmingly in French. He grinned to himself and forgot his exhaustion for the moment as he urged his horse down the slope toward the gleaming palace.

The next morning, Shan T'u went to the bathhouse. Her ladies-in-waiting took her silk robe and she stepped naked into the great jade basin. Water splashed from the mouths of nine carved dragons and drained away through the mouth of a tortoise. The water was heated by fire. Even so, she hugged herself tightly and shivered deliciously for a moment, enjoying the goose bumps on her skin.

The night seemed very far away to her. A dream. Yet he was so real, that phantom warrior, that even now she felt she could run outside and see him riding into the garden. She fought a fresh bout of crying, as servants unpinned the flowers and gold and silver ornaments that dressed her hair. Black tresses cascaded down her smooth back, and she lowered herself to her throat in perfumed water.

A few moments later, Lady Feng joined her. Her husband was visiting Prince Chang Hu. "Good morning," Lady Feng said with a smile. "You're up early."

"I couldn't sleep."

"Oh?" Lady Feng was taller than Shan T'u, and paler. Servants took her robe and hair ornaments and helped her into the water. Shan T'u admired Lady Feng's willowy grace, her artfulness—and of course her tiny lily feet. She carried herself haughtily, her breasts milky and pink tipped and her chin tilted in aristocratic contempt. Shan T'u still behaved like a spirited girl. With her big feet, she often sprinted across a pavilion, or rode a horse barefoot. Her father had ordered her beaten more than once for willfulness.

"What awakened you?" Lady Feng asked. The water rippled gently around her shoulders, and her body beneath the surface seemed to break apart and glint in pale green sections.

"The morning breeze," Shan T'u said.

Lady Feng's laugh rippled like the water. "And nothing more?"

"Is something the matter?"

"No," Lady Feng said. "I just wonder at your whims and fancies. I don't know how you'll manage to settle into court life in India."

"I'll have to try."

"Yes, I would say so." Lady Feng regarded Shan T'u with disdain. "You may not run in the gardens when you wish, or take your lord's best horse and ride through the hills until the animal's legs are bleeding." She laughed nastily. "Your father only had you stripped naked and whipped for that. Your *husband* will have your skin peeled back and cut into ten thousand pieces."

Shan T'u tossed her head, trying to act unconcerned. Servants came into the water to scrub her back. "Well, Father has not found a guide yet to lead my wedding caravan over the mountains. I still have time to study my graces."

"What nonsense! You know, you really *are* Ma-ku, my dear, and you will wind up in the hills eating crickets."

Shan T'u winced at the servants' rubbing. Ma-ku was a fairy of legend who took pity on her father's

9

laborers, then quarreled with her father and fled to the hills as a hermit. "I'd rather eat crickets than dine with an old prince," she said daringly.

Lady Feng's beautifully painted eyebrows seemed to rise. "Oh? Are you going to defy your father?"

"Maybe I will!"

"And run away? On his best horse? And fight his warriors?" Lady Feng laughed.

"You mock me," Shan T'u said.

"Never," Lady Feng said, between peals of laughter. "I do enjoy you, Shan T'u. Your head is unbound, as well as your feet. You take stars from the sky and you fill your mind with them. You refuse to be in proper balance with life, and you will suffer for it. Sometimes I wish, just a little, that I could be as strange and childish as you are."

"And sometimes," Shan T'u said hotly, "*I* wish I could be like *you*, Lady Feng. Married to a nobleman right here, and not shipped like a cask of spices to India!"

Lady Feng looked reproachfully at Shan T'u but said nothing. Shan T'u's face tingled and she regretted her outburst. Lady Feng's husband was a powerful prince, and Lady Feng was a scurrilous gossip who loved to make trouble.

The servants finished scrubbing and Shan T'u dipped low in the water. Her eyes closed for a moment, and in that moment, she saw the moonlit hill again and the man on the horse. A sadness came over her, like the rushing of clouds to cover the sun on a stormy day. She opened her eyes again and looked at Lady Feng.

"Lady Feng," Shan T'u said softly, "don't you ever dream of going *somewhere*—to Persia, to the stars? I dream of someplace wild, where the mountains are steep and waterfalls crash in the mists, where the moon is like white jade, and a dark warrior takes the clothes from my body and unclasps my jewels . . ."

"Shan T'u!" Lady Feng's voice cut like a sword. Shan T'u stopped, regretful. Lady Feng spoke in cold, clipped words. "You go beyond foolishness. We are aristocrats, Shan T'u. We do not dream of being raped by soldiers. We dream of service to a noble lord. And *your* service will be to a potentate. There's your travel, Shan T'u. There's your exotic land, your adventure. Your *only* adventure. You must never again speak this way."

Shan T'u's face burned under the tongue-lashing. She longed to strike back at Lady Feng, but she dared not. "It is only a dream . . ." she said weakly.

"Yes, I know. And one day you will go to live in the southern land where there is no heat or cold, no sun or moon, no day or night. Where the people do not eat or wear clothes, but only sleep, and awaken once in fifty days. They believe that what they do in their dreams is real and what they do when awake is false. Is that where you wish to live?"

"That's a fairy tale," Shan T'u sulked.

"With a great deal of truth," Lady Feng scolded icily. Her lips curled into a smile. "You are so badly behaved I oughtn't to tell you of the great surprise."

Shan T'u's heart paused. "What surprise?"

Lady Feng chuckled. "For a princess who cannot sleep, you miss a great deal. You heard no commotion last night, no horses, no voices?"

"Horses . . . ?"

"Close your mouth, silly girl. What's the *matter* with you? We have a visitor. Last night—"

11

The high, piercing shriek of a servant girl struck down the words of Lady Feng. Shan T'u gasped and tried to follow the path of the scream. There was a patter of damp feet on marble. "What's wrong?" Shan T'u asked.

"I don't know," Lady Feng said tensely. "I heard—"

The man appeared so unexpectedly that for a moment Shan T'u was not certain she saw him at all. He was monstrously tall, or so he seemed, and he was hidden in a brown cloak with a cowl that shadowed his face. Shan T'u's hand flew to her naked breasts, and her eyes grew wide. Lady Feng drew a sharp breath.

"Oh, dear!" The man boomed in Chinese. "I *am* sorry. What an embarrassing error."

Shan T'u could not make her throat work. She became keenly aware of her nakedness in the water, but strangely, did not feel ashamed. A tremulous excitement scampered down her spine like a centipede. "Who are you?" she asked in a whisper.

The man nodded politely. "Friar William De Rais."

Lady Feng spoke now, and Shan T'u was astonished to see the lady stand erect and proud in the water, her wet nakedness exposed from head to waist. "Leave *now*," Lady Feng commanded. "Or you will be quartered like a thief."

"Yes!" Shan T'u said quickly as she found her voice. "Please go. My father will have you tortured if he finds you here. It won't be very pleasant . . ."

Lady Feng turned an exasperated eye to Shan T'u. "Stop whimpering," she hissed. "Behave like a princess."

The friar laughed, a deep-throated laugh that made Shan T'u shiver. With a graceful hand, he flung back the hood and revealed his face. His thick, unbarbered hair was the pale yellow of sand, and his beard was the same hue. His nose was straight and chiseled, his brow high and patrician. But his eyes—his eyes were the most beautiful and astonishing thing of all. They were blue, as blue as the lake when it reflected the sun. And the sun seemed to be in those eyes, fiery and blinding.

He was strong; Shan T'u could see that. Even hidden by the rough folds of his cloak, his body strained with power. Yet he did not look thick or boulderlike, as some of her father's warriors did. He moved with the grace of an acrobat, and the quickness of his hand reminded her of the magicians and story-tellers who entertained at banquets.

But the eyes—they held Shan T'u now, more than anything else. Shan T'u dropped her own eyes, for they burned from the light of those twin suns. Never had she seen such eyes, never . . .

It was true, she thought ecstatically. *I wasn't dreaming last night.*

But of course she was being ridiculous now. This man enthralled her, no doubt. He was a foreigner, a splendid stranger who had stumbled into the bath-house. But he was alien, a distant prince who came to pay tribute to her father, and no man for her to dream about.

In fact, what made her think he was not here to *harm* her? To kill her, or to split her as raiding Mongols split captive women?

"Ladies," De Rais said with a disarming smile, "I thought this was the summer house. Forgive the intrusion. I am an innocent child seeing two fawns, no more. Good day."

13

Lady Feng sniffed furiously and turned her ivory back, but Shan T'u saw her shoulders quiver. She looked, despite herself, at the man, and his eyes captured her, as a hawk snatches a squirrel. He murmured, "Your friend is more of a woman, but you are more desirable." And then he said to himself in a language Shan T'u could not comprehend, *"Quel idiot que je suis! Il ne vaut pas la peine s'occuper d'une telle barbare!"*

He laughed to himself, and disappeared with breathtaking quickness among the marble arches. Shan T'u felt intensely cold, and listened to the splashing as marble animals spewed fresh jets of water. She could hear birds and horses outside. A summer morning, but nothing was the same.

"Come," Lady Feng said in a shaken voice. "We must tell your father of this."

"No," Shan T'u snapped, and Lady Feng stared at her. Shan T'u saw her ladies-in-waiting return, scuttling like terrified children. She signaled for her silk robe. To Lady Feng, she said, "He is not one of us. He made a mistake and he is a guest in my father's house. Say nothing."

Lady Feng regarded Shan T'u for a long moment with inscrutable eyes. Then a small, wicked smile upturned her lips. "As you wish, Princess. As you wish."

14

Chapter Two

SHAN T'U DID NOT SEE THE STRANGER AGAIN THAT DAY,
and would not see him until tonight's great feast. The
daughter of a warlord was not invited to spend a day
with the men. They would go riding on her father's
Dragon horses, review her father's troops, play *liu po*,
or perhaps drink grain liquor.

Shan T'u sighed. She sat, with Prince Chang's
concubines, on a woven mat in an ice-cooled room.
She imagined what the friar was doing now. Then she
considered what *she* was doing, and sighed more
wretchedly.

Around her, her father's concubines primped and
gossiped. Liu Ch'e exquisitely arranged the hair of
Liang Hsum, who sat with her hands in her silk
sleeves. Tzu Ch'un knelt archly before a mirror and

painstakingly painted her eyebrows. Sometimes, one of the concubines would address a remark to Shan T'u or ask her a question, but the ladies of the court had learned not to bother with Prince Chang Hu's headstrong daughter. Shan T'u barely knew the names of the aristocrats who were gossiped about. She adorned her face only when necessary; in fact, the concubines giggled about *her* when she was not present.

The Imperial Instructress, Hsueh Wei, entered the chamber and glared with stone-cold eyes at the ladies. "Another day wasted," she complained. "You fritter away your time adorning your faces, but you don't know how to adorn your souls."

There was a girlish chorus of groans and sighs from the women. "Good afternoon, Instructress," Tzu Ch'un said dryly as she stroked her eyebrows.

The Imperial Instructress was a tall and slender woman with a reposeful face, her lips red against pale skin. She wore a brocaded silk robe sashed at the waist, and her hair was pinned with ivory clips and small gems. It was her task to train the ladies of the imperial household.

"And *you,* Shan T'u," the Instructress said, "what are *you* doing to improve yourself today?"

Shan T'u pouted. "I'm observing these ladies so that I may learn to be a master of brushwork."

This brought a shocked murmur from the wives and a hiss of disapproval from Hsueh Wei. "Shan T'u, your sarcasm is disgraceful!"

"I apologize," Shan T'u said unapologetically. "But you urge us to adorn our souls. How better than by painting the lotus? Or by learning to read and write? We need books—"

"That will be enough!" the Instructress cried. The

room seemed to vibrate for a moment, and the concubines looked away in perfect silence, pretending to continue their preening, but clearly delighted.

Shan T'u flushed. The Instructress walked to where she sat and looked down at her with blazing eyes. "I teach the ladies in the court of Prince Chang Hu to be dutiful and humble. The wives and concubines of a great lord are expected to be models of decorum. And you, Princess, must provide the model for the rest."

"Yes, I've been told so," Shan T'u said angrily. "But your admonitions are ignored by everyone!"

"How *dare* you say that to me!"

"I dare say more! These ladies are only models of vanity and intrigue! I alone have the desire to improve myself, but for that I am scolded. Hypocrite!"

The concubines uttered shocked exclamations. The cheeks of Hsueh Wei darkened. Shan T'u realized that she had better run fast. She uncoiled swiftly to her feet and fled from the noisy chamber.

She ran from the palace itself, toward the mighty gate. The summer heat slapped her down like a burning hand after the coolness of the chamber. Still she ran, her legs lithe and strong. Not for nothing had Lady Feng once remarked, "Your big, strong feet would be wonderful for your father's battalion of lady warriors."

Shan T'u stopped at the towering bronze gate. She commanded the brawny guard, "Open!"

"Princess," the guard admonished, "it's too hot to be outside—"

"*Open!*" Shan T'u cried again, with a stamp of her foot.

The guard's face furrowed with worry. "Princess, if you wish to be outdoors, at least the garden—"

Shan T'u pummeled her thighs with her fists. "Shall I scale the wall?"

The guard shook his head and slid open the heavy gate. Shan T'u slipped outside. She ran more slowly now, her hair undone, her silk gown damp against her skin. Dark storm clouds rode over the lake. The hills in the distance were dark green masses, the further hills blue and violet.

She could hear the rapid beating of her heart as she crossed a bridge over a stream and emerged into a mulberry grove. The trees showed a deep green and it was cooler here, damp and rich with the smell of earth. She stopped, pushed back tendrils of hair with her fingers. She shut her eyes and tried to quench the fire in her lungs.

"Shan T'u?"

The voice did not startle her; she had expected it. "Yes, Master Po." She smiled when she saw the old man. He sat at a lacquered table, set incongruously on the loamy forest floor. Ghostly light filtered through mulberry branches and dappled his fragile body so that he seemed a delicately brushed painting.

The old man regarded Shan T'u curiously. He wore a silk robe of sapphire blue, signifying that he held a degree, and on his wizened head he wore the mortarboard of a scholar. "Why were you running?"

She had regained her breath now. "I spoke hastily," she said, "to the Instructress. I asked why women did not use the brush or read, and I called her a hypocrite."

The old man's eyebrows rose, and his eyes, deeply sunken in their sockets, seemed to burn. "That was foolish."

18

"I know," she said, chastened. "But sometimes I get so angry I can't stop myself."

"That's hardly exemplary," he scolded. "I risk my life to teach you forbidden arts, for I believe you may do special deeds in this life. But I waste my time if you cannot learn self-control."

Shan T'u felt her eyes sting with tears. The Imperial Instructress, at her most fearsome, could not strike guilt into Shan T'u's heart as this ancient scholar could. Po seemed a porcelain carving, his skin nearly translucent, his hands gnarled. Yet when he used the brush, he spoke poetry on rice paper, imparting delicate irony or quiet truth with each stroke.

He was also a master of the important fields of knowledge: astronomy, geography, classics, historical texts. He had been surviving in poverty in a hut when Prince Chang Hu conquered this province by force from a fat and lazy prince whose corrupt magistrates abused the citizens. Chang had flushed Po out of the hills, half-starved, and installed him in the palace to teach all the male members of the royal household. Po had been a fixture in the palace for as long as Shan T'u could remember.

And, for as long as she could remember, Po had brought his table and his brushes out here to the mulberry grove rather than to the formal palace gardens. It was here that Shan T'u had found him the first time she'd bolted from the house. He had given her small cakes and sweetmeats and had first suggested that she, alone of all the girls, might learn to read and write. His eyes—ancient even then—had blazed as he'd sworn her to secrecy.

"And now you've threatened that secrecy," he said in a high, whispery voice.

Shan T'u dropped to her knees on the cool earth and bowed her head. "Master," she said, "I deserve your anger. I have no excuse. I'm frightened—"

"And willful and disobedient," Po said sternly. "You don't want to get married. You're curious about the friar. You're bored by the women. And you cannot hide any of your childish feelings. What good will your skills be to you if they are not controlled?" He leaned across the table. "Shan T'u, I have taught you what few *men* have mastered. My princess of the unbound feet, you have been singled out by destiny. I sense that somehow you will have a hand in . . . changing things."

Po stopped, but his rheumy eyes continued eloquently. Shan T'u understood, a little, what he meant. It was at the feet of Master Po that she'd learned the terrible history of the empire of the Khans. How, over a hundred years ago, Yesukai the Strong was presented with a son named Temuchin who became a fighter and a hunter. How Yesukai was murdered by Tartars and how Temuchin took the Kiut, the nomads who lived in tents in the snowy steppes, and raised them into an invincible army. How Temuchin came to be called Genghis, the leader of the united Mongolian nation, and creator of the most fearsome army in the world.

Shan T'u had listened to the tales of torture and murder, to the story of the reign of Genghis, and of his sons, and of his grandson, the wily Kublai Khan who now ruled all of China from his mighty palace in Kanbaliq. She had heard the grief of the subjugated Chinese people who waited for real warriors to rise up and crush the Mongol hordes.

The tales, cunningly told by Po, had inflamed Shan

T'u's heart. Po had arranged for Chang's best archer to teach her to be skilled with the bow, and for Chang's finest horseman to teach her to ride like the wind. "Still," Po had told her, "you are merely a girl and cannot be a warrior. But should the Mongols sweep further south and destroy everything of our lives, you may survive and preserve our knowledge. There may one day be no palace here. Who can predict? If you can ride and shoot, if you can write and read, you may live, and pass on the history and culture of our land."

"But I want to fight," Shan T'u had always said.

Po had always smiled and said, "You cannot accept what cannot be, Shan T'u, and that will break your heart one day. None of what I say may come to pass, not in your lifetime, not in a hundred lifetimes. But what is one lifetime? Chaos is upon us, and order will come again. If ten thousand generations must return to the earth before this happens, it is nothing so long as balance is restored. My knowledge will not die with me; it is in you, and in the others I teach. Your knowledge will pass to others still. It is the knowledge that matters, the truth that is immortal."

Shan T'u had always left the secret grove bursting with sadness and joy, not truly comprehending but overflowing with the splendor of learning. Yet this taboo knowledge had made her restless and angry, for she could tell nobody what she knew.

And so today, Shan T'u knelt before her master to be chastised. "I'm sorry,' she whispered once more. "I won't let it happen again."

"You will *try* not to," Po corrected. "You are not yet such a master that you can promise rashly." He glanced up at the shivering canopy of leaves. "The storm threatens, Shan T'u. Return to the palace. Deport yourself like a princess. Listen well at the feast tonight. I want to know about this man who comes at night from the wilderness."

Shan T'u nodded eagerly. "I will. But . . ." She glanced longingly at the pots of pigments and white lead powder for painting the lotus, at the inkcake and the porcelain and jade brushes for calligraphy. "There's no time for a lesson . . . ?"

Po smiled and began to close the pots. "No. It would not be helpful to write characters in the rain. Hurry now. And *behave*."

Once again, his visage was stern and grandfatherly. Shan T'u rose to her feet and nodded again. Then she turned and ran from the grove. As she ran, the storm broke and spread curtains of rain before her. The pelting drops slashed at her face, drenched her gown, streamed from her hair. At this moment, Shan T'u felt gloriously alive. She opened her mouth and tasted the rain on her tongue.

But she had reached the gate and she refrained from further displays. She called out and the gate opened for her. The guard looked relieved that she was alive, and helped her negotiate the slurry of mud created by the rain.

As Shan T'u reached the palace, the storm abated. The dark clouds became fringed with white and let through the crimson rays of evening sun. In a moment, the earth was aglow in vermilion light, and the cupolas and turrets of the palace were aflame. The sky unfolded like a great flower. Birds made a racket and the wind came fresh and strong.

Shan T'u cried out impulsively at the beauty of the

moment, and her throat constricted with longing. Then she went inside to prepare for the feast.

With rare gusto, Shan T'u adorned her face and hair. She sat before her mirror, and from her small compartmentalized box took rouge colored with safflower for her lips and cheeks, rice powder for her face and shoulders, and blue grease to create illusory eyebrows. Then, after they had draped her body with silken garments in the latest Persian style, her ladies-in-waiting dressed her hair with gold and gems and set on her head a tinkling golden crown decorated with pearls and precious stones.

Feeling womanly and beautiful, Shan T'u appeared in the huge banquet hall, which was filled with sculptures and paintings and hung with draperies. Already, wine and liquor were being dispensed, and the crowded hall rang with laughter.

Prince Chang Hu sat impressively on his royal throne at the head of the table, his great bulk swathed in an imperial robe of yellow silk, embroidered with dragons. On his head he wore a topknot held in place with elaborate hairpins. The ends of his moustache and goatee were waxed to razor points. He laughed uproariously, and his small, bright eyes glittered.

"Well, Friar!" he shouted. "How do you like a *real* feed?"

Shan T'u's eyes swiftly fastened on Friar De Rais, who sat at Prince Chang's left hand, on a lower level. Dressed in his cloak, he seemed stunned by his surroundings. Shan T'u sat at the far end of the table with the wives and concubines, but even at a distance, she was pleasantly disturbed by De Rais's height and blond handsomeness.

"Your Highness," De Rais said, "I'm impressed. We have great banquets too, but our castles are stone, and hot in summer. Our tables are boards laid over planks. We have nothing like this. Not even the king of my country dines in such majesty."

With that, De Rais raised his carved golden goblet and drained his liquor. Prince Chang chortled with delight as he emptied his own cup. He encouraged cheers and applause from the assembled guests. He wiped his wet lips with a napkin and said to De Rais, "I keep cool on summer nights, you see?"

Shan T'u's father referred to the whirling fan that sprayed water behind the throne. From the water fan came a steady, cooling breeze that reached even to the rear of the banquet hall. De Rais, and other noblemen, sat on stone benches cooled by ice from within. Curtains of water fell along all four sides of the room.

"I must tell His Holiness about this air cooling," De Rais said. "And about your cold drinks!"

Chang laughed again. "You never thought of putting ice in your drinks?" he taunted. "And you come from such a cold climate. I'll send some ice back with you—but don't lose it in the desert!"

This struck Prince Chang as so hilarious that he nearly fell sideways from his throne. The male guests, deep in their cups, hooted along with their lord, though at least half the men had not heard the joke. De Rais smiled politely, but Shan T'u could see that he was stung by the mockery. *You'll get to know my father's humor,* she thought.

The banquet lasted for hours, and Prince Chang had spared no expense to provide a pleasing array of dishes. There were imported pistachio nuts from the far west, and almonds from Turkestan. There was white carp marinated in wine, steamed pig in garlic sauce, dumplings shaped and flavored to resemble twenty different flowers. There were snow babies made of frogs' legs and beans, snails in vinegar, and a dish that Prince Change especially urged De Rais to try.

"How do you like that, eh?" he demanded, as he watched the friar struggle with chopsticks made of jujube wood.

De Rais chewed carefully and regarded the prince with cool eyes. "The flavor is unusual, but not unpleasant."

Chang began to rumble with laughter before he spoke. "Those slices of meat are seasoned with ginger," he said.

De Rais nodded.

"And topped with *ants' eggs!*"

De Rais paused, the chopsticks an inch from his lips. Shan T'u could not see clearly, but his face must have paled, for Prince Chang brayed with laughter and repeated the joke to each of his nobles. "Ants' eggs!" he shouted again and again, each time collapsing into helpless mirth.

The nobles cackled and guffawed and regarded the stranger with vast amusement. But De Rais had not changed his posture. He remained with the chopsticks poised, his eyes steady. His immobility caught everyone's attention and the laughter died down. The nobles became curious, surprised that the man had not gagged and run from the table. In moments, silence enveloped the room and Shan T'u could clearly hear the soft rush of water. Prince Chang Hu looked down at De Rais with dangerously narrowed eyes.

Be careful, Shan T'u prayed silently.

De Rais knew he held the attention of the entire assembly. With no further word, he brought the chopsticks to his mouth, took the food, chewed slowly, and swallowed. He laid the chopsticks by his porcelain plate and lifted his goblet. He flooded his mouth with grape wine.

"Prince Chang," De Rais said in a strong voice, "it makes me even more humble to know that you think so highly of me that you offer me a dish that earns your highest favor. Thank you!"

The guests remained silent, watching Prince Chang for a sign of his displeasure. The joke had been flung in his face. Chang Hu was not known for his good sportsmanship. Shan T'u caught the movement of bowmen in the room and kept her hands in her sleeves, praying.

Chang sat impassively for a long moment, regarding De Rais. He seemed to be making an important decision. For an instant, his black eyes went to Shan T'u and she felt a chill pass through her. Then a sudden grin split Chang's sweating face and he cried out, "That's the spirit! This man has got guts!"

The rolling thunder of Chang's laughter broke the tension as a surgeon's lance breaks an infection, and at once the room was riotous with laughter and talk. Men raised their goblets, and beer and wine ran down bearded chins. Chang signaled for an orchestra of eight serving girls to begin playing.

The night became a blur of color and music. Shan T'u barely heard the chatter of the women around her; she looked shamelessly at De Rais as he ate and talked with Chang. Her father and the friar seemed to be in earnest conversation, and once or twice De Rais looked at Shan T'u.

Dessert was a chilled mixture of milk, rice, and camphor, and after that, the entertainment began. There were drums and bells and flutes, harps and lutes. Dancers performed the wild steps of the Turks and the Persians. There were Sogdian twirling girls, who wore green pantaloons and crimson robes and danced on huge rolling balls.

De Rais sat cross-legged next to Prince Chang and his eyes glowed brightly. He clapped his hands and shouted with the other men. Now and then, Prince Chang would lean over and whisper something to De Rais and the friar would nod and smile.

Shan T'u felt her bones ache with tiredness as the night wore on, but the feast seemed destined to last forever. The wine fogged her brain and she grew sad as she watched De Rais. It was a moment before she realized that her father was addressing the guests and that *her* name had been spoken.

Prince Chang said, "As you know, my daughter, the Princess Shan T'u, is to be wed to Sultan Akbar of India. I needed only a guide who knew well the mountains and plains along the difficult journey. Only that kept my large-footed daughter from the one prince who would bed her!" He snickered and Shan T'u flushed angrily. "Now, give praise! A stranger has reached our gates who has crossed the deserts and mountains and lives! His holy mission is our omen of good fortune.

"I consider this a sign from the heavens. This friar has been sent to guide the princess safely. He has agreed to lead Shan T'u's caravan on the long-postponed wedding trip. Tomorrow, we celebrate with a royal hunt. Tonight, we drink to the nuptial journey of Shan T'u across forbidden lands!"

Prince Chang raised his goblet and roared his approval. The room resounded with the approbation of the drunken guests. Chang signaled for more dancing and there were audible groans from exhausted nobles. But the prince was flaunting his stamina, and challenging the friar to match him. De Rais seemed capable of keeping up the pace.

But Shan T'u was stunned and bereft. She no longer felt her throbbing head or leaden eyes. Her throat flamed and her hands had gone cold. So her wedding journey was here—and her wonderful stranger, this man of her dreams, had come to betray her and end her life.

No, she swore. She wouldn't let this happen. The moment of decision was now, and it took the heart from her body. She trembled as she sat in the din of music and reveling.

Goodbye, Friar, she thought bitterly. And quietly, she rose from the cashmere carpet and left the banquet hall.

Chapter Three

SHAN T'U FOUND THAT, ONCE HER DECISION WAS MADE, she moved quickly and confidently. She realized that deep in her heart she had been planning this moment all along. She went from the banquet hall to her bedchamber, where she shed her royal robes, unpinned her hair, removed the gold and gems. She belted on a simple silk tunic and brocaded jacket, and covered her feet with riding shoes.

With her hair loose and flowing behind her, Shan T'u kept to the shadows, alert to the distant noise of the feast. She avoided servants and guards and moved like an assassin from pillar to arch, until finally she was outside.

The moon rode full and brilliant in a sky the color of oysters. Shan T'u hurried to the stables, and quieted the nervous animals as she untethered a white mare. She petted the horse's nose, and led the beast along a paved path through the gardens. She passed a pond where lotus blossoms floated like ceramic sculptures on water of dark glass. The wind was hot and damp, and smelled of rain.

When she was beyond the light thrown by torches in the palace, Shan T'u swung up and into the saddle. She gripped the reins tightly to still the jingling of the ornamented bridle.

She looked sharply at the night-veiled shrubs, and saw the wooden statue of Buddha streaming with water that spumed from the mouths of jade dragons. Her eyes blurred as she recalled the solitude of these gardens. All she had ever wanted was to stay here and find a nobleman to wed.

No. She lied. What she truly wanted was not possible. Shan T'u urged the mare forward. She would jump the gate at its lowest point on the western side of the palace. She had daydreamed this escape many times, felt her thigh muscles tighten against the flanks of the horse, imagined herself hurtling over, riding like summer wind past the lake, toward the tantalizing hills.

Goodbye, Father, she thought. She felt no love for him. He'd had no use for her, except as a stick in a cryptic game of *go* to aggrandize his power. Rage firmed her jaw as she rode. A few more yards past the garden, then over the gate. The nightingale would fly from her cage.

Master Po, she thought guiltily. *I pray you'll understand.*

The mare's hooves sounded like dropping rain on

the stone path. The moon seemed to wait for her beyond the gate. Shan T'u threw back her finely chiseled head and her nostrils flared. *Now,* she thought.

She dug her knees into the mare's belly and felt a surge. And then she was flung backwards as the horse stopped!

"What—?" Her cry was a startled whisper.

"Be quiet!"

Shan T'u gasped as she saw the friar. He gripped the mare's bridle in one iron hand and grinned up at her with mocking eyes. She said fiercely, "You're inside, at the feast."

"As you can see, I'm out here," he said. His voice was gentle but taunting. *"I* came for fresh air. But where are *you* going? It's almost dawn."

Shan T'u's heart fluttered and her skin felt chilled. "I may ride if I wish."

"Were you running away?"

"That's none of your business, Friar."

He smiled. "Oh, but it *is* my business, Princess. If you run, your father will have you beaten and your journey will be delayed. Or you may die out there and *never* make the trip. Your wedding is important to me; I'm to be rewarded."

"Rewarded!" she said contemptuously. "What reward could a holy man wish?"

"Why, the chance to bring God to the barbarians in this land. I burn to do good work."

She regarded him coldly but curiously. He was closer than he'd ever been to her, though she could barely see him in the darkness. Yet she could smell the musk of his skin and hair, and she could hear his breath. The moonlight carved his face, and his eyes shone with reflected light. The suns had become moons.

"You're a liar," she said. "And for someone who's been so long in this land, you speak abominable Chinese."

"I apologize. Your tongue *does* crack the jaw."

His propinquity was making her blood watery and she didn't like it. She felt naked again under his gaze. "What are you, really?" she asked.

"Really? I don't understand."

"You are no monk. You ride fearlessly at night. You have crossed the land where yin and yang do not interchange, yet you did not become trapped forever in your dreams. You crossed the northern hills where people do not sleep at all. You drink as hard as my father does, and you stop one of his Dragon horses with one hand. Our monks do not possess such skill."

"I'm not one of *your* monks," De Rais said. "In my country, even holy men must fight bravely. Everyone must. We do a great deal of it."

Even though the man's syntax was atrocious, his slyness was evident. Her blood quickened, but pride brought ice to her heart.

"You're swift with words," she said. "Now please let me pass. It's not your affair if I stay."

"It's your father's affair."

"My father sold me to an old bag of guts."

"So you *were* running away," De Rais said. "How far did you think you'd get?"

"There are others. Nobles, scholars. They'd help me run."

"Run where?" De Rais gestured with his free hand.

"Your father owns this province. His soldiers will slit the throats of anyone who hides you."

Shan T'u looked away. "I have some cunning too."

"Yes, I can imagine." His voice softened. "And you are a brave girl. But you're a baby. You'd be captured inside a day." He smiled abruptly. "At least your hair isn't weighed down with armor."

She flushed hotly. "I made myself beautiful tonight in your honor, Friar!"

De Rais's eyes widened in comprehension. A broad grin split his face and he laughed sharply. *"Mon Dieu!"* he murmured. "You were trying to flirt with me!" His eyes twinkled. "I prefer your hair like this, not with trinkets. And I like your face fresh and windblown, not painted like the face of an ugly old duchess."

"You dare much, Friar," she said tightly, "to speak to the daughter of your host this way."

"My host and I get along famously," De Rais said. He tugged on the bridle and brought down the mare's head, forcing Shan T'u to slide forward. She clutched at the reins to right herself.

"Let me tell you what's out there," De Rais said intensely. "There are no magic lands where people dream or don't dream. There's a land to the north with forests and mountains, and land to the south with rivers and lakes. There is a river so mighty and long I don't yet know the ends of it, and there is a wall that I think divides one half of the earth from the other. It's hot as hell in summer, and it's endless, and there were days I thought I'd go raving mad.

"I've seen bazaars with acrobats and gem dealers. I've been cheated by Turkish pawnbrokers, arrested by petty officers, beaten and robbed. There are only two other friars in all of the Far East. Only two who had the guts to come *that* far, and they lost their courage when they saw China. I went further. I contracted a killing fever and rode until I reached Balkh and the cool winds. I recovered for a year, and studied the native languages. I climbed to the plateau of Pamir—at the top of the world—and looked east to Kashgar and Yarkand. Lands we haven't even mapped in Christendom. I saw a desert that made me sink to me knees and cry like a girl. Tribesmen warned me not to dare to cross it."

He released pressure on the bridle and the mare shook her great head. De Rais was breathing hard. "I dared. I know more than your father knows. I know you're a tempting morsel and I'd like very much to slake the thirst in my blood. But I'll pass up the chance for something more important. Passage through your father's province. Trade routes from France to where no Christian has been. You can't imagine it, Princess."

Shan T'u shivered in the dawn chill, crushed and excited by his voice. "I say again, you are no friar."

"Of course I am," he said. "Now go back and do what your father says. I've got too much at stake to lose because of your silliness."

"You make a mistake to treat me like a child."

"Do I?" he said. "Then I'll treat you like a woman."

His hands moved like serpents and lifted Shan T'u from the mare's back. She was suspended for a moment, weightless. Then just as suddenly, she was standing on the stones, and his hands were around her waist. She looked up into his shadowed face and his eyes flickered with the flame of sunrise. Then his lips pressed hers, parted hers, and his hand cupped her breast. And then his lips and hand were gone.

The instant passed like a dream. He stood a few feet away from her, his eyes impudent. Shan T'u hugged herself, ashamed and afraid. Her breast burned where he'd pressed it.

"You're not a woman yet," he said. "But you'll be a tempting one. Your Indian lord will eat you up." He laughed, and seized the bridle again. "To bed, Princess. I'll take back your father's horse."

The mocking cadence of his voice angered her. She could smell the wine on his mouth. "You think *we're* barbarians," she said. "You have it wrong. My father is a subtle man."

"I hope so," De Rais joked.

"*You* are the barbarian!" Shan T'u cried in sudden fury.

"What's got your back up?" De Rais asked innocently.

"Your presumptions." She caught up the bridle in her own tiny hand. "I'll return the horse myself."

"You expect me to trust you?"

"I expect you to release my horse."

He scrutinized her, considered, then let go. He gestured grandly. "After you."

The anger burned low now. "You'll soon understand what we are," she said churlishly.

She turned the horse with a yank of the bridle and saw the horizon lightening. Her head spun from wine. *Only* from wine, she told herself petulantly.

The day caught fire, the forests and hills lit by the sun. The sky throbbed like a drum beaten with copper sticks. The hunt was prepared early in the morning, and before the sun was halfway up, Prince Chang Hu sat astride his great black mount in saffron hunting robes. His eyes flickered as he watched his minions bustle and sweat to serve his pleasure.

Shan T'u joined the ladies but rode her white mare, whereas they were carried in litters. Twenty servants in brightly colored robes carried a great canopied litter ornamented in gold and silver. This was Prince Chang's hunting litter, with a couch that revolved to let him shoot from any direction.

Ranks of hunters gathered near the palace gate on stamping, chafing horses. There were archers with long mulberry bows, their topknots clasped with ivory pins. There were falconers lightly bestriding their mounts, golden birds perched on their forearms. The beaters assembled on foot, each with a long bamboo stick for flushing game.

Shan T'u petted her skittish horse and shielded her eyes from the burning sun. The servants alone were an army: grooms helping lords and ladies onto their horses, maids-in-waiting cooling the concubines with great beautiful fans, bearers carrying food and drink. The paved courtyard swarmed with humanity and rang with noise. Musicians played drums and flutes. Shan T'u's blood sang with the splendor and color of the scene. She loved the hunts as much as the men did, a feeling she dissembled. She barely heard the ladies chattering and even remained aloof from Lady Feng, who occupied her own canopied litter.

The friar appeared on his own sorrel mount. Shan T'u felt a pang of disappointment. He was still imposing in height, but with his cowl shielding his face and the coarse brown cloak making him shapeless and drab, he looked a poor match for the hunters. The friar's horse was unadorned, dull next to the gaily caparisoned mounts of the warriors.

Shan T'u's mouth tugged into a rueful smile. The man *did* have a quick tongue—and a disrespectful one. And he must have courage and strength to travel from Europe to China. But he was no luminous prince, no lord with suns in his eyes. He was a conniving friar with lecherous hands. And she, despite her dreams, was a princess with a duty to uphold.

Chang Hu signaled for the hunt to begin, and the party rode ceremoniously through an inner gateway into the prince's private hunting gardens. Shan T'u loved to ride through these landscaped acres with their miniature mountains, glades, valleys, plains, rivers, and lakes. The topographies of six countries were carefully reproduced in this verdant preserve that sparkled against the dun hills and sere grasslands outside the palace. Shan T'u tingled with anticipation of the friar's reaction to the lions, wild boar, wolves, and bears that her father kept here. The lakes were stocked with game fish from seven nations. As the hunting party rode, the trees erupted with clapping and the sky darkened with brilliantly colored birds.

Prince Chang took great pride in these hunting gardens; only an extremely rich and influential warlord could maintain such luxury, and the estate of Prince Chang had been spoken of in the palace of the Great Khan himself. Shan T'u looked at the friar, who scanned the artificial countryside with wonder.

Barbarians, are we? she thought vengefully. *Think again, holy man.*

Now the hunt was joined by the animal tamers, who

restrained cheetahs, lynxes, and dogs on silken leashes. The friar gaped at these exotic stalking beasts, and at one point locked eyes with a sinuous cheetah. The glance caused Shan T'u to catch her breath. The eyes of the friar had, it seemed, glowed scarlet like the cat's.

More imagination, she thought disgustedly. The sun created mirages. The musicians kept playing, with the eerie effect of chimes on the hot wind. Shan T'u thought briefly of Master Po and of her attempt last night to run.

The friar was right; she wouldn't have gotten far. She *would* have vaulted the gate and galloped across the dawn. But she would have returned. The longings that tormented her, the forbidden skills that made her unique—all of these had to kowtow to the princess, to the obedient royal woman.

Shan T'u banished her dead dream with an impatient toss of her head. Her heart felt crushed. The beaters crashed their sticks into the brush and Chang Hu dismounted and was helped into his litter and handed a black bow and a quiver of arrows. The twenty servants, sweat streaming down their faces, lifted the litter with visible strain and carried it, while a groom led the prince's horse.

De Rais rode next to the litter and listened as the prince spoke. Shan T'u suddenly wished the hunt were over.

Then, a commotion! The dogs barked savagely and the cats crouched low, snarling. Great shouts went up and horses were spurred into motion. The archers fanned out in two squads to flank the brush, while the falconers stayed behind. This was big game, not for birds.

Shan T'u whispered to calm her horse and felt her face tauten with excitement. The other ladies were not in sight, having paused for refreshments. Shan T'u bit her lip to resist calling for a bow and a quiver of arrows. She would not embarrass her father any further. Her childhood was over.

A sudden braying and crashing alerted Shan T'u. The servants bearing Chang's litter surged forward with a frightening groan of effort, and the litter was borne toward the racket, leaving the friar stranded near a precipitous shelf of rock. The mounted archers had surrounded a glade on three sides, their bows taut, arrows nocked. Shan T'u wondered what it was. A stag, perhaps, or a bear . . .

She gasped, then cried out. Her horse reared and Shan T'u tugged the reins. A monstrous wild boar exploded from the brush into the open. The creature was horrendous, a great charging machine of hulking shoulders and tapered back, bristling with dark fur, snorting hideously. Its grotesque face sprouted yellow tusks. The huge beast was clearly enraged.

The canopy on Chang's litter was pulled back and the couch revolved, bringing Shan T'u's father into full view. He'd drawn back his bowstring and followed the boar with his poised arrow. Yet he did not shoot, nor did the other archers.

Why don't they kill the beast? Shan T'u wondered.

She had steadied her horse, though the animal still whickered piteously. She looked behind her, making sure of a clear path out of the animal's charge. Blood pulsed in her veins, and her heart beat wildly. Suddenly, she remembered the friar.

Frightened, she scanned the area. Her eyes found him—astride a nearly hysterical horse, backed against that shelf of rock. The jagged stone glistened with falling water.

Shan T'u's throat constricted in horror. The friar was trapped, unable to control his mount. And he was directly in the path of the charging boar!

Her eyes swung back to the animal, which was now about fifty yards from the friar. The grunting beast plowed up translucent clouds of red dust that hid the sun and made the light momentarily scarlet. Shan T'u's horse shied, and she gripped the reins tightly, looking desperately for a servant with weapons. She would reveal her secret skills to save this man; her royal obligations meant nothing now.

Still the boar came, inexorable in its speed and savagery. Its tusks lowered to rip the stomach from the horse, to gouge the flesh from the friar's thigh, to bring down the mare, to thrust upward into the monk's belly, to lift the gutted man and dash him against the ground, plunging again and again into the mauled corpse . . .

She felt cold, as if the beast had gored *her* and let gush the warm blood. But there was no servant.

And the boar was only a few feet from the cringing friar. The man's cowl was flung back, his face white. His eyes were fixed on his approaching death.

No, she screamed silently.

And then, out of the pluming dust came her father's litter, borne by the soaked arms of the servants. And out of the red dust came ghost horses bearing the archers. Prince Chang let fly an arrow and the steel tip blazed in the half-light, then buried itself in the boar's humped back. More arrows hissed into the air like angry locusts, thudding into the boar. The animal stuck its razor-toothed snout straight up and uttered a shrieking cry of agony. Again it squealed, and the black fur glistened with blood. Chang's couch spun, and from each angle he released an arrow, and each arrow found its mark in the torn body of the boar.

Insane and strong, the boar staggered a few more steps, still intent on killing the friar. But the arrows had been dipped in numbing poison, and the animal spilled blood from fifty wounds. It faltered, swayed, then dropped with a shuddering thud.

The air was suddenly quiet, and Shan T'u heard only the panting of the horses. The red dust thinned, letting through the sun, and the sky became blue again. The steady trickle of water over the rock sounded refreshing.

Shan T'u watched two archers detach from the squad and ride to the friar. They spoke to him and he nodded. He seemed badly shaken. One archer took the horse's bridle and led the friar to Prince Chang.

It was at that moment that Shan T'u understood what had happened, and a flood of fury burst the dam of her control. She nudged her mare with her knees and rode to her father, bypassing the slain boar, which lay petrified in a widening pool of blood.

Chang Hu glanced up at the new set of hoofbeats and regarded his daughter idly. She knew that look. "My daughter," he said in a honeyed voice. "How did you become lost from the other women? You could have been hurt."

"Thanks to *you*," Shan T'u said. "Didn't you see me?"

"I saw nothing with all the dust," Chang said. He gestured to the friar, who had dismounted and stood by his horse, one hand loosely holding the reins.

Shan T'u's eyes went to De Rais, who met her gaze.

He smiled bravely at her. Shan T'u said to her father, "Why did you wait so long to kill the boar?"

Chang Hu pursed his lips and stroked the oiled bow. "I think the boar would not wait for *us*."

"You *had* him. You could have killed the animal in the brush. You let him escape; your beaters left the path open."

"As we always do," Chang said with an edge in his voice. "It's sporting."

Shan T'u paused, biting back harsh words. It would not do to openly accuse her father of trapping the friar, making the holy man look into the mouth of his death and then saving him at the last moment. She knew that's what her father had done, but not why. The answer to that unspoken question came a moment later.

Chang Hu looked lazily at the friar and said, "My daughter was worried. See how pale she looks, how her eyes drop, how her mouth quivers? It is seemly for the girl to fear for your life, holy man."

"Not as much as *I* feared for it," De Rais said.

Chang laughed. "Of course. You are no hunter."

"I *do* like to hunt," De Rais said with a weak smile. "Rabbits."

This caused Chang to guffaw. The prince handed his bow to a servant and placed his great hands on the knees of his robe. "I am glad, Friar. This weakness is what I seek in the man who will guide my daughter to her husband. I have armed warriors enough to protect her, and her purity is safe with them. Now I know I can trust you, that you are what you say."

Chang smiled at his brilliance. He signaled, and his servants lifted the litter once more, nearly cracking their bones with the effort on this brutal day.

Shan T'u watched the litter borne off, and her eyes reflected the bright sunshine. She turned back to the friar, looking down upon him from her mare. "I warned you," she said. "My father is not the buffoon he pretends to be. He is descended from a wandering shepherd, but he is a skilled hunter . . ."

"Thank God," De Rais said dryly.

She smiled. "He also designed the bathhouse and pavilion you saw. He writes calligraphy and paints and plays music. Yet he is also deeply superstitious. He left my feet unbound because an old astrologer made a prediction."

"Unbound feet are bad?" De Rais asked.

She dropped her eyes. "They are not considered beautiful as lily feet are."

"I think your feet are divine."

She felt herself blush. "Enough! We were discussing my father and his treachery. He played the drunken barbarian to lull you and *arranged* for you to be trapped by the boar. He was testing you."

De Rais looked thoughtful for a moment, then gracefully mounted his horse. The litheness of an acrobat, she had thought when first she saw him. The hands of a magician, the strength of a warrior, the wit of a courtier. Yet he had waited to die horribly, too frightened to save himself.

"If he was testing me," De Rais said, as his eyes looked directly into hers, "do you think I passed the test?"

He smiled, then galloped away with superb riding skill. And Shan T'u realized, slowly and terribly, that she *and* her father had been outwitted. That this man possessed a courage and daring she had not imagined. To *wait* for death, to depend on the equal daring of her father . . . And what if De Rais had been wrong; what if he'd misread Prince Chang?

Shan T'u had never seen a deadlier game of wits than the one just played. She looked at the dead boar with a deep shudder and her skin burned with the memory of the friar's touch.

The afternoon passed in splendor as she watched the flight of the falcons, the fluid charge of the cheetahs, the skill of the archers. Much game was dragged back to the palace at sunset, but Shan T'u kept her eyes on the friar, who was framed in the glow of the dying day.

Her body quivered with reckless hope and excitement, and for the first time, she looked forward to her wedding journey. Once more, taboo dreams dared to play in her heart.

Chapter Four

IN THE DAWN MIST, A FEW DAYS LATER, A RED-CLAD figure made her way over a stone bridge to a pagoda that stood on a small island in Prince Chang's estate. The still waters of the lake mirrored temple and bridge in shimmering green reflection, and ghostly fog slipped past veiled mountains.

The figure was Lady Feng in a scarlet gown, her hair coiffed but unadorned. She swayed, and cursed her lily feet, bound from babyhood to make her alluring.

The pagoda's brick walls dripped with moisture, and Lady Feng's nostrils recoiled at the stench of rotting vegetation. She darted glances like daggers right and left, searching the mist.

At last she heard a shuffling on the bridge. She

waited just inside one of the four gates of the pagoda. In her sash rested a small jeweled knife. Her hand closed over its haft. If she was discovered, she would know what to do.

The figure stumbled out of the fog, in the sashed tunic and jacket of a nobleman. His brocaded slippers were splashed with mud. Lady Feng laughed.

"Who is it?" the man demanded.

Lady Feng stepped out of the gateway and confronted him with her hands on her hips. "You are quite a hero, Wei Ku."

The man exhaled windily. "Thank the gods. I was so frightened coming here. If your husband had followed me . . ."

"I would have been gone," Lady Feng said. "Do you think I'm that much of a fool?" She swayed toward him with a seductive smile. "Come, my love, let's not think of fear now."

She caressed his neck and her mouth strained to kiss his lips. Wei Ku threw his arms around her waist. Her practiced tongue flitted like a captured bird in his mouth. Then she stepped back and gripped his hands.

"Has your courage returned, love?"

He gulped, and Lady Feng giggled. "How could I betray my warrior husband with *you?*" she taunted. "You are a poet. Not one drop of soldier's blood flows in your veins."

"I'm not ashamed of being a poet," Wei Ku said with wounded dignity. "I don't envy the filthy Mongol warrior who drinks blood from the veins of his own horse."

"Yes, but that's why the Mongol warrior does not die of thirst on a long march and conquers a nation."

The palest hint of rising sun glowed against the

silken wall of cloud. Wei Ku glanced up at the increasing light. "Enough. You did not ask me here to extol the virtues of Khan's soldiers. What did you want?"

Lady Feng dipped her head becomingly and rubbed the silk of his embroidered collar between her thumbs and forefingers. "Wei Ku," she murmured, "I beg your leave if I seem forward or presumptuous."

Wei Ku cleared his throat. "I forgive you."

Her lips plucked at the skin stretched over his collarbone, and nipped at his throat. Wei Ku sucked in a breath and held her face in his trembling hands. "No more," he pleaded.

Lady Feng's eyes shone like green jade as she smiled. "Wei Ku, I want to arouse you to watchfulness. You know my husband, the Prince Tuan Lei, walks in the courtyards with Prince Chang Hu. And what are they discussing?"

Wei Ku shrugged miserably. "Court matters. They never tell me."

"No, they never tell you. But I get close to my husband when he is filled with wine. And I touch him so expertly that he speaks . . ."

Lady Feng's hands slipped beneath Wei Ku's tunic and slid down his ribs. Wei Ku worked his tongue over his lips to moisten them. "What have you learned?"

"That my husband is a fool," she hissed. "And that Prince Chang is a bigger fool." Suddenly, the cooing dove was a coiled, scarlet snake.

"How are they fools?"

"They plot, and they plot, and they plot to ally their lands and their armies against Kublai Khan," she said bitterly. "They will regain the southern lands, they think. Meanwhile, Chang Hu fawns on Khan, and dribbles compliments, and sends him gifts. He even sells his daughter to an Indian potentate to do Khan a favor. All to turn Khan's head. Pah! Does Chang really think he can fool the lord of the Yuan Dynasty? Wei Ku, it is doomed!"

Wei Ku's eyes bulged with fright as he listened to her passionate words. Now her hands gripped his with white-knuckled desperation. Wei Ku's voice was a rasp when he spoke. "What can I do?"

"We," she urged him. "Right now, we can do nothing. It's hard to know if Khan is suspicious. But I have been told of Mongol hordes sweeping down into the southern mountains. I have heard of marauding bandits who provoke the Mongols, trying to rouse the peasants to revolution. If the Khan becomes angry enough, he will crush Prince Chang with one mighty stroke of his sword.

"Wei Ku, I am frightened for my life. I was chosen to marry Tuan Lei, but I dare to choose you. We must be ready for the worst."

"Yes, of course," Wei Ku stammered. "How?"

A serpentine smile lifted Lady Feng's lips as daylight swathed the island in teal blue. "You, my love, are more valuable than the warrior princes. You have journeyed to the court of Kublai Khan, and you will journey there again. He dotes on the entertainments you provide. You can gain his ear."

Wei Ku blushed. "I'm not as close to him as that. I . . ."

"You are close enough!" Her eyes blazed. With visible effort, she regained control. "You anger me so. The time is momentous, Wei Ku. When you next journey to the court of Khan, bid him keep a watchful eye on Prince Chang Hu, and on Prince Tuan Lei.

When our princes make a fatal misstep, we can administer all these lands for Khan. There is much tribute to be exacted."

"It seems treasonous," Wei Ku mused.

"No! The Mongols rule our land. It is our own princes who plot treason. We must serve our masters."

Wei Ku nodded. "I suppose so."

"It *is* so." The sun broke the moist clouds as a child tears a spider's web, and radiant morning light flooded the lake with blue fire and set the tiles of the curved pagoda roof aflame. A flock of lake birds thundered out of the brush and winged southward.

Lady Feng glanced up and cried out softly. Daylight drove her to the cool shadows of the women's apartments. She folded her hands over Wei Ku's arms and gripped him with her eyes. "Believe me," she pleaded. "We will triumph together."

Wei Ku embraced her awkwardly with boyish desire. His lips wetly mashed her cheek. "I'll do as you ask."

He kissed her unyielding lips one last time, then turned and ran over the stone bridge and down the path leading past the river to the palace. Lady Feng drew a scarlet sleeve across her mouth to wipe away his kiss. But her eyes flamed with triumph and her heart raced with anticipation.

Shan T'u often came down to a riverside pavilion to watch the sun on the water and to let her thoughts fly free. It was not a formal pavilion, and Shan T'u liked it for that reason. There was a simple bamboo structure with an intricately woven roof, and there were pathways for walking. Musicians sometimes played on a small island near the pavilion when the moonlight poured onto the water and the mulberry trees filled the air with fragrance.

Shan T'u walked sadly down the path now as summer heat rose from the leaves and the grass. She could hear the gentle lapping of the river even before she came to it. She brushed at green flies with her saffron sleeve and felt her eyes fill with tears.

She sighed. She couldn't bear to be around the palace these days. Everything was bent toward preparing her wedding journey. Warriors trained with bow and arrow, servants packed clothing and provisions, horses and camels were groomed. So much excitement!

Very few of the concubines or lordlings would miss her. She was the shame of the family, a disgrace to Chinese womanhood. Well, maybe the courtiers in India would welcome her. Right now, the princess felt very sorry for herself.

Shan T'u sniffled back her crying and emerged at the pavilion. A heron stood gracefully on one leg in the water and darted its slender beak beneath the rippled surface. Here there was no sign of palace or prince. Here there was only nature, the nature that Master Po enshrined in shades of black ink. If only *she* could paint this riverbank . . .

But that was another forbidden dream.

She stamped her foot petulantly and then stopped, as an animal bellowed a reply.

Shan T'u held her breath, her eyes flickering back and forth. Not an escaped tiger or bear . . . ?

There it was again!

Shan T'u wet her lips and wondered if her thudding heart could be heard. She moved cautiously around the screened side of the pavilion and poked her head past the bamboo pole to see.

She gasped. There, in the blinding water of the river, floated the friar's head!

Shan T'u shut her eyes and sorted out her thoughts. Of course that couldn't be possible. How could the friar's head float right side up like that?

She opened her eyes and there was the head still, but it was very much alive, and it was singing. That was the strange bellow she had heard—the barbarous doggerel he'd been chanting. She kept herself hidden and listened, smiling. He sang lustily, whether in tune or not she couldn't know because the tune itself was such a caterwaul. No doubt the words were in his French language. As she listened, she admired the shape of his head. His darkened hair clung wetly to his skull. His beard dripped as he sank under the surface and came back up again, still yelping.

Shan T'u had tried hard not to think about the maddening friar since the hunt. She'd failed. Every night she'd stood by her window and sighed at the taunting moon, wondering where he'd ridden from, dreaming of how his lips tasted. Yearning for him to put her in the saddle with him and spur his horse over her father's wall and into the green mountains.

Even after she reluctantly lay down, she stared into darkness with sleepless eyes and remembered the boar charging in the red dust, and the friar awaiting his awful death, risking his life on his judgment of a foreign prince he'd only just met.

Why?

To gain Prince Chang's trust, to become a holy chaperone on Princess Shan T'u's wedding journey.

And again, why?

Who was this friar and what did he want? He'd said something about trade routes, but it made no sense to Shan T'u. She had heard that Kublai Khan tolerated other religions and trusted foreigners over Chinese for his administrators. Could the friar be planning to desert the wedding party for the perilous ride to the emperor's palace at Kanbaliq? Then why begin the journey in an opposite direction?

And so passed the wretched nights of Princess Shan T'u. Only the promise of the friar's company made the wedding trip bearable to contemplate. But the knowledge that he would ride away once her Indian prince claimed her made Shan T'u close her fists and sob.

Now Shan T'u ventured to the other side of the pavilion, where she secreted herself behind the screen. She was much closer to the friar now. The heron glanced at her, cawed, then flapped its tremendous wings and lifted clumsily into the steaming air.

The friar looked at the bird and cried, *"Ah! Oiseau doux! Retournez avec ma princesse!"*

Whereupon he began yet another bout of terrible singing. Shan T'u giggled, then clapped a hand over her mouth. The friar stopped singing and glanced toward the pavilion, shrugged, and sang again.

Shan T'u leaned dreamily against the bamboo pole that supported the pavilion's roof, and rested her cheek on her hand. Her hair was elaborately pinned up with ivory clips, and for a moment she considered unpinning the tresses and letting them flow past her shoulders, as he liked. But that was folly, of course.

Her skin seemed to swell with longing as she thought of pleasing the friar. Dear gods, how wicked she was, and how undisciplined in thought. A deep sorrow crushed her throat. How would she survive a lifetime with a prince she did not love?

Her eyes flew open wide. The friar had stopped singing, and now he shook his head vigorously to hurl away droplets of water. He began to rise from the river, and he was naked!

Shan T'u was frozen. To run now would call attention to herself. To step forward would be too bold. She gripped the bamboo pole with both hands and her eyes remained fastened to the friar. He stood now with water eddying about his belly. Shan T'u flushed with the heat of her own desire as her eyes lovingly caressed his sinewed neck, his deeply molded shield of a chest, and his flat, rippled stomach. His muscles moved beneath his coppery skin with oiled smoothness, catching glints of sunlight. When he sucked in a breath she saw the skin pull taut over his ribs. His arms were powerful . . . from what? Praying? Surely more than that! And what were those scars? That ugly white slash from his neck down across his collarbone, and that livid pink memento curving from his back around his left flank? They looked like sword wounds, inflicted in battle. Quite a friar, this William!

Shan T'u trembled as her body betrayed her. She quieted herself and feasted on his beauty. He scooped water in his cupped hands and splashed it on his face, shutting his lovely blue eyes. She smiled at his playfulness.

And now he was walking out of the river—moving up toward the bank!

Shan T'u, shut your eyes!

But she could not. Her eyes were his prisoners now,

forced to watch as he revealed his manhood, encircled by matted black hair, and his thighs, bulging with the muscle of a hard rider. Shan T'u gulped. Her palms felt clammy against the bamboo. A green fly buzzed around her face.

He is magnificent, she thought wildly. *He is all I've dreamed about. But I am a princess of China, and he is a barbarian and a holy man. I am promised, and I can never know him.*

So that was how it would end. After all her young years of disobedience and willfulness, after all her fantasies of a rider come to pluck her away, she would, finally, be true to her father and to her training. She had grown up.

The friar stepped onto the riverbank and retrieved his green dalmatica and his brown cloak. She saw the whiteness of his rear, and the stringy tendons of his legs as he bent. He rubbed himself dry with the cloak. He seemed so content and unafraid to be alone.

Of course he was. He had braved the deserts and mountains to come this far. He only toyed with her. He thought her a child, a curiosity. He played with her heart, not caring about the torment she suffered.

She became angry with him. She would watch him no longer. She had other things to do today.

The green fly thudded into her nose. Shan T'u's eyes flamed. Her hand struck with an archer's speed and the hapless fly was crushed against the bamboo pole.

Shan T'u turned her back on the river and hurried around the pavilion onto the path through the mulberry trees. But her eyes burned with the outline of the friar emerging from the river like a god, and her heart thumped helplessly. She had never seen a sight that wonderful. It was a forbidden sight, a sinful sight, but at least it could be kept as her delicious secret.

Shan T'u was so wrapped in her reverie that she didn't see the man step into her path. She cried out, and her hand flew to her mouth. Then anger replaced shock as she recognized the simpering poet Wei Ku.

"Why don't you announce yourself?"

Wei Ku eyed her strangely and spoke without his usual timidity. "My apologies, Princess. I was entranced by your beauty, and words would not come."

Shan T'u expelled an exasperated breath. "I never knew words to fail you, Wei Ku," she said scathingly.

"The princess is quick-witted," Wei Ku said unctuously. "What brings you to the riverbank?"

"A need to escape the stale air of the court," she said. "And you?"

"A need to commune with nature."

"Not with the Lady Feng?"

Wei Ku's face paled at the cheekbones, and Shan T'u could not stifle a merry laugh. "Why so struck, Wei Ku? You and Lady Feng are friends, are you not?"

Wei Ku recovered his composure and bowed stiffly. "Yes, we are. I felt faint for a moment. The summer heat."

"Of course. Excuse me, Wei Ku. I must return to my apartments."

She brushed past the poet, but Wei Ku's arm snaked out and held her fast. Shan T'u's head snapped around, and her eyes smoldered.

"You take liberties, poet!"

Wei Ku's eyes glittered unpleasantly. "So do you, Princess."

"Meaning what?"

"Meaning that a naked holy man is not a fit object for the lustful eyes of a princess—especially a princess about to be married."

Shan T'u's breath stopped and the blood rose in her cheeks. "What are you talking about?"

"Don't be coy, Princess. I've been watching you for some time."

He was hurting her arm. "Well, and what of it? I didn't know he would be here."

"You could have warned him."

"*You* might have warned *me*."

Wei Ku laughed, a high-pitched giggle that sent shudders through Shan T'u. "I think *I* had better reason to keep silent. Your father won't like this. In fact, I suspect he'll have you flayed raw."

Shan T'u shivered at the thought of a severe whipping. Surely Wei Ku was right. "What do you want?"

"Are you suggesting I would take a bribe?"

"Let's not waste each other's time," Shan T'u said. "How much will seal your lips?"

Wei Ku seemed to consider. His small black eyes bored into her, and his face, not at all unattractive, curved into a wicked smile. "I am already a nobleman of some personal wealth," he said, "although a few hectares of your father's estate might be a nice addition." He laughed at her reaction. "But that *would* be awkward, wouldn't it? So why don't we dispense with baubles and speak of more romantic things?"

"What are you talking about?"

He seized her other arm. A film of perspiration coated his upper lip. "Surely you know how deep my feelings run for you, Princess. Soon you will be gone, across the green mountains to far India. The bride of a very fortunate prince. But before that, Princess, before the final farewell, perhaps we can share just a moment, a bird's flight, of passion."

Shan T'u's throat tightened. "Wei Ku, this can't be serious!"

"The needs of the flesh are always serious."

"You could be executed for saying this!"

"If anybody heard me say it."

"*I* hear you."

"Yes," he hissed, "a desperate, sinning princess trying to avoid a beating. But your father will believe me because you have trespassed before. You will be stripped naked and bound, and your velvet back will be striped with blood. And possibly you'll die before your wedding night. A virgin sacrificed to her own lust."

"You pig."

"Names will not change the truth."

"Get away from me."

His hands tightened on hers, making her skin tingle. "I don't think you ought to turn me away."

"I'll scream."

"You'll summon your torture."

Fury overwhelmed her, and Shan T'u spat into Wei Ku's face. She wept as spittle dribbled down his glistening cheek. But his eyes only glowed more brightly. "You were never docile, Princess, but surely you're sensible."

She shook her head. "No . . ."

"Only a morning's delight."

"*Please . . .*"

"Ah, you're weakening."

She shut her eyes. His arms slithered around her

back, and like the tentacles of a great octopus, they pulled her closer and closer to his thin, panting body.

Then she heard a twig snap, and her eyes flew open. She saw the friar, dressed in his robes. His sunbright eyes were shadowed, but she could see the gleam of rage in them.

"What is the meaning of this?" De Rais demanded.

Wei Ku's lips twisted into a leer. "The meaning may not be clear to a holy man, but our business is private."

"I don't think so," De Rais said. "I know very well what you're up to, and where I come from, that's good reason for me to run a sword through your eyeballs."

Wei Ku visibly blanched. "But of course, you have no sword."

The friar held up his hands. "But I have these, and they are strong from traveling. My fingers could crush the bones in your neck."

"Ah, so violent for a friar . . ."

"And so repulsive for a poet!"

Wei Ku licked his lips feverishly, glanced at Shan T'u, then at the friar. "The daughter of Prince Chang Hu has committed an act of lust and sin—"

"Demanding one in return?" De Rais asked archly.

"She ought to be punished!"

"She ought to be judged in the eyes of God," De Rais intoned. He pointed dramatically at Shan T'u. "The princess came to a riverbank to revel in the joys of a summer morning. If, by accident, her child's eyes lit on my undraped form, then she, as innocent as uncorrupted Eve, gazed sweetly upon the body of Adam. There is no sin in this."

Shan T'u's heart burst with relief. Wei Ku's hands

slid reluctantly from her body. "You're twisting words," he said.

"And you twist your soul!" De Rais roared. "Your sin is an abomination in the eyes of the Redeemer. Get thee gone, adulterer, and pray that your wretched guilt does not betray thee before thy prince."

Wei Ku's lip was trembling. He darted watery eyes at Shan T'u, then snarled and lumbered up the path, nearly tripping over the roots of a tree.

Shan T'u turned to the friar. "Thank you," she said.

De Rais nodded deferentially, but his eyes twinkled. "No thanks needed, Princess. Was he right?"

"What?"

"Did you watch me bathe?"

Shan T'u's ear tips grew hot and she cast down her eyes. His laugh boomed delightedly. "Well, I hope you saw something worth getting pawed over."

Shan T'u looked up and imagined his body without the cloak. "I saw something very beautiful, Friar."

He laughed again. "Now you make *me* blush. I think you'd better get home before you get us *both* in trouble."

"Yes," she murmured. She glanced up the path. "I don't think we've heard the last of him."

De Rais chuckled. "I know his kind. Generally harmless. Go on, Princess. Scoot. My *own* thoughts are becoming impure."

Shan T'u nodded and turned away with an effort. She hurried gracefully up the path, and her heart beat madly with excitement and foreboding.

As Prince Chang Hu contentedly lounged on a low couch playing a flute, Lady Feng entered the dim chamber and prostrated herself. Chang and his concubines looked up languidly. Chang seemed a great golden Buddha in repose, save for the satanic beard and conniving eyes. "Yes, Lady Feng?" he said.

"With Your Highness's indulgence," Lady Feng whispered, "a moment or two. There is something very terrible you must know about this friar, and about your daughter, the princess."

Chang's eyes narrowed. With two handclaps he dismissed the concubines. He wanted to hear this news in private.

Chapter Five

SHAN T'U AWOKE TO A CLATTER AND SHOUTING AND THE neighing of a thousand horses. She tumbled out of bed and ran to her window. A camel lumbered past, its fur matted and its beard dripping. A servant stood atop a cart waving his hands frantically and screaming orders. Retainers scurried everywhere. Shan T'u shook with rage at the sight. How dare her father prepare her wedding caravan without waking her up!

She performed her morning toilette quickly, snapping at her servingwomen. After breakfast, she dressed in a yellow *cheong sam* and angrily pinned her coiffure. Then she strode outside into the fearsome heat. The din of screaming voices, braying animals, and creaking machinery deafened her. Everywhere, half-naked laborers tied bundles onto carts or draped them over the backs of animals. Shan T'u stood in the courtyard and despaired. Nobody even noticed her! She might be trampled by a bullock and the packing would go on.

Shan T'u looked toward the towering gate, its red-tiled roof jeweled in the sunlight. Soon she would pass through it for the last time. And beyond that gate lay the green hills, the treacherous mountains, the mighty river—and perhaps bandits, wild animals, and marauding Mongols.

She looked back at the courtyard and saw her gleaming, elaborately decorated cart being hitched up to a massive camel. Her camel driver wore a brocaded coat and ivory hairpins, and draped the beast in its own finery. Shan T'u felt her throat closing. A sense of destiny crushed her.

A camel nearby stumbled and fell to its knees, dumping porcelain ewers and cups from an untied bundle. Servants cursed and one man thrashed the hapless beast with a stick. Shan T'u could not bear to watch any more. She needed, for the last time, to be alone in the gardens. She needed to seek the peace and balance of mountain and water, as landscaped by Prince Chang's designers.

She moved impatiently through the crush of people, imperiously ordering servants aside and sometimes striking out with her arm. Eyes flew open at her approach and the poor wretches dropped to the earth in prostration. Shan T'u took no notice of their obeisance. She hurried over a zigzag bridge to a quiet courtyard, then passed through the gates of a pavilion into a lovely arbor with white rocks and bamboo. A stream rushed softly past stone walls draped with creepers. From the eaves of the pavilion a waterfall splashed. A white lotus floated on a glassy pond, and red pomegranate grew on the pond's bank.

Shan T'u breathed in the delicate beauty and banished the noise of the caravan from her ears. She knelt by the pool and with her right hand made ripples. She watched the ripples spiral outward and rock the lotus.

"Are you redesigning?" an ancient voice asked.

Shan T'u cried out in surprise and stood. Her wet fingers tingled with cool air. In the shadow of the pavilion sat the withered form of Master Po. He sipped from a cup of tea.

"Master," she whispered, and kowtowed gracefully.

"Get up, get up," he said. His voice sounded more ethereal than ever. "No formality. All that you know ends today. All that you *are* to know begins."

"I am aware," she said dryly. "I didn't know you were contemplating the pool."

"I rarely discuss contemplation while I'm doing it," he said. "But you were never hesitant, Shan T'u. It is like you to crash into a garden like a drunken Mongol and agitate the waters of a pool. Perhaps you would like to uproot some trees or hurl the rocks about."

"Master Po, I surely haven't sinned so grievously . . ."

He laughed. "You *never* see what calamity you bring. The garden is a work of art. Would you scrawl caricatures over my scrolls?"

"No—"

Master Po gestured with a translucent hand. "But you disturbed *this* painting."

"*You* designed this garden!"

Again he chuckled. "Yes, this was my design."

"I've been foolish again," she said.

"Headstrong," he amended. "As you always are."

She sat next to him. "You must spend many hours here."

"So I do, Shan T'u. Lost in admiration for the beauty around me."

Her throat swelled, and her fist closed. "Oh, Master Po—and I have to leave this!"

Her tears blinded her. When his voice replied, it was like the dry rustle of paper. "We enter many gardens and we leave many gardens. I shall have to leave this garden soon."

"Don't talk of your death."

He smiled thinly. "My death folds into your life. It is all illusion, as Buddha teaches us."

"I can't bear to leave you."

"Of course you can—and the moment has come for you to stop whining and become a princess."

Shan T'u felt faint with inspiration. "I'll try," she promised.

"Remember the pond, Shan T'u," Master Po murmured, "and the rock. All of nature is in one stone. All of China is within you. You are a stone from this garden and you *are* the garden."

She looked at him with shining eyes. "I love you, Master Po."

"Sentimentality is pleasant but not useful."

"And you would never confess to feeling a little of it yourself?"

"That is for the melodramatic novels that seem so popular today."

Shan T'u laughed affectionately. "I will accept my duty, Master Po. I shed my girlhood as the caterpillar sheds its skin. I am the butterfly. China will not die."

His old eyes glistened with helpless tears, and Shan T'u' squeezed his hand wordlessly.

Their silence made the sudden noise more startling, as the friar appeared wildly, his cloak swirling about him. His dark hood was thrown back, baring his blond head.

"*There* you are!" he said to Shan T'u. "Your father is looking for you."

"And you, too?" she teased. "Mustn't lose your reward, eh?"

De Rais flushed, but kept his temper. "*Touché.*"

Master Po watched carefully. "This is a day for disruption."

"I apologize," De Rais said. "I didn't mean to interrupt your conversation."

"It isn't the conversation," Shan T'u said, "it's the garden."

De Rais cocked an eyebrow. "I interrupted the garden?"

"You wouldn't understand," Shan T'u said wearily.

"Teach me."

Shan T'u looked at him with surprise.

He spread open his hands. "We have some time before the caravan departs. Why not walk with me and instruct me in the pleasures of the gardens?"

Shan T'u's heart leaped, but she rejected her feelings. "You assuredly can't be serious."

"I intend to be utterly frivolous!"

"Friar!"

De Rais chuckled and stepped lightly into the

garden. "You, old man, must be Master Po. I've heard about you."

"I am Po."

"You're the resident tutor here?"

"I instruct the young nobles in the classical arts and sciences."

De Rais looked around with curiosity. "So much learning in this country. Back in France, almost everybody is ignorant. The nobles especially. The king *most* especially."

"Are you proud of that?" Po asked.

De Rais laughed. "If I were proud of it, *vieux père*, I wouldn't be halfway across the world. I'd be snug in my manor with some peasant wench, waiting for the next crusade."

Shan T'u caught her breath as De Rais realized his mistake. Master Po said softly, "Strange occupation for a holy man."

De Rais coughed. "My error. The syntax of Chinese is difficult to master. I was speaking of the typical knight of my country. My *own* life would be one of poverty and prayer."

Master Po nodded. "I understand." He turned to Shan T'u. "Why don't you walk with the friar? I need a nap."

"Master Po! I'll never see you again."

"Prolonged farewells are empty and distressing. The caravan will leave whether I sleep or wake."

He rose, and Shan T'u got to her feet as well. She kowtowed to Master Po, then impulsively embraced him. "Goodbye," she whispered.

"No unseemly displays," he said hoarsely. "Find happiness with your prince."

"Never."

"Shan T'u! Even at the last, must you be willful?"
She kissed his wrinkled forehead and smiled at him.
"You would not want to remember me otherwise."

She reluctantly left the pavilion to join the friar.
She looked up at De Rais with brave determination.
"Since you searched so hard for me, you may have
your walk."

De Rais studied her with ill-concealed interest.
"You confound me and enrapture me," he said.

Her pulse fluttered. "I thought you wanted philosophy and contemplation."

"At least."

Shan T'u nodded deferentially to him and led him
out of the garden. Under the pavilion, Master Po's
eyes blazed defiantly like the sun flaming atop a
mountain before sinking into night. He'd probed
deeply into the heart of the friar, and of Shan T'u, and
he was not displeased with what he'd seen there.
These were two people who did not fear the forbidden, and who possessed uncommon courage and skill.
But he could suggest nothing, and advise no more. All
would be as destiny demanded.

Master Po sighed and sipped his tea. He returned
his senses to the soothing beauty of his garden. It was
important to contemplate deeply, for there was little
time.

Shan T'u showed De Rais several of the finest
gardens in her father's palace. They walked under the
Pavilion for the Contemplation of the Moon, which
was set in a shimmering lotus pond, then crossed a
long zigzag bridge to the shore, where a willow

overhung the bamboo railing. They entered a vast garden where Prince Chang had built rock mountains and a pond with islands joined by bridges. Beyond a dwelling area was a wood of pines and bamboo.

"Father likes the wilder side of nature," Shan T'u said. "He loves valleys filled with mist, mountains against the sky, cliffs and gorges and storms. Master Po's garden is too prissy for him. This is more to his liking. See those huge, gnarled rocks?"

De Rais nodded. "This is more to *my* liking, too."

The pond water rippled in a warm breeze, and the tree leaves shivered. Shan T'u said, "The bamboo symbolizes strength and friendship. The water lily stands for purity. And the rocks display the awesome powers of nature."

De Rais observed her as she spoke, enjoying her small yet strong frame, with hip outthrust and young breasts swelling against her silk *cheong sam*. Her throat was long and slender, her ears exquisite.

"Beautiful," he said. "Poetic."

"We are a poetic people," she told him. "Or we were, until the Mongols came."

"No more?"

Her voice stiffened. "They crush all that is beautiful. Poetry does not flourish under tyranny."

"It does sometimes," De Rais said. "In songs of patriotism, in tales of heroes and deeds."

Shan T'u lowered her eyes. "Our poets are not warriors."

"A poet doesn't have to swing a sword to write about it," De Rais said. "He needs only to imagine the whistle of the blade, the stink of the enemy's sweat, the pounding of his heart as he slams his steel into bone. . . ."

"And this is *poetry?*"

He laughed. "Well, maybe that was a bit savage. But yes, there is poetry in blood and honor. In fighting for Sweet France, as Roland did, in celebrating the glories of paladins."

"Are *you* a paladin?"

This brought a great guffaw. "Not me, Princess. A paladin is a fine knight. I'm not a fine knight at all. And anyway, most of our knights are foul-smelling ruffians who would just as soon burn a village and rape the women as earn their booty in combat."

She sniffed haughtily. "Your people sound like Mongols."

"Maybe so. But *your* people sound like women who put out their necks to be stepped on."

"Don't you think we want to fight?"

"You're not doing much of it."

"Against the Mongol hordes? Their armies can ride three hundred miles in a night, turn their horses in one motion . . . they are the most brutal war machine invented."

"Yes, I've heard these things said about the Tatars. They certainly kicked the derrieres of the Poles and the Teutonic Knights. A nasty crowd."

"Then why do you mock us?"

"Because these villains took your country. I'd be damned before I'd let a pack of nomads take France from under my nose."

Shan T'u shook her head. "This is idle talk. You only want rewards. And to convert those nomads to your God, or so you said."

"Oh, of course, of course."

"Well, do so. Maybe they'll leave us alone."

De Rais seized her arms gently. "Don't wait for that to happen, Princess."

Her face tilted up. His yellow beard and hair made his head seem like a second sun. "We need a great hero," she said dreamily, "to rise up and lead us."

"You need some good soldiering."

"A hero," she insisted. "A second Yi."

"Who?"

"The great archer whose arrows shot down the children of the Supreme Ruler. They were ten suns, and each day one of them rode across the sky. When they all rose in the sky together one time and burned the crops and seared the earth, Yi shot them down. They fell to earth as crows and only one sun remained."

He smiled charmingly. "You remember the stories of your childhood."

"Another Yi will come," she said, "with a magic bow."

"No, Shan T'u. There is no magic."

Her eyes smoldered. "Do you like to crush belief?"

"No. I like to face reality." His head blotted the summer sun. His lips brushed her own, then pressed hard. She resisted, but the small fires shooting through her body weakened her. His lips parted hers, and his moist tongue darted into her mouth.

For a moment, madness possessed Shan T'u. Her small arms flung around his massive body, lost in the rough folds of his cloak. She pressed urgently against him, her breast tips hard against the silk of her *cheong sam*. She could think only of his nakedness. She heard herself moan with pleasure.

His hands kneaded the small of her back and then

encircled her slim hips, rubbing the silk against her aroused skin. Then his hands came up to her excited breasts, molding to their budding shape. She hissed as her nipples pushed between his fingers.

And as quickly as the forbidden desire had flared, it cooled. The bray of a camel shocked her into realization. This was her father's palace! This was the friar!

He stepped away from her and looked searchingly into her wide, terrified eyes. "Your gardens have a dangerous effect, Princess."

Her throat was shut, and words barely escaped. "I don't know what made me . . ."

"Yes you do." He folded his palms soothingly around her feverish neck and his fingertips stroked her chiseled jawline. "And so do I."

"But you're a holy man . . ."

"A man."

"You can be executed for what you did."

"I'd die smiling."

"How can you jest about this?"

"Because in my land a man may kiss a woman without incurring the wrath of God, and two lovers may laugh on a sunny day in a beautiful garden."

Shan T'u shook her head. "No. I sinned. Lady Feng was right about me. I cannot be a true princess."

"Does a princess have to be a nun?"

"Stop taunting me!" Her face tingled under his touch and she wrenched away. "You don't understand our customs. Here a woman is inferior; nothing else is held so cheaply."

"Even a princess?"

"Yes. Women are prostitutes, or midwives, or bearers of children. If we are of royal blood, we can be bartered to foreign potentates. We are forbidden to talk of outside affairs inside our apartments. We are forbidden to sit together with men, or look beyond the palace walls. We learn obedience—to our fathers, our brothers, and our husbands."

De Rais's eyes were round with astonishment. "But surely this is madness. A woman may be created to become a wife and mother, but a man may still welcome the company of a pleasant maiden."

Shan T'u took his hands in hers. "But we are not in your land. I have walked with you, and spoken of political matters, and shared intimate pleasures that are only for concubines or wives."

"And this makes you a sinner?"

"Yes."

"Even if you *liked* it?"

Shan T'u blushed. "You truly don't understand. It is bound up with yin and yang, with the elements of sun and moon, depth and height, light and darkness, strength and weakness. We are yin, and you are yang; and we cannot take on your traits, nor must you take ours, or there is no balance."

"But there is love! And that means being *out* of balance."

She let his hands drop and turned away. "No. Perhaps in France a holy man can embrace a princess and speak of love. Not here. In my life, I have defied my father and done wicked things. But today I threw off my childhood ways and took the responsibility of a woman and a princess. I cannot go further in this flirtation."

"I don't believe you. You're just afraid."

"Yes, I'm afraid!" Her limbs were trembling and

she hugged herself to still her tremors. "Friar, why do you pursue me? I am a princess, and a woman, and I carry all of Chinese civilization within me. In these dark times, I am bound to preserve that civilization."

De Rais snorted. "I see. You've been listening to that old tutor."

"Yes," she whispered. "The fates brought him to me and let him show me the truth at the last moment. He has bound me to a destiny more important than my appetites."

"You can pursue your destiny, Princess, *and* slake your appetites."

"*No.*" She spun and faced him with a breaking heart. "You shunned me at first, Friar, when I was all too willing to be wicked. You laughed at me for being a child and said the rewards my father will give you are more important than my kisses. Why do you court me now, when I have forsworn such behavior? Why do you break your oaths to your God? You are no better than Wei Ku. At least he didn't spout holy lies."

De Rais glared mutely at her, restraining a great fury. Shan T'u feared for her life in that instant as she imagined those powerful hands around her throat. Instead, the friar thrust an arm to the ground and scooped up a gnarled white stone. With a howl of rage and anguish, he hurled the stone across the pond and into the wood. Shan T'u heard the stone crash among the pine branches.

De Rais faced the pond, heaving great breaths. He clenched his fists and threw back his head so that his eyes challenged the sun. Then he turned to Shan T'u and the sun remained in his eyes, blinding her.

"Get back to your father," he said in a deadly voice. "And to your customs. Child? You are a baby. *Go!*"

She winced at his shout and tried desperately to think of a reply. But her insides crumbled and her eyes filled and she could only turn and hurry from the desecrated garden. He had merely thrown a rock and disturbed the artistic beauty. She had nearly surrendered to her desires and disturbed the universe.

But more vital—she had resisted. She had been true to Master Po. And she burned with his kiss and yearned for the friar more than ever.

No greater parade had been mounted by Prince Chang Hu than the caravan that majestically plodded beneath the mighty gate of the palace. Bearded soldiers led the way, mounted on caparisoned stallions. Next came horse-drawn catapults. Following them were bullock carts, groaning under provisions. Then came wagon after wagon of foodstuffs, clothing, and dry goods interspersed with camels whose humped backs swayed under their loads.

Arrays of mounted huntsmen followed, their horses plumed and blazing with pinpoints of golden light. Falconers rode with their birds perched on their wrists. Behind the hunters, the groaning, proud camel pulled Shan T'u's curtained, ornamented cart surrounded by a sweating royal guard.

More soldiers rode behind the cart, and behind the soldiers rode Friar William De Rais in the company of berobed Buddhist monks. The shaven heads of the Chinese monks contrasted with De Rais's sun-washed locks and beard.

Still more wagons followed the royal procession, some of them carrying priceless gifts of gold, pottery, and jade for the Indian potentate. Musicians played frantically as they brought up the rear. The remainder of Chang's household lined the caravan route, clapping and chattering.

Prince Chang Hu sat astride his coal-black horse, swathed in salmon robes. His face, beneath his elaborately pinned topknot, glistened in the afternoon sun. A soldier detached himself from the caravan and guided his horse to the prince. The horse dipped its head and whickered softly as the soldier bent close to Chang.

"We are ready to kill the friar," the soldier said.

"Good." Prince Chang nodded without changing his expression. "Remember, let the holy man guide you to the river crossing where the prince's minions will meet you. Once there, kill him swiftly. If he makes a wrong move before that, kill him on the spot."

"It will be done."

Chang smiled with satisfaction. "A very clever fellow, this false friar. But a man's lust will betray him every time. So he wants to steal my daughter away? Well, he'll have no ransom." Chang raised a brawny arm in salute as his daughter's cart rumbled past. "Only his head on a stake in the middle of the desert."

With a wave of his hand, Chang dismissed the soldier, who rode back to the procession. Chang walked his steed to where Lady Feng sat beneath a parasol held by a servingwoman. Chang looked down at Lady Feng, who was elegantly bedecked in silk brocade.

"I suppose you want a fat reward for telling me about the little scene at the riverbank," Chang said.

Lady Feng's lips curled into a crimson smile. "Only the reward of your trust and friendship, my prince."

"Indeed," Chang said. He laughed, showing yellowed teeth. "A serpent may be useful for catching rats, but it is not a beast to be trusted. Sleep cautiously, Lady Feng."

Lady Feng retained her cool expression and nodded in bland deference. Prince Chang urged his horse forward at a trot until he rode alongside the royal cart. *"Daughter!"* he bellowed.

The silk curtain was pulled back and Shan T'u's shadowed face looked out. "Father!"

"I know we made our farewells, Daughter. But one final glimpse of your face."

Shan T'u's eyes glistened. "I beg you for the last time, Father. Don't send me to this prince."

"Stop sniveling!" Chang snarled. "Even at the last, you defy me."

"No," Shan T'u whispered. "I do not defy you. I will wed this prince and bear him children. I will raise your name high in foreign lands. I will bring the glories of our people to India and await the day when we conquer our own land again."

Chang's eyes widened and a reptilian grin split his face. "Well! Finally, the talk of a princess. Good fortune, Daughter! Good fortune!"

Prince Chang roared with laughter and pivoted his horse away from the cart. He reviewed the majestic scene as it wended its way past pavilions and reflecting pools. In the cart, Shan T'u let the curtain drop back and wept silently, her tears drowned in the stamping hooves, the music, and the shouts.

And far behind her cart, William De Rais rode expertly, his lips warm with the impress of Shan T'u's mouth, and his arms tingling from her body. And all at once, his plans were changed and his destiny was rewritten.

Chapter Six

THE WEDDING CARAVAN WOUND SINUOUSLY ACROSS THE grasslands, silhouetted against a vast sky. Dense white clouds spread over the heavens, and a hot wind blasted the savannah.

From her cart, Shan T'u watched the long miles pass by. The great, gilded wheels were meticulously balanced, and only now and then did she feel a thump or bump. She looked with sympathy at the camel driver as he became slicked with sweat beneath his ornamental tunic. The rippling of his back muscles reminded her of the friar.

Buffalo grazed near streams, their shaggy bodies aswarm with flies. A flock of birds veered toward the west. Shan T'u looked back over her shoulder to see her father's palace, but the angle was not right. She settled against the cushions and shut her eyes to lessen the cruel heat.

The caravan made camp at evening, and Shan T'u was helped from her cart. She stood in a great meadow, near a pond bordered with elms and mulberries. This was still her father's province. She knew that treacherous mountain passes would come after the rolling green hills.

The encampment became busy as servants set up cooking pots and hunters watered their horses and sharpened their weapons. Soon there was the smell of tea and the hum of idle chatter. Shan T'u strayed from her personal retinue with a decorated parasol over her shoulder. She smiled and spoke kindly to the hunters, soldiers, and retainers she passed.

She reached the grassy summit of a sloping hill and gazed down into the sunken meadow. She saw the friar combing the mane of his horse. Near him, a wrinkled porter sat cross-legged and played a mouth organ called a *sheng*.

In a sudden, thrilling commotion, the hunters mounted their horses. Shan T'u's heart rose as she watched them wheel their mounts and gallop off with a thunder that shook the grass. The friar stopped grooming his animal to watch the hunters. He held his horse's reins, and even though he was too far away for Shan T'u to make out his features, his gaze was clearly one of deep longing. Shan T'u felt the wind blow her robe and threaten her coiffure. For a moment, she imagined herself alongside the friar, both of them riding like the wind.

Shan T'u turned away and watched the hunters. They rode toward a wooded area. Meanwhile, near the princess, two porters whipped an exhausted bullock who pulled a creaking cart up the hill. The whistle and crack of the whip blended with the shouts of the hunters and the drumming of their horses.

Dry rations of cooked grain were being passed around and eaten by retainers. The smell of frying leeks sizzled against the scent of pines. Shan T'u wondered what the concubines were doing now at court, or what pleasures her father was pursuing. Her heart ached with homesickness. She walked back to her cart, barely glancing at a circle of soldiers playing cards. But suddenly there were triumphant shouts from the woods, and Shan T'u spun to see.

Her eyes caught the sudden, startling clap of wings as a trained Korean falcon whipped through the air. Two hunters exploded from the brush, bows drawn. Arrows geysered into the evening sky and there was a crash in the woods. Members of the caravan shouted and pointed. Shan T'u leaned forward, her lips parted in excitement.

The horses burst from the forest and hunters held aloft their trophies: pheasants, foxes, and rabbits. The hunters seemed frozen against the shimmering green-wood as they pounded up the hillside. Then, abruptly, they were upon the princess in a melee of flying hooves.

Shan T'u stood her ground as the mighty horses reared and stamped around her, snorting and dribbling foam from their black lips. She grabbed the bridle of one horse and spoke soothingly to the beast. The hunters were smeared with dust. "A good catch," Shan T'u said.

"These are well-stocked woods."

"Yes," she agreed. "I wonder whose they are."

The hunters laughed. As Shan T'u waved, they

rode toward the great bronze cooking pots and dropped the bloody carcasses on the ground with loud thuds. Priests in saffron robes scurried forward to claim part of the kill for sacrificial purposes, and chattering women flailed at the rest, plucking feathers and skinning.

Shan T'u returned to her personal entourage, well apart from the others. A spacious tent had been erected for her, and she ducked inside and sat on cushions. Two porters sat at the tent's opening with great fans, keeping insects away. Two servingwomen prepared a makeshift bath for Shan T'u by boiling water in iron pots and pouring it into a bronze tub decorated with golden dragons. The servingwomen then added fragrant oils to the water.

Shan T'u shed her kimono with a hiss of relief and unpinned her hair. She shook her head gloriously to let the glossy ebony waves whirl free. Grime coated her velvety skin and she sank gratefully into the warm, scented water. She rested her neck against the curve of the tub and looked lazily at her body, pale gold beneath the surface. Her hand traced the contour of one breast, causing her to gasp a little. Her fingers wandered over the tender mound of her stomach and up one raised thigh. Her heart beat faster and her nostrils flared as she recalled the friar's hands.

Shan T'u stood, dripping. The servingwomen washed her thighs and calves, her backside and her belly, her breasts and between her legs. She lifted her arms sensuously and draped handfuls of hair over her forehead. Her lips curved into a dreamy smile. Her nerves leaped to joyful life at the touch of the sponges. She could smell cooking meat in the heat of the evening, and the sap of pine. She could smell the excrement of camels and horses and the stink of unwashed porters and soldiers. She liked all of these smells, for she was a child of nature.

Shan T'u lowered herself into the water to rinse one final time and her hands languished over the sides of the tub. Idly, she watched a salamander creep up the side of the tent. The servingwomen, splashed with water, turned to prepare Shan T'u's garments.

For that reason, they did not see the tent flap suddenly yank upward. Shan T'u's eyes widened in horror as the friar ducked inside!

"Princess . . . !" he began, and then paused. His mouth tugged into a grin. "Well!"

Shan T'u ignored the screeching of her servingwomen. "Friar, this is becoming a bad habit."

The friar bowed, but he couldn't stop smiling. He backed out of the tent and Shan T'u heard his bellowing laughter and the scuffle of approaching soldiers. She stood up and allowed her servingwomen to dry her. She stepped out of the tub, tingling, and was dressed in a fresh *cheong sam*. She refused the repinning of her hair, which caused consternation and wailing among the servingwomen.

"Be still!" she snapped. "He is a holy man, not a Mongol."

This only reduced the women to whimpering and hand wringing. Shan T'u left the tent and stepped into the sunset. The sky was aflame with vermilion light, and the clouds were fringed with luminous white. The tips of the trees swayed in the breeze and cattle lowed on distant hillsides. Shan T'u's still-damp skin shivered.

Near the campfire, the friar was being detained by

four burly soldiers, each with a crossbow aimed at his throat. De Rais held a book.

Shan T'u approached the tense scene. "At ease, officers. This holy man won't harm me."

The soldiers hesitated, then lowered their weapons. De Rais said to Shan T'u, "You look lovely."

"Thank you. Soldiers, you may have your dinner."

There was relieved murmuring among the four guardsmen as they moved away into the gathering darkness. Shan T'u faced De Rais across the leaping fire.

"Just once," she said, "it would be pleasant if you begged entry and waited until I gave permission."

His smile returned. "You would never believe me, Princess, if I told you that I was excited about *this*." He held up the book.

"Ah," she said. "Let me see."

He handed over the book. She examined it, careful not to reveal her ability to read. It was a book of Confucian philosophy, printed and bound in a big city to the north. The book was several years old and well thumbed. "Where did you get this?"

"One of the priests. I didn't know what it was."

She laughed pleasantly. "It's a book, Friar. Don't you have books in France?"

"We have illustrated books of great beauty, but nothing that looks like this. How did the scribe print it so perfectly? And why so small?"

Shan T'u stared at him. "Do you truly not understand?"

De Rais shook his head.

"My dear Mongol from Europe," she said teasingly. "This was not printed by hand. It was printed mechanically, by means of clay blocks that can be moved about to form words."

De Rais's eyes narrowed suspiciously. He snatched the book from her hand and looked closely at it. "Clay blocks?"

She nodded.

"That move about?"

She laughed delightedly. "Not by themselves, you donkey. The printer must move them. He has a machine that presses the inked blocks against the paper and makes impressions."

"Paper . . . ?"

"That's what the book is printed on!"

De Rais looked again at the book, flipping the pages. "It is smoother than our paper."

Shan T'u looked at the firelight on the friar's face. "You really have no books?"

"Not printed books. I have heard stories of printing devices, but I've never seen one."

"We print many things. Books, money—"

"You *print* money?"

"Yes, also on paper. One can use it in many provinces and engage more freely in trade."

De Rais held the book almost reverently. "Paper money. Printed books. I am continually humbled by this land."

"You think better of us now?"

"Or worse of myself," De Rais said archly. "You know how to live in comfort. And how to fight, too, if your weapons mean anything."

"Our bows?"

"To hell with your bows. You've got multiple ballistas and some fancy catapults that don't hurl rocks."

"Oh, the exploding stones."

"Exploding stones?"

"I can't explain it," she said. "Perhaps the soldiers will show it to you."

"I'd like that."

She turned toward the meadow and saw many fires outlined against a red sky. The haunting strains of music drifted across the field: bronze bells and stone chimes, drums and flutes, harps and lutes.

"Friar," she said, "the priests will be offering prayer. And there will be entertainment. Perhaps you wish to walk?"

The wind danced between them. His eyes were phosphorescent in the dusk. "Yes."

His fingers closed around her hand and at once she felt the sweet tremors that his touch produced. But she would not succumb. *He*, after all, was the barbarian, and she the civilized princess. Everything was in balance now, though it tore her heart in pieces.

They walked together through sifting grass, she with small dancing steps, he with a soldier's strides. She sensed his muscles moving beneath his cloak, and his brave heart beating in his chest. She remembered his narrow hips and naked sex, and her hand grew damp in his.

The priests had gathered around their own fire, in the midst of which stood a gleaming bronze ritual vessel decorated with silver dragons. On carts nearby, stone figurines had been set out.

"That peaceful one is Kasyapa," Shan T'u whispered to De Rais as she pointed out a figure. "And the fierce-looking statue is a King of Heaven who protects Buddha from evil spirits."

"Nasty fellow," De Rais commented. He watched

the priests at meditation, the firelight casting eerie shadows on their shaven heads. Shan T'u bowed her head and whispered her own prayers and De Rais fell into rapt wonder at the marvelous perfection of her forehead and cheekbones, the wetness fringing her closed eyes, and the swell of her moving lips. Everything about her was exquisite and carved, yet she possessed an inner strength. She was so different from the maidens he'd bedded in France, so much closer to the chivalric ideal of womanhood. The wenches of De Rais's homeland *could* be innocently lovely, but they tended to be bigger boned and often afflicted with blemishes and bad teeth. And the lustiest of the village lasses had much to learn about bathing.

A smile touched his lips as he thought of his past adventures and contrasted other nights, in barns or on battlefields, with this night in an exotic land. The surging lust that had overcome him at the nearness of Shan T'u transmuted now to something more reposeful.

The spell lasted for a long time as the music chimed and tinkled in the wind. The sky darkened to violet and luminous blue, through which the first stars of night sparkled. Shan T'u at last looked up and clasped her finely wrought hands together. Her eyes, agleam with reflected firelight, seemed to dance.

"Are your prayers done?" De Rais asked.

She didn't turn. "It is easier in a monastery. There is a beautiful one near my father's palace. There are pine trees and jade images of Buddha and libraries of holy scriptures all bound in lacquer cases."

"Then Buddha is your god."

She seemed to consider. "There are three ways for

us. The way of Buddha, the way of Confucius, and the way of the Tao." She smiled.

"Which way do *you* follow?"

"In truth, I follow all three. Confucius gives me the wisdom of the sages to know what I must do among men in this world. The Tao bids me know the innermost secrets of nature and my place *within* nature. And Buddha offers me the holy scriptures to learn that all I see and feel is illusion, so that I may know the path to salvation."

She looked at De Rais and her eyes glowed with faith. De Rais could not speak; his mercenary heart had been touched by her sweetness and devotion. He grasped her hands impulsively. "Shan T'u . . ."

She smiled girlishly. "Has my philosophy silenced you? Have *you* no religion, Friar?"

His eyes turned cold for a long moment as they journeyed far from this fragrant hillside. When he returned, he was quiet and sad. "As a Christian, I seek salvation through our Lord Jesus Christ and the Holy Roman Church," De Rais said. "But I find my Mother the Church very cold. Sometimes . . . sometimes I want to find my Lord in the deep woods, or on a cliff, or in a flowered meadow."

Shan T'u seemed entranced. "That sounds like the way of Tao."

He laughed. "But it should *not* sound that way, Princess. If I ran about France prattling of finding God in the woods and not in the Church, I would be put to the torch."

"They would *burn* you?"

"As a heretic. And probably touse me a bit on the rack first."

"How horrible. But you are a holy man . . ."

He laughed a second time, more hollowly. "The robes of a friar do not always ensure safety from the Inquisition. One wrong word, one syllable chanted without conviction—or what *they* think is conviction . . ."

"Brrr, what a bitter place you come from, Friar."

"Well, your Mongols don't seem a great improvement from what I hear."

She withdrew her hands and sighed. "That is something not Confucius nor Buddha nor the Tao can help."

"But those weapons can help. And your soldiers seem brave and strong."

"Nobody can fight the Mongols!" she said fiercely. "No Chinese battalion can overcome their hordes."

"Sounds to me like you've all talked yourselves into it. No soldier's got magic on his side. I'd like to meet some of these Mongols."

"Haven't you?"

He shook his head. "I spotted some riders, and I think once or twice, at night, they surrounded me. But they never challenged me, and I haven't journeyed far enough north to encounter them in great numbers." He smiled. "Besides, they like foreigners."

"Yes," Shan T'u agreed. She turned back to him. "I wish you were not a friar, William De Rais. I wish you were a warrior sent from Heaven to raise up an army and defeat the Khan."

"More fairy stories," he chided. "Don't depend on legends, Shan T'u." He smiled cryptically. "But don't believe what you see, either. *Cucullus non facit monachum.*"

88

"I don't understand French . . ."

"That was Latin, Princess. I'll translate it before you meet your prince."

Shan T'u stiffened and walked quickly away. De Rais followed. He caught up with Shan T'u where several girls were playing instruments and dancing. Shan T'u stood with her slim back toward De Rais and her arms crossed.

On the ground, around a fire, four seated girls played bamboo mouth organs and strummed lutes. The three dancers turned and whirled. A sizable audience had gathered to watch them.

De Rais's eyes mirrored the movements of the dancing girls. He put up his cowl to ward off the wind. "Shan T'u, why did you run?"

Her eyes brimmed with tears. "I did not wish to be reminded of my fate just then."

"I apologize."

"It's my own fault."

"For enjoying yourself?"

"Please leave me."

He exhaled in frustration. His hands folded over her shoulders, causing her back to arch. "I liked being with you tonight, Princess," he whispered. "I don't give a damn what your customs say. You're as good company as any man. I hope your Indian prince treats you better than your father did."

Her tears flowed more rapidly now. "Thank you," she said. "You have cheered me."

"Good night, Shan T'u," the friar murmured, and he softly kissed her cheek.

The thudding of a horse's hooves stopped De Rais from melting into the night and forced Shan T'u to blink back her sadness. The horseman rode into the firelight and dismounted. He was a soldier in the caravan, and he slapped dust from his trousers.

"Princess," he gasped, "I ran into some bargemen from Tien-Chin, the city to the east. They say that the red masks are marauding the mountains as close as ten miles from here."

There was much murmuring. The music and dancing had stopped. "Who are the red masks?" Shan T'u demanded.

"Bandits," the soldier said. "Fierce bandits who have killed travelers and taken their belongings. Their leader's name is Kung. He can send an arrow through a man's throat at a hundred yards."

This brought gasps. Shan T'u whirled to face her people. "Listen to me! We have a battalion of my father's finest fighting men, and fifty of my father's most skilled huntsmen. Surely we should not fear bandits in the hills."

De Rais had returned to the fire. "You ought to fear them if they attack first."

Shan T'u's eyes blazed as she looked at him. "You don't make military decisions, Friar."

The soldier said, "Now wait a minute. He's been through those mountains. Maybe he knows what he's talking about."

"I say he does not!" Shan T'u's words silenced the chatter and brought a frightening stillness, interrupted only by the nickering of animals. "We will go on. We will be watchful. We will speak to the officers of this city tomorrow when we pass through it. I must meet my prince at the specified time."

There was a good deal of residual grumbling. The soldier looked from Shan T'u to De Rais, then kowtowed. He led his horse away. Shan T'u and De Rais were alone by the guttering fire.

"Why so determined?" De Rais asked.

"I will not be frightened by bandits."

He studied her. "Maybe you *wish* to be attacked, Princess? So you can escape in the fighting and avoid your fate? For all your pious devotion to principle, you're still a fighter."

Shan T'u pushed back her blowing hair. "You make rash assumptions, Friar."

"Sound ones, I think." He wrapped his cloak more tightly around him. "But you risk the lives of all your entourage. Bandits like this will shoot from cover, cut your soldiers down one by one. They can do this day after day, night after night, until you've got nobody. And then they'll take *you*."

"Ah," Shan T'u whispered. "And you care about that because your reward is at stake."

"Exactly."

"Then protect me, Friar. Make sure I don't die."

He smiled. "Shan T'u, I care about more than my reward. If the situation is right, *I* might carry you off."

"Oho," she said. "The *real* bandit unmasks."

"And I wonder," he said, "if you would fight me."

He laughed impudently as she turned away in haughty rejection. Then he was gone, swallowed in darkness. Shan T'u remained near the dying fire, shivering in the night wind. Tonight had been more frightening than the other encounters with him; tonight she had felt something stir deep in her heart, beyond fleshly desire and beyond defiance. She wondered how truly the friar had read her just now.

Chapter Seven

EARLY THE NEXT MORNING, THREE HORSEMEN RODE UP
to the soldiers at the head of Shan T'u's caravan.
They were aristocrats, clothed in brocaded gowns and
hats of marten fur. The horsemen brought greetings
from the county magistrate and offered to conduct the
caravan through the city of Tien-chin. Shan T'u's
captain agreed, and the caravan, under escort, majestically rolled over the grassy countryside under a fresh
blue sky.

Soon, Shan T'u's cart rumbled over a wide bridge
on the banks of the city's moat, and passersby lined up
along the railings to watch this fabulous sight. Two
workers urged their mule to haul a wheelbarrow out
of the way, and laborers whipped their oxcarts into

side streets. A great shouting and commotion went up, and soon there were running feet, waving arms, and a blur of color as the town turned out to watch the caravan of the princess.

Shan T'u filled her senses with the activities of the city. She watched a herd of pigs driven across the road, and she felt her heart catch when she saw the hobnailed double doors of a Buddhist temple. What would Master Po think of the mingling of sacred and profane when she clasped the friar's hand before the priests?

Shan T'u pushed away the conflict and waved to the ecstatic onlookers. The arrival of the caravan had flushed out the wealthy inhabitants of the city, who now trundled up in sedan chairs and astride horses to proudly join the procession. They passed beneath the great gate of the city into a world of noise and color.

Peasants looked up from a letter writer's stall at the commotion, and at a *cheng tien* festooned with hangings, the affluent wine drinkers stopped socializing to point and gossip.

Now a clatter of hoofbeats alerted Shan T'u and an imperious nobleman rode up beside her litter. He sat astride an Arabian horse that flicked its ears haughtily. "I have heard," the nobleman said, "that you are the Princess Shan T'u, daughter of the Prince Chang Hu, and that this is your wedding journey."

"It is so," Shan T'u acknowledged.

The nobleman smiled. "Then I offer you congratulations, and on behalf of the magistrate I throw open the hospitality of Tien-chin to you and to your retainers. Our wineshops and bathhouses are at your disposal."

Shan T'u nodded. "My gratitude to you."

"Wang Wei is my name," the nobleman announced. "My family owns many acres of land adjacent to the city. We are most proud to greet the daughter of our prince and benefactor."

"And I likewise am honored to be greeted by one of my father's loyal subjects," Shan T'u said.

The caravan wound tortuously through the center of town amid open-air shops. Everywhere, citizens stopped their business to gather and talk excitedly. Fireworks cracked nearby and music played. The stink of human sweat, rotting produce, and unwashed animals made a pungent mélange. Flies swarmed about the cart and Wang Wei flailed at them with one brocaded arm.

"Princess," the nobleman said, "there is something I must say."

"Yes?"

"I have heard that our officials warned you last night of the mountain bandits."

"They did."

"And you paid no heed to the warning."

Shan T'u smiled. "I heeded the warning. I chose not to be frightened by it."

Wang Wei sighed, clearly searching for words. A scholar in a wide-brimmed hat and stiff beard rode his horse past a medicine dealer.

"Princess," Wang Wei said, "I urge you to divert your caravan some miles to the south to avoid the mountain passes."

"Are these bandits so fearsome?"

"They are cutthroats. Already, some of us have suffered irretrievable losses. It is said that these red masks want to raise an army against the Mongols, and so they take the purses of the rich to build a treasury."

Shan T'u smiled. "I see. So these bandits must be peasants."

"Undoubtedly," Wang Wei said. "Now your caravan, Princess, is laden with rare gifts. These jackals will feast upon you."

The caravan had passed out of the raucous main square and onto a shaded, tranquil street. Pale green willows dropped their supple branches. Off-duty soldiers dozed at the doorway of their quarters, and the wineshops and restaurants were empty of customers. Sedan bearers sat and talked under the willows.

"Wang Wei," the princess said, "I appreciate your fears for my life. But a detour to the south would consume many more days. My prince awaits me. My soldiers are brave and skilled. A friar guides us who has made the journey through the mountains. I will take the chance."

Wang Wei shook his head as his horse's tail switched at insects. "I despair at your decision."

Shan T'u laughed musically. "I know, Wang Wei. You fear that I will be ambushed and all our treasure lost. You fear that word of this will reach my father. You fear that he will wreak vengeance on you for failing to warn me. You see your lands seized and your heads cut off. My own safety pales beside your own."

Wang Wei blanched at her words. "I take exception to your implications, Princess."

"Nevertheless, you don't deny them."

Now they moved along the banks of the Tien canal, where massive barges laden with produce were rowed or pulled from the shore. The stench of stagnant water came up hot from the canal, and royal retainers hurried with fans to repel black clouds of mosquitoes. Cormorants and gulls dove from slanted rooftops.

"I am sorry you feel this way, Princess," Wang Wei said. "I think you are being unreasonable."

"Perhaps it amuses me to think of how you will fret until my caravan passes safely through the hills."

Wang Wei sniffed. "Very well, Princess. I wish you a safe journey."

Wang Wei snapped the reins and dug his thighs into the belly of his horse. The animal whickered, and plunged into the crowds, scattering laborers. Shan T'u laughed to herself. *That*, she longed to tell De Rais, was why the Chinese did not challenge the Mongol. The Mongol offered his life at all times to his Khan. The Chinese noble hugged his moneybags.

Finally, the caravan wound through the outskirts of Tien-chin, past shops, rice paddies, and small raised pavilions. Workers unloaded sacks of grain from a barge as their overseer shouted directions. Ahead, Shan T'u could glimpse the green countryside.

A horseman rode up beside her, and for an instant she wondered if Wang Wei had returned with a second appeal. But it was the friar. His cowl was pushed back and his hair was matted with perspiration. "No refreshment in the city?" he asked.

She smiled. "I did not want to lose time or retainers."

"A beneficent ruler."

"A fit queen of India, do you think?"

"No." He peered into the distance. "Yonder lies the greenwood. And the mountains beyond that. Are your bowmen ready for the red masks?"

"Have they been filling *your* ears with stories?"

"I believe the stories," De Rais said sharply. "And I intend to remain close to you. Your folly may cost a few lives."

A shiver of anger rippled through her. "So, you also think me a fool. We shall see, Friar."

"No doubt." He urged his horse ahead. Shan T'u let the curtain drop and sat in the hot, cushioned shadow of her cart. Her heart raced with worry. She had made the first royal decision of her young life, and perhaps had endangered her caravan. Had she decided impetuously, out of spite?

The sounds and smells of the city receded behind her, replaced by the call of birds, the buzz of woodland insects, and the rush of summer wind. There was no turning back now.

Two days later, the caravan came to the end of the rolling hills and began its torturous journey through the mountains. With each hour, the pathways plunged more treacherously into rock. Scrub trees grew crazily from boulders that jutted over swirling rapids. Massive stone shelves loomed over the road. Foaming cataracts crashed and plunged to the boiling river below. The blue sky turned slate gray. Lightning flickered eerily, and peals of thunder reverberated back and forth between the twisted cliffs.

The soldiers, their horses skittish, craned their necks as their sharp eyes looked for signs of bandits. They saw wild mountain goats and frightened birds wheeling over whirlpools. The caravan crossed rotting wooden bridges and passed through a valley that reflected lurid light as night approached.

The rain began as pelting drops, then quickly became a hissing torrent that drenched man and horse. Still the caravan pressed on. The sky heaved with black, roiling clouds. Servants wore straw rain cloaks. Heads were bowed under the downpour and exhausted animals smelled of rain as they pulled groaning wagons. Shan T'u huddled and prayed, starting at peals of thunder.

Suddenly, she felt the cart plunge noseward, and there were shouts and curses. She pulled aside the curtain and saw two of her servants, knee-deep in surging gray water, yanking at the reins of the camel. The beast raised its soaked head to the sky and brayed woefully as its eyes rolled. The cart was so badly tilted that Shan T'u had to grasp the wooden doorframe to keep from tumbling.

"What's wrong?" she shouted.

"We're stuck!"

Shan T'u could see, by looking to her rear, that the huge spoked wheels of the cart were mired in water and mud. The rain clattered on the canvas roof of the cart and squalled through the parted curtains. Soldiers urged their horses into the whirlpool to help.

A tremendous clap of thunder and a blinding fork of lightning sent the camel into paroxysms of fear. The beast reared back and spat viciously, tearing the reins from the servant's hands. The servant fell backwards into the roaring current.

Shan T'u's blood raced as she tried to think. The entire mountain pass could become flooded soon. "Ropes!" she cried. "Bring ropes and tie them to the camel's bridle!"

Soldiers spurred their horses in response. Shan T'u leaned out of the cart and sheets of rain battered her face and pasted her hair along her neck. Her robe molded to her drenched skin.

"Shan T'u!" The voice was weak against the wind, but she recognized the friar.

"Yes!"

He rode up, his cowl pulled over his head. "Are you all right?"

"So far."

He surveyed the situation. The camel howled and snarled at the servants as the water eddied higher and higher around its legs. The cart jolted, and dipped even more precariously. Shan T'u gasped.

"We must pull you out," De Rais said.

"I've sent for ropes."

"Good."

The friar urged his horse forward. The camel turned its head and spat with drooling lips at the friar. The beast's eyes rolled back in terror.

The soldiers returned with coiled ropes. The friar grabbed one rope and tied an end around his wrist. Shan T'u bit her lip as the cart slid deeper into the sucking mud. The friar walked his horse cautiously through the rising water. The camel tried to back up. *"Non,"* the friar coaxed. *"Calme, calme, mon doux animal."* He continued to talk to the camel as he gauged the distance to the bridle. The rain washed over him and the thunder cracked and boomed. The sky blackened into night.

De Rais now held a loop of rope in his soaked hand. The water hissed around them, up to the animals' bellies now. The camel paused, confused by De Rais's soothing voice.

De Rais coiled, then struck. With a hand as quick as a loosed arrow, he looped the rope around the camel's bit. He cracked a command to his horse and the obedient animal backed up swiftly. De Rais pulled the rope taut and the camel's head shot forward. The beast shrieked in protest.

"Now!" De Rais screamed over the din of the storm. "More ropes! *Vite!*"

The soldiers responded. Each looped a rope and moved in on the immobilized camel while De Rais strained every muscle to keep the beast from shaking loose. Shan T'u could see the veins on his forehead popping and his mouth pull back in a rictus of pain.

The soldiers looped their ropes around the bridle on all sides and urged their horses backward as De Rais had done. "Pull!" De Rais commanded. "Make the hairy bastard move!"

De Rais turned his horse, holding fast to the coiled rope. The soldiers did likewise, and each man spurred his mount. The horses whinnied and stretched out their heads, ears flattened. They pawed and scrabbled to gain an inch of rocky ground. The camel's neck went taut, and then the terrified beast lurched forward with flailing hooves. The cart scraped against rock and shuddered.

"Again!" De Rais shouted.

The men dug their spurred bootheels once more into the bloody flanks of their horses. The horses struggled forward, and pulled the ropes as their muscles cracked. The camel pawed and bleated, then yanked. The cart suddenly lunged up, water cascading from its frame. Shan T'u was thrown violently back onto the soaked cushions.

De Rais kept shouting encouragement and flogging his horse. The soldiers followed. The horses skidded and moved sideways against the swollen current. Each time, the camel was forced to pull, and now, finally, the great creaking wheels began to turn. Water spumed from the gilded spokes. The cart jerked and rolled and moved forward as rain sliced into it. The soldiers cheered and redoubled their efforts. The horses strained, and the camel dragged the cart through the water, up and up, until at last the path beneath them was muddy earth. De Rais looked down at the flood below and then ahead at the sheer cliffs.

"We can camp just around this bend," he told the soldiers. "There are caves. We can light torches and dry our clothes."

The soldiers wearily voiced their approval. The caravan continued up the treacherous path, the horses pulling the camel, and the camel pulling the cart. Thunder smashed the mountains and the lightning was the only illumination. A great, echoing crash made the men look down, and they saw huge boulders come loose. The giant stones plummeted, bounced, and sent up fountains of raging water.

De Rais shut his eyes and crossed himself.

Shan T'u sat in her damp cave as torches cast a flickering red glow on the walls. She shivered miserably in her wet kimono and listened to the hiss of rain outside. For the first time on this journey, Shan T'u was lonely and frightened. She didn't know how high this mountain was, or if they would be able to go on tomorrow.

Her eyes searched the dimness and her nose recoiled at the dank, rotting smell. She sat on the soggy cushions her serving women had set out. Those faithful servants slept now at the mouth of the cave, and outside, two soldiers snored. Shan T'u could not tell if everyone in the entourage had survived the storm.

She blinked back tears and vowed to be brave. At least no bandits would attack tonight.

Her eyes flew open wide. She held her breath, wondering if she had truly heard something. The sound came again—a scrabbling of dirt and a rustling of clothing. And now she heard the harsh rasp of a man's breath.

Her throat shut and her pulse bounded. "Who is it?"

"Shut up," came the familiar whisper.

Shan T'u shut her eyes and exhaled in relief. De Rais crawled into the perimeter of the light and sat beside her. He smelled wet. His cloak was torn and stained.

"Friar," she said softly, "you saved my life."

"I told you I'd look out for you."

Her eyes shone as she looked at him. "You are indeed a hero."

He smiled, and his eyes were like green jade in the dimness. Cave shadows carved deep clefts in his craggy face. "You persist in making a legend of me."

Shan T'u shifted her body on the cushions. "And have you no legends at all, William De Rais?"

For a long time, he didn't answer. Then he nodded, and rested his bearded chin on his upraised knee. "We have many legends, Shan T'u. My favorites are about Charlemagne and his paladins."

"You've mentioned them."

"Especially the stories of Roland, the nephew of

King Charlemagne. He is our greatest hero." De Rais looked intimately at Shan T'u. "When Roland was only fifteen, Princess, he proved himself a knight. Charlemagne had called together all his brave noblemen and challenged them to a quest: to find the Robber Knight of the Ardennes, a knight who could not be defeated, a knight who took what he wished and whose sword carved a path of blood."

"Like the Mongols," Shan T'u said.

"Well, like a very bad knight. And this Robber Knight had in his shield a priceless jewel, so pure that it blinded a foe when its facets caught the rays of the sun. Well, Charlemagne wanted that knight dead, and he wanted that jewel, and he told his nobles to go one by one into the forest, each with a page as escort, to challenge the Robber Knight and win the jewel.

"Now one of the knights was Milon, Roland's father, and of course, Roland was Milon's page and armor bearer. Milon looked and looked and looked and found neither hide nor hair of the Robber Knight. So he gratefully stripped off his heavy armor and fell asleep under a shady tree. Roland was ordered to keep watch."

De Rais leaned closer to Shan T'u. "Roland watched for some time, but he itched to be a knight himself, and he was a very impatient young fellow. So he put on his father's hot, heavy armor, and he rode clanking into the forest to search for the Robber Knight.

"And wouldn't you know it—where every trained paladin had failed, young Roland succeeded! There, only a few feet away, under the mighty oaks, rode the Robber Knight himself, plumes a-flying, armor a-gleaming, horse gigantic and snorting smoke—" De Rais made snorting noises and wiggled his fingers in his ears to imitate a charging horse. Shan T'u giggled.

"And there, right smack in the center of the knight's gleaming shield, was set a magnificent gem. It caught the sun and the blinding light spun out, blue and green and amber and white. And the Robber Knight laughed, as deep as the thunder you hear, and challenged the boy to fight. And while the knight was laughing, young Roland charged!

"Imagine the surprise of the Robber Knight to see this foolhardy youth in all that clanking armor thundering at him on a horse two times too big, with a lance he could barely lift! The Robber Knight readied his own lance, but by then Roland's horse had covered the ground between them and—*crash!*—the Robber Knight was sitting on the earth.

"Roland dismounted and drew his father's sword, which he had to grip with both hands. The Robber Knight swung his own sword with great strength, but Roland parried the blows, and he returned those blows with a courage and might far beyond his green years. The bravery and strength of the lad confounded the Robber Knight, and at last, Roland's sword sliced through flesh and muscle and bone. Blood gushed forth and the Robber Knight fell to the forest floor, dead."

Shan T'u clapped. "Wonderful!"

De Rais smiled. "Of course, when the boy produced the jewel before the court, King Charlemagne made him a paladin, and before long, he was the most renowned of all. *There's* a legend for you, Shan T'u."

Shan T'u felt deliciously sleepy, no longer cold or

afraid. "What an exciting tale, Friar. In so many ways, *you* are a legend come to life. I will be very sad when I leave you."

"Then why leave?"

Her heart bounded. "Please. No more."

"Shan T'u, I've known many women. I thought my jaded heart could never be serious about any. But I can't get *you* out of my heart."

"Liar."

"I do *not* lie!"

Her temples pounded. "How do you dare to ply me with romantic words when you know what you are and what you want? You made a bargain with my father to see me safely to India. In return, he will reward you. You toyed with your life at the hunt to convince my father of your timidity. Whatever you want, you want very much. You even told me that you wouldn't try to seduce me. Now you change your mind. Why? Because we are far from my father's palace?"

De Rais breathed raggedly. "I can understand why you think that, Shan T'u. I told the truth when I first met you, and I tell the truth now. The truth has simply changed. I burn with wanting you."

"So did Wei Ku."

"*No.*" He lowered his voice and moved very close to her. She could see the pearls of perspiration on his forehead and cheeks. "Shan T'u, I thought of you as a child. I thought of you as a barbarian."

"Well, you are honest *now.*"

"Listen to me!" His hands were on her shoulders. "I've been humbled, Shan T'u, by your science and art and poetry, and by your beauty and innocence and

105

courage. You are no child, Princess. No child could heat my blood as you do."

She shook her head even as he pinioned her wrists. "No. Please, Friar . . ."

"Don't call me friar!" he cried.

Her eyes flamed up as they locked with his. "I will not give myself to you."

"I don't seek surrender. I want your love, Shan T'u . . ."

"Never." Her voice cracked across his face like a bullwhip. She trembled like a leaf in a storm. "I cannot love you. Yes, I was tempted. But I accept my destiny."

"We're in the mountains, Shan T'u. High up in the mountains, and there is no palace and no prince and no China."

"Fool. China is everywhere I am. Oh, Friar, I denied what I was. I rode horses, I refused to practice the womanly arts. Even my feet were not bound. The astrologer told my father I'd be crushed by a great red snake because I could not run away. So he left my feet unbound so I could run—"

"Then let's run, Shan T'u!"

"I've stopped running, Friar." She cried freely now. "My feet may not be lily feet, but my soul is bound and my life is bound. When you came, Friar, I had forbidden dreams. I even tried to flee alone, the night you stopped me. But Master Po had planted the seeds of my destiny, and just as my wedding journey approached, the seeds sprouted. I became a princess and left the foolish, wicked girl behind."

De Rais drew her body close. His voice was thunder and his look was lightning. "Shan T'u, I also knew what my destiny was meant to be. But I could *not* be what my destiny proclaimed. And you, too, are meant to defy your destiny."

"I must not—"

"*Why?* Great God in Heaven, I know I speak heresy and I know I damn my immortal soul, but you're the most important thing in my wasted life. I defy everything. My Church, my father, my own greed. Defy your father, Shan T'u. Defy your prince. Defy Master Po."

"I cannot."

"You *will* not."

Her voice was barely a breath. "Very well, then. I will not."

His hands tightened, and his face turned dark. His lips curled into an animal snarl. "You little fool. Can you tell me you don't want me? Can you tell me *this* means nothing?"

Without warning, his mouth sought hers and forced her lips apart. She tried to scream, but the scream died in her throat. Her hands strained against his grip, her fingers spread wide. His tongue pried apart her teeth and combed the hot inside of her mouth, and it burned, oh, how it burned! Helpless, her own sweet tongue answered.

"No . . ." she sobbed, but there was no denial left. His lips were on her tender throat, moving down, leaving fiery souvenirs of his passion. Now his mouth kissed the ridge of her collarbone and journeyed across her chest. Her fingers quivered, then curled over his hands. He released her, tore at the folds of her kimono, and wrenched the damp silk from her shoulders. He looked at her naked breasts heaving in the torchlight.

Tears streamed down her flushed face, and her body

seemed to wither under his gaze. His words came thick and slurred. "Can your body say no, Shan T'u? *Can it?*"

His hands forced her down against the cushions. Her bare back felt the wetness. Her nipples peaked in the dank cave air as his head descended like the head of a wolf. He suckled at each breast, swirling his tongue over the pink blossoms until they felt as if they'd burst. He kissed the pillowed underside of each breast, bringing her again and again to a dizzying peak of desire.

Her hands trembled in the air, uncertain. Her knowledge of what was about to happen stifled her breath. She couldn't stop it now. Her fingers plunged, found his matted hair and tangled there. His tongue licked at her velvety stomach and swirled in her navel, causing her to utter a deep groan. Roughly, his hands parted her quaking thighs.

She threw back her head, her body arching like a drawn bow. Her fingers strained to touch his eartips. His lips found her pulsing womanhood, delicately curled like the folds of a spring flower. His tongue parted her and slipped in, igniting white-hot fires. The shocks spiraled upward through her limbs and she sobbed.

Now he bestrode her, this mighty, steel-muscled man whose great brawny arms had pulled her cart from watery death. His cloak was gone. She saw his golden beard, and his sculpted shoulders glistening in torchlight, and his massive chest like a god's bellows. Her hands raced across his naked skin, rapidly and hungrily, and she panted deliriously.

"How principled are you now?" he husked. "Where is your damned destiny?"

Shan T'u could not reason. Her brain had clotted, and her senses pummeled her. Her skin hissed for him. No words were possible. She felt his weight bear down on her, weight that could crack all of her ribs and crush her bones into her heart and lungs. Her fingers kneaded the muscles in his back and found the sudden, shocking curve of his rear. He was once again without covering, as she'd seen him in the river, but now he was so close, so close to her own naked treasures, so close to shaming her for eternity.

Her nails dug with instinctive defiance into the skin of his back and she felt them draw blood. Then faintness overspread her. The cave whirled. She felt herself go limp and lifeless as his bronze thighs rudely scissored between her legs. He arched, poised over her throbbing purity.

Her eyes flew open and looked into his as if from a deep, deep cavern. He seemed to be falling away from her. She tried to breathe, and to her horror, no air came.

Then, suddenly, as if she'd dreamt it, he was not there. She turned her head weakly and saw him rise to his feet like a vengeful giant. His tawny body glimmered in the torchlight, and he was, for that instant, unutterably beautiful and absolutely barbarian. And for that instant, her very spirit left her body and yearned toward him.

But now, from deep inside his chest, came a long, piercing howl of fury and despair. *"Damn you!"* he cursed. *"Damn you to hell!"*

He swept his cloak from the rotted cave floor and whirled it about him. In a moment, he was covered, and his cowl was over his head. He looked at her only for a second, with ice-cold eyes, then flung himself from the cave. She heard the alarmed voices of servingwomen and soldiers, and she heard him say that the princess had suffered a nightmare.

Shan T'u lay shaking against the cushions for a long time. Her fingers touched her heated face and she wept bitterly, with great, wrenching sobs. Mercifully, perhaps, she did not know that outside the cave, in the glistening rocks, other eyes were watching from the rain-swept darkness.

Chapter Eight

DE RAIS RODE AHEAD OF THE CARAVAN THE NEXT DAY. His cloak stank of rain, even though the sun blazed high in a white sky. Below the mountain trail, a swollen river surged and foamed. Trees stood bent and broken.

De Rais's cowl lay at his back, and he ruffled his hair with his fingers to help it dry. He'd slept last night under an outcropping of rock, with a hissing curtain of rain around him. His bones ached today.

His eyes searched the terrain ahead. His tempestuous emotions had calmed into a brooding bitterness. He'd done what he'd sworn never to do: he'd bared his heart and let desire rule his head. Had the wounds of his youth not taught him better? This fickle princess had turned his good sense inside out and brought him to his knees.

Duty to the last. Oh, her flirtation had been delicious: her downcast eyes, her quick kiss, her sly peeking at the riverbank. Feminine tricks to inflame a man. And when he'd come to her for the love she promised, she'd slapped him with her fan.

De Rais spat onto the soaked ground. He felt chagrined. He'd fought many fights, loved many wenches, and escaped death by his chin whiskers more than once. He'd ridden across Christendom, through Arabia and halfway across Cathay. And a child-woman with almond eyes and a porcelain face had made him a gibbering idiot.

"Aux enfers, Princesse," he growled. His horse's ears perked up and De Rais scratched the faithful animal's mane. He guided the horse beneath an overhanging ledge, determined to avoid this troublesome princess. But deep within his powerful chest, William De Rais desperately longed for the love of Shan T'u.

He sighed and blinked away the sunlight. It was not his first heartache.

In her cart, Shan T'u sat glumly on the cushions, with her chin pressing the knuckles of her right hand. She gazed bleakly past the tied-back curtains at the panorama of wild rock and rushing water. Her head throbbed. She knew her soldiers and huntsmen and servants were tired also. And there were so many miles to go.

Shan T'u turned away from the scenery, and her mouth was a thin line. Had it really happened last night? Had the friar come into her cave like a great dragon? Had he declared his love for her in words that inflamed her heart? Had he torn the clothes from her body and had he touched and kissed her most intimate places, bringing tongues of fire to her skin? Had his mouth possessed hers and had his warrior's body threatened to take her maidenhood?

She shuddered with the memory of it. She knew it was true. She had not fought, not until the very last. She knew that he had not consummated his lust. He'd left her, and cursed her from the depths of his fevered heart.

Left her undressed, cold, and suffering spasms from his lovemaking. Never had her body known such sensations; never had her nerves sung with such ecstasy. He had awakened in her all the mysteries of her womanhood, this profane holy man.

Well, she thought darkly, *you proved your mettle.*

She remained pure for her Indian prince. She would *not* defy her father and ride off with the friar. She had banished the dream that had sustained her in youth. This proved her a princess.

And pain marked her royalty. Her heart wept for him. She loved this friar with a fresh love that unfurled like a flower. A flower that a woman trampled underfoot when her father announced her husband-to-be. A flower that bloomed only once, that the friar had stooped to pluck. And in his adoring hand, the blossom had withered. *Does this mean eternal paradise, Master Po?* her heart cried. *Does this save our land?*

She closed her eyes and leaned back. How dare she ask such questions? How dare she challenge the wisdom of the sages? She had conducted herself properly. Heartaches were children's ailments, and she was no longer a child.

A piercing scream roused her. She sat bolt upright and looked outside. Before she could see anything, soldiers surrounded the cart.

"What is it?" she demanded.

"Bandits!" a soldier cried.

Shan T'u's blood stopped. She heard more screams, and a storm of hoofbeats. "Where are they?"

But the soldier never replied. An arrow sang through the air and pierced the man's throat. He was jerked back in his saddle and his hand groped for the shaft.

"No!" Shan T'u cried.

The soldier slid from his horse, and the animal bolted. More arrows flew past the cart. Shan T'u tried to think. How could the bandits have gotten past the soldiers at the front of the caravan? How many were there?

An arrow thunked into the side of the cart, and Shan T'u screamed. More soldiers rode past. The dust swirled and Shan T'u could no longer see valley or mountain, only a choking fog and the phantoms of men and horses.

But the sounds she heard chilled her blood. There were the piteous screams of dying men and the thuds of arrows piercing flesh. And now another soldier rode up next to her cart . . .

No—a bandit!

Shan T'u recoiled in terror as glittering eyes peered in at her over a red silk mask. A hand reached for her, fingers snapping like claws. Then the bandit gasped and fell backwards. She glimpsed the arrow sticking out of his back.

Shan T'u shut her eyes for an instant. The bandits were going to massacre the caravan. They would murder her, or perhaps carry her off and ravish her as they divided up her treasures.

What an imperious fool she'd been. Princess, indeed!

Her rage overcame her fear, and with a mighty wrench, Shan T'u flung open the door of the cart and stepped onto the rock-strewn path.

When the attack came, De Rais had been several yards ahead of the caravan, enjoying the solitude of his ride. For a moment, it was as if he were crossing Cathay for the first time, his senses aroused and his greed hungry for a rich prince.

He sensed the attack before he saw or heard anything. Experience had trained him to smell a strange horse, or hear a vibration in the earth. He stopped his horse and wheeled, looking back at the caravan. The mounted soldiers and the endless line of bullock carts and laden animals seemed to dance in the shimmering heat. Birds cawed. Water dripped from rocky eaves. The air itself seemed to be plucked, like the strings of a lute.

And then, as suddenly as death itself, the ledges above the caravan swarmed with bandits. The first wave of attackers came on foot, springing up from behind boulders. They wore dark, belted tunics over trousers and boots, in military style, but their hats were those of Chinese peasants. Each man covered his nose and mouth with a red silk cloth.

The bandits waved swords over their heads as they

boiled up in front of the soldiers. Horses reared and whinnied at the invasion. Soldiers vainly reached for their bows. The swordsmen spun and their blades sank deep into legs and ribs. Wounded soldiers fell, and were hacked to death on the ground.

This was the signal for the mounted bowmen to appear on the ledges themselves. The bowmen shot cleanly and accurately, and one after another of the princess's guard tumbled from his horse with an arrow through his throat or chest.

The stunning swiftness of the assault threw the servants into panic. Horses shied, throwing off bundles. Camels brayed and sank to their knees. Servants and teamsters tried to hide behind carts and fell on one another in their desperation to escape.

De Rais tried to assess the situation. The bandits had waited until the caravan was trapped on a narrow pathway between cliffs. The soldiers could neither turn nor regroup. They were easy targets for the bowmen, who could cut them down at will.

Those soldiers still on horseback had gotten to their bows and wildly shot arrows all about them. Some of the shafts found their marks, and bandits pitched forward and thudded down the rock walls. But many soldiers lay heaped on the ground, interfering with the movement of the horses. It was only a matter of time before the bandits picked off the rest.

A bandit had fallen among the soldiers, and his sword lay in the dust near his outstretched hand. De Rais made his decision. Their only chance was to return the surprise and mount a counterattack. He spurred his horse and lowered his head as he rode toward the melee. Arrows whistled past his head. De Rais kept his eyes on the sword, never wavering.

He timed his move with precision. A few feet from the bandit, De Rais gripped the reins and leaned out until he was nearly at right angles to his horse. As the ground rushed beneath him, he stretched out his fingers and scooped up the sword.

De Rais wheeled his mount and swung the sword over his head. He rushed at the soldiers and whacked a riderless horse on its rump with the flat of the blade. The animal shrieked and plunged down the path. De Rais smacked another animal and a third, urging the beasts to run.

The soldiers realized what he was doing and joined in the shouting. The horses kicked up plumes of dust that half hid the soldiers and also opened up the logjam. De Rais's eyes swept the rocks and spotted a steep pathway. He dug his knees into his horse's flanks and the animal shouldered its way into the rocks. The powerful hooves dug deep, kicking up pebbles.

When he reached the bowmen, De Rais wasted no time. He whirled the gleaming sword around and around, screaming curses in French. A bowman turned and loaded an arrow. De Rais was faster. He brought the blade down sideways and sliced through the bowman's neck.

As the headless body crumpled, still holding the bow, De Rais galloped deeper into the stronghold. The bandits were confused. De Rais gave them no time to consider. His sword wove a red path of destruction as he swung and slashed again and again. Another head flew from its body. A bowman collapsed with a geyser of blood gushing at his side. A bandit clutched in horror at the space where his arm had been.

More soldiers now followed De Rais up into the rocks and let loose a flurry of arrows that quickly found their targets. The bandits spun to defend, but had no time. They pitched forward in agonized death as the princess's arrows thudded into them.

De Rais wiped the drenched sword blade on his cloak and reined up his horse to look below. Straining to see through the red dust, he noted that some of the soldiers had managed to guide their mounts over bodies and past carts, and to move toward the rear of the caravan. Other soldiers and huntsmen engaged the bandits on foot and were cutting them down. De Rais looked far down the length of the caravan but could not make out what was happening.

The stench of blood and steel stung his nostrils. The thrill of battle coursed through his roused blood. His yellow beard glowed like the sun. But horror gripped his throat. He thought of Shan T'u in her cart. Had her soldiers reached her in time?

De Rais yanked at the reins and rode madly over the treacherous rocks, past battling bandits and soldiers. His sword whistled and slashed through flesh and bone as bandits tried to unseat him. A rage was upon him now, and his strength was prodigious.

At last he could make out the cart through a haze of yellow dust. The cart tilted downward, and the camel that had come through the flood lay in a massive, furred heap, with arrows bristling like quills from its bloody flanks.

"Merde," De Rais cursed. Without thought or pause, he snapped the reins and kneed his horse. The animal leaped into space and crashed down onto the path only a few inches from the sheer rock wall on the other side.

De Rais calmed the beast and looked at the carnage around the cart. Dead soldiers lay twisted, some under their fallen horses. Bandit corpses mingled with the bodies of royal guardsmen. But why was the cart not surrounded? Why were the soldiers not here?

De Rais dismounted, still gripping the blood-soaked sword. He kicked aside one corpse and leaped over bodies until he reached the cart. His eyes brimmed as he saw the cushions, ripped and slashed by swords and stained deep with blood. Blood splashed the wooden frame as well, and the wood was nicked and splintered.

But the cart was empty.

"Non," De Rais sobbed. Tears stung his dusty face and streamed down his cheeks. He looked around, breathing raggedly.

"Shan T'u!" he shouted. *"Shan T'u!"*

But he doubted that his cries could be heard in the hubbub. It seemed as if the bandits were retreating back into the rocks. There was still the clash of steel on steel, still the thwack of arrows being loosed, still the scream of a struck soldier or red mask. But the dust was clearing and De Rais saw fewer of the attackers. The mounted bowmen were gone completely, and those on foot were clambering up the rocky paths.

The soldiers were shouting now, and loosing volley after volley of arrows onto the rock ledges. Yes, the bandits were routed. De Rais let his sword sink to the drenched earth. His right arm shrieked with pain. His body quivered with numbness. He threw back his head and uttered a wracking sob. What a fool he'd been. He could have ridden away when they attacked.

Instead, he'd returned to fight for a princess he could not win.

He bowed his head as moans and wails replaced the noise of battle. "Shan T'u," he said brokenly. "Shan T'u . . ."

"Up here, William," her voice said.

His head snapped up and his lips curled in shock. His eyes blazed. "Where in hell . . . ?"

"Not in hell, William. Up here. And move carefully."

De Rais whirled. He saw her now, up in the rocks. She'd belted her robe so that it exposed her bare calves and feet. The torn silk hung in flaps that tantalizingly exposed her breasts and ribs. Her hair fell dusty and matted to her shoulders.

And she held a mulberry bow, with a steel-tipped arrow aimed at his heart!

De Rais gulped. Slowly, a smile of astonishment and delight spread over his face. "You live," he said.

"Yes."

"You surprise me again, Shan T'u."

De Rais stepped toward her, and she pulled back the bowstring. "I warned you not to move."

He stopped. "They were not my bandits, Shan T'u."

"I'm not certain of that."

He could see now that she was not as icy as she wanted to appear. While her aim was true, her lip trembled and her eyes glistened. The princess was shaken by the carnage.

"How can I reassure you, Shan T'u, before your hands grow tired and release that arrow into my chest?"

"Who are you, William?"

He hesitated and glanced at the sword he held. He raised the gruesomely stained weapon and twirled it in the hazy light. "You observed my unholy actions."

"I observed that you saved my caravan and that your sword is blessed with magic."

He laughed. "Well, this is a bandit's sword. It all depends who uses a weapon."

"Stand where you are!" she warned again. "Until I know the truth, I can't trust you."

He sighed. "Princess, I estimate that the weight of your bow will break your lovely arm in two minutes. You may be a sharpshooter, but that weapon was carved and strung for a big soldier."

She tossed her hair and kept her stance, but her eyes wavered. "You are no friar."

"No," he admitted. "I am no friar, nor have I ever been."

"Then what are you?"

"I am a knight," he said, without pride. "A nobleman of Burgundy, banished by my family and hounded by outraged fathers all over Christendom. I am a thief and a swindler, a violator of maidens, and a murderer of perfectly decent young louts who tried to defend their wives and sisters."

Shan T'u was silent for a long time. Her arm quavered, no longer able to hold the bow. With a cry of despair, she lowered the arrow and let the bow clatter to the rocks. Her hands flew to her face and she swayed.

"Princess!"

De Rais lunged in time to catch her plummeting body as she fell. He flexed his knees and folded her into his arms. For a sweet moment, he gazed down on her grimy face and pigeon-soft body in the tattered kimono. He could feel her shattered heartbeat.

Her eyes fluttered open and looked up at him in surprise. Quickly, he set her on her feet and steadied her. She passed a hand in front of her eyes to banish the faintness, then raised her head proudly. But she could not conceal her grief.

"I was a fool, William," she wept. "I refused to heed the warnings. I am unworthy."

He shook his head. "Shan T'u, you spend so much time hating yourself. Mother Mary, if I thought about the errors I've made, I'd take my own life." He cupped her face in his hands. "You couldn't know there'd be so many of them. This is no clumsy band of thieves. This is an army in training."

"And you defeated them."

He smiled. "I stirred things up. Where I come from, Shan T'u, you have to think fast and fight hard. Knights wear beautiful armor in my land, and strut about and talk of chivalry, but in truth, many of them are scoundrels and cowards. We do not train, nor drill, nor plan attacks. We gather in a field, sweating our backsides off in our armor, and face a bunch of knights from another land who are sweating *their* backsides off. We trundle up to each other and whack about with our lances until one of us falls down and can't get up. Then we put a sword through the poor wretch's eyes and go home and brag to our ladies."

She smiled. "You mock yourself."

"And we learn, Shan T'u, to be resourceful and tricky. Because it's every man for himself. I became strong as a youth, and quick-witted. And larcenous and immoral, I'm afraid. The De Rais manor was well thought of in France. The duke, my father, was kind to his serfs and brought much tribute home for the king. He supplied knights for battle and tithes for the Church, and a few tapestries into the bargain." De Rais smiled in reminiscence. "But he also supplied me, and I was a rapscallion."

"Not like young Roland?"

He laughed aloud and took her hands. "Oh, hardly. In Roland's situation, I would have stolen my sleeping father's armor and sold it."

"No!"

"Yes. I sold a number of my father's treasures on the sly, usually to pay off an infuriated father or priest. From the age of thirteen I found myself unnaturally . . . thirsty, and I was always digging new wells."

Her eyes showed disapproval. "William!"

"I was trained, of course, in manners and knightly codes and chivalry. But I used my sword to start scrapes and brought no less than six blood feuds against my father's manor. When I made love to a duke's daughter in his own bed, and began yet another blood feud, the bishop ordered a church interdict against the De Rais manor. So the duke, my father, set me on a horse, poked a lance tip in my butt, and told me that if I ever showed my face again in France, he'd have me quartered."

"Banished?" she said with mockingly wide eyes. "What did you do, sir knight?"

He exhaled tiredly. He plunged the sword blade into the dirt to clean it of guts and blood. "I wandered," he said. "I traded and tricked my way through

Christendom, and became a pretty fair merchant. I increased my fortune by swindling and got a taste for riches and fine ladies. They were much cleaner and better smelling and much more imaginative."

"You try to shock me."

"Well, you wanted the truth. I grew stronger and ever more artful with sword and bow, which got me out of not a few scrapes. Many was the dawn that I galloped across a border with ten or twenty horsemen breathing down my back. I used to ride into some brush, turn around, and charge back at the bastards, shooting arrows. Surprised the hell out of them." He laughed, then grew solemn. "Death was my companion. I grew less devout, and began to scorn the Church, and chivalry, and morals, and all that men prayed for and died for. I wanted only to become the richest trader in Europe and the Near East."

"Is that why you came here?" she asked.

He nodded and rested on a boulder. Dust creaked in his joints. "There was no great fortune to be made in Europe, with the Church owning everything the feudal barons didn't own. So I passed through the world of Islam to the borders of the Mongol Empire. And I found storied wealth, and stupid Tatars who welcomed trade. Still, a man with his eye on someone else's gold is not a man who travels safely. So I assumed the guise of a friar. Meanwhile, I searched for a prince influential enough to grant me a route through Cathay, a route by which I could transport jade and gold and silk to the West to sell for enough money to build my own palace. I planned to live on a lake somewhere in Arabia in royal splendor."

Shan T'u watched him as the last wisps of dust floated to earth. Everywhere, survivors tended to the dead. The threnody of wailing and weeping made the princess shudder.

"So that was your scheme," she said. "Deliver me to the Indian prince in return for trade routes. But you made my father believe you were a holy man."

"He would not have trusted a greedy merchant with his daughter." De Rais smiled ruefully. "He should not have trusted a friar. But it doesn't matter now."

"Why? I'm alive. The caravan will go on."

He sensed the bitter edge to her voice. "But I have changed, Shan T'u. You have transformed me."

She turned away. "If you think that saving my life has bought you a privilege . . ."

"Don't flatter yourself," he said acidly. "You made your choice clear. But I have no stomach now to cheat your father. I will see you safely to India if I can, and hand you to your prince."

"You won't pursue your dreams of plunder?"

He smiled, though his shoulders slumped with weariness. "Don't make me promise too much, Princess. I may plunder again. But I won't use you as barter. Even though *you* were less than candid with us all."

His eyes indicated the discarded bow and arrow. She blushed. "Nobody knows that I learned archery. But my soldiers were fallen, and I was threatened . . ."

"No explanation needed," De Rais said. "Your skill saved your life. Did you kill any of them?"

She nodded, overcome. "I think so."

He sighed, stood up, and held her gently as she shook with sobs. "The first time is hard," he said. "When you don't know what it's like."

"I am no longer a princess . . ."

"*That* refrain again! Shan T'u, if you will not blab to everyone in Cathay that I am a thief, I will not let your prince know that you can shoot like a hunter."

She gazed up at him with shining eyes. His beard was dust caked and bloodstained, like his skin and his cloak. She said, "William De Rais, there is still a part of my soul that would ride away with you."

He stroked her matted hair. "It wouldn't matter, Shan T'u. I wouldn't take you now."

"No?"

"You're not ready; and to give up everything you were for a new life, you must be ready. You're still too confused about being a princess. You could not be happy with me."

Her lips quivered and her eyes filled again. "Oh, William. I wish it were not so."

"But it *is* so."

Her head bowed. "Yes," she breathed.

He lifted her head and kissed her mouth with exquisite tenderness. "We must move on. They may regroup and attack again."

She nodded and ran from him, looking wildly lovely on the rocks: half-naked, boyishly slender, begrimed with battle. De Rais cursed and wrenched his eyes away.

Chapter Nine

By THE NEXT NIGHT, THE CARAVAN HAD REACHED THE summit of the mountain range. Nearly half the princess's soldiers had been killed, as well as many of her huntsmen and servants. Many others were wounded, and had to be transported on carts or horseback.

The dead were prayed over and left behind. A fresh camel was hitched to Shan T'u's royal cart. Teamsters took over the work of dead horses, pulling wagons and shouldering loads.

The caravan made camp that night in a barren, windy pass. Shan T'u was bathed and dressed by her servingwomen, but she did not venture forth. She was ashamed over the ambush, and stayed in her tent, meditating. De Rais kept watch for most of the night, too keyed up to sleep. He saw the gibbous moon flirt with black clouds. He smelled the ozone in the air and thought fleetingly of France.

The following day's journey was long and arduous. The caravan inched up, past spiring pikes and bleak plateaus. Meals were taken in cold weariness. Many of the wounded grew worse. A few died along the way.

Now it was night once more, and De Rais stood on a precipice. He looked down upon an outcropping foliated by a hardy oak tree. There the princess's tent was pitched, luminous in the moonlight. Below the outcropping, along the bluffs, the rest of the caravan slept. A few fires guttered, and dozing animals snorted. De Rais had suggested this arrangement. He could see the approach of a foe from here, and the princess was in her own natural fortress.

De Rais chewed on a rice cake and lifted his booted foot to a rock. After the battle with the red masks, he had openly confessed his identity to the soldiers and had taken the clothing of one of the fallen guardsmen. It felt good to be rid of the coarse cloak. The cotton liked his skin, and the belted tunic and trousers fitted his sinewy body well. This afternoon he had bathed in a mountain stream and washed off the blood and filth.

Now he tasted a sweet sadness for Shan T'u. She had played a game and caused a bloodbath. Not her fault, the poor child. She'd been sheltered in her father's palace all her young life. She certainly wasn't ready to plan strategy.

De Rais hefted the sword he'd taken from the fallen bandit. He twirled the blade slowly and it seemed to catch fire from the moon. *Strange sword for a peasant,* he thought. The blade was forged of a fine steel, strip-welded to make it tough. The process gave the blade a damascened look, and the hilt was decorated with gold.

Where had this hill bandit gotten it? De Rais wondered. No doubt these bandits had marauded other caravans and slain noblemen. Now, this souvenir of a past raid had fallen into the hands of a rogue from Burgundy. A smile crossed De Rais's face. He would keep the sword. It had been lucky for him.

His eyes narrowed as he glanced down at the oak tree and the tent. He thought he'd detected a movement among the rocks, but all was quiet. He finished his rice cake and sat down on a rock, as the wind rushed over his face.

In her tent, Shan T'u tossed on the cushions. She flung one slender arm over her head. She could hear the mountain breeze outside, and a distant rush of water. She felt, for a moment, as if she were floating over the peaks, to the land of Immortals.

Tears welled in eyes that were already red. She could not shake the memory of the attack. Again and again, her restless sleep was tormented by visions of arrows in the bodies of her soldiers. They hated her now. She'd led them into death.

Only William had proved heroic. William, who looked so thrilling in the garb of a soldier. William, whose golden hair caught the flame of the sun as he rode. William, whose mighty arm had turned back the red masks.

Shan T'u turned on her side and curled up, sniffling. Her arms trembled as she recalled snatching up the bow and arrows from the dead soldier. She could still feel the palsied shaking of her fingers as she slipped the quiver over her shoulder while arrows whizzed past her head. What had given her the courage to slide the first arrow into the bow, pull back the string, and shoot?

The arrow had gone true to its mark, piercing the bandit's throat. The red mask had gaped in stunned horror at the princess in silk gown and coiffed hair, holding the weapon that had ended his life. After that, Shan T'u did not think. She shot again and again, then found a niche in the cliff where she hastily unpinned her hair and ripped the hem of her gown to allow her to move. Horses stampeded past her, and dust burned her eyes and tickled her nose. She kept loading the bow and letting fly.

Until, finally, her soldiers prevailed and the bandits turned and fled back into the rocks. And she stood, torn and bleeding, as De Rais appeared like a wizard from the sky.

Shan T'u sat up now. How long would the nightmares go on? When would she know peace? She knew only that Master Po's foresight had been magical. Her training had saved her life. But she did not want the life of a warrior. She wanted only to fulfill her duty and for this journey to be over.

There can be no other desire, she told herself fiercely.

But other desires were aflame within her, kindled by the attack. What had Master Po done to her? Piously, he had instructed her to be an obedient Chinese princess. Meanwhile, he had taught her arts and skills that could only make her despise what she was.

Shan T'u covered her eyes with her hands. She

needed time to heal the wounds of this journey. All would balance.

A pebble skittered outside, and Shan T'u held her breath. In the distance, a horse neighed. Nobody could be there—her guardsmen slept outside the tent. De Rais watched from the ledge above her.

But more pebbles rattled. Her heart fluttered. "William . . . ?"

The tent flap whipped open and the bandit leaped at her like a wolverine. Shan T'u would have screamed, but before the breath left her lungs, a strong hand clapped over her mouth. Shan T'u clawed at the hand, and a silken, muffled voice whispered, "I will slit your throat if you try to scream."

A gleaming blade wavered in front of her face. Slowly, the bandit slid his hand from her mouth. Shan T'u gulped and moistened her parched lips.

"Good," the bandit purred. "Now lie back, Princess, and fold your hands in your lap. Very slowly, please."

Shan T'u felt the blood racing through her veins as she obeyed. The bandit now sat at her side, looking down at her. His entire face, below his brimmed peasant's hat, was covered with a red mask into which he had cut slits for eyes, nostrils, and lips. He wore the cotton tunic, trousers, and boots of a warrior. But he was no simple peasant. His Chinese was too classical, though he worked to disguise his voice. His eyes were like the eyes of a crocodile, heavy-lidded but watchful.

"You are exquisitely beautiful," the bandit said. "With your tresses unpinned like that, you might be a goddess."

Shan T'u tried to think clearly. She was paralyzed

with terror, but she was also fascinated. "Who are you?" she demanded.

"Ah, an imperial question! Then I *must* answer." He held up the knife blade. "My name is Kung. I am the chieftain of the red masks."

"How did you get in here? My soldiers . . ." Her heart leaped to her throat. *"No!"*

"Be still!" The knife blade flashed and the razor tip pricked the skin of her throat. She hissed in terror. "I didn't kill your stupid guardsmen—not yet. I struck each of them with a rock. They will awaken with headaches."

"Why . . . ?"

"More questions. Princess, right now *I* am in a position to ask questions, not you. Neither your soldiers nor your huntsmen could stand against my red masks."

"We drove you off," Shan T'u retorted.

He smiled. "You had a few surprises up your sleeve. Your own prowess with bow and arrow was unexpected. And your friar proved to be a splendid knight."

"And a match for *you.*"

She heard his sharp intake of breath and regretted her perversity. "That isn't wise," he said. "I am very sensitive to insults."

"I apologize," she whispered.

"Very good. I like princesses to be humble to me. I like them to kowtow and beg me to spare their lives." He gripped her by the hair, yanking her head back and exposing her white throat. He laid the knife blade flat across her neck. Her pulse throbbed.

"One stroke," he hissed, "and your royal blood will pour like red wine from your torn throat. Or I can disfigure your face so that no prince will ever look at you. Would you prefer that?"

He touched the knife blade just under her eye. She looked wildly at him. "Scarred and hideous," he taunted. "To become a crone and live an outcast. Who is king here, Shan T'u?"

"You are," she managed to whisper.

"And who is the slave?"

"I am."

"Very good, Princess." He took away the knife. "Your heart flutters like a captured bird," he said. "Your breasts heave. Your belly shivers. Your face pales." He grinned. "Do you take offense at my intimate words?"

She shook her head.

"I may speak of your body with impunity?"

"Yes."

"And I may uncover your royal flesh and gaze upon it?"

"Yes."

He seemed aroused by the glistening tears on her cheeks. "Ah, what a magical night," Kung murmured, "when a humble peasant may touch the body of a princess and not be executed!"

"Who are you?" Shan T'u demanded. "You speak too well for a peasant."

"And you shoot too well for a princess!" His voice sounded tantalizingly familiar but at the same time coldly alien. "We all make assumptions, do we not? We look to the classical scholars for truth. As it has been for ages, so must it be forever." He leaned closer now. "But did the scholars tell us of the Mongol Empire that now subdues China and slowly destroys her?"

"So you fight the Mongols by slaughtering Chinese?"

Kung bristled at her words. He spoke with controlled fury. "Understand, Princess. The rebellion is growing all over China. The Khans leveled whole cities and sent thousands of homeless ones to the hills and mountains. Most of the refugees starved to death in the wilderness, and thousands more wander in ragged hordes of beggars. There, Princess, is our army of vengeance."

"A beggar army?"

"You assume it is impossible because you don't consider beggars to be human. I do. They were once merchants and farmers. Their farms are now Mongol hunting parks. And the rest of our peasants are forced to labor in the fields to pay taxes so Kublai Khan can finance his wars."

"Were you a farmer, Kung?" she asked.

He lifted a tress of her hair with the knife blade, and idly examined its sheen. "No, my life was—let us say in the civil service. Khan did away with that, too. His civil service posts are filled by Arabs and Persians and Turks. Few of them can read or write Chinese. Most of them can't even understand it. Of course, they *all* speak Mongolian, and even write the barbarous tongue."

King sat erect, his eyes passionate behind the mask. "Do you understand, Princess? The end of our language. The end of our culture. The end of our history."

"I have heard all of this," Shan T'u said with annoyance. "What can be done?"

"*This* can be done," Kung said savagely. With a

flashing stroke of the knife, he cut a lock of her hair. She gasped as he held aloft the shining prize. "Tress by tress, we hack at the Mongol Empire until it is bald. We draft the beggars, the peasants, the rusticated civil servants, the priests, the poets. We train them to fight. We turn on our Mongol masters. We begin a new dynasty in China."

Shan T'u sat up, her arms wrapped around her knees. "It sounds fine, Kung. But what are you *truly* doing? Attacking caravans? Robbing merchants? Is *that* rebellion against Kublai Khan?"

"That is how we begin," Kung said. "This is not a child's game. All of us, Shan T'u, were honest men. We were forced into this life by the Mongols, and yes, we have become murderers. We kill for treasure to buy weapons and horses and food."

"I wonder if you kill for such noble reasons . . . or because the blood is in your heart. There are dying men in my camp tonight. I watched them fall, with arrows in their throats . . ."

She collapsed into sobs, overcome. Kung simply observed her, without visible emotion. When at last she quieted, he said, "You are a silly little girl. You knew nothing of death. Now you know. Your soldiers would not have willingly handed over your treasure. Now you *will* hand it over, as we attack your caravan again and again. Word will spread of our fearsome band, of the fate of the wedding caravan of Princess Shan T'u. Perhaps the news will even fly to Kanbaliq and to Kublai Khan's ears, and perhaps other bandits will seek us, and we will forge an army. An army with banners flying. An army whose swords will cut down the Mongols."

Kung's words rang in the tent. Shan T'u said, "And the murders of innocent Chinese will sit well in your souls?"

"You murdered!"

"I defended my life!"

"Just so." His face pressed close to hers. "And we are defending *our* lives. If a few Chinese die, their blood is spilled with honor. Come, Princess. Surely you understand?"

She shook her head. "No. I will never understand."

"But you will." His hand reached out and touched her face. She looked up, startled. His lips, behind the mask, seemed to quiver.

"What do you want?" she whispered.

"I risked my life," Kung hissed, "to come here alone. I had not expected you to be mistress of the bow. I had not expected you to affect me as you have."

"I don't understand . . ."

"Princess, can't you see? If *you* join us, if Shan T'u, daughter of Chang Hu, dons the red mask, it will be a sign from Heaven. A miracle. You will be a legend. We will rally warriors from all provinces of China."

Her breath caught in her throat. "Join you? Surely you are mad."

"Isn't this already madness, Shan T'u? Your caravan attacked, decimated? Why wed an alien prince when a blazing destiny awaits you in these hills? Be *my* princess, Shan T'u. Rule the red masks with me, and learn what a royal life can be had in the mountains. Ride with me, and be marked down in the scrolls as a deliverer of China."

His words inflamed her soul and found a secret

longing so forbidden that she had buried it deep. But it was not this sinewy bandit chief she wanted to ride with, it was William De Rais.

"No," she said. "I understand your pain and your anger. But I have no wish to live in the hills like a wild animal, not with a man who murders the innocent."

Kung ran the ball of his thumb down the knife blade. "Your morality is offended."

"It cannot agree with yours."

"Perhaps not." His eyes seemed to pierce her skin. "But your morality is flexible enough for the European."

So he was jealous! "You have no right to speak of these things," she said.

"Don't I? I've observed this devil from the West. He is a liar, is he not? And a ravisher of women, if I observed correctly."

Her hand flew to her mouth. "You watched . . . ?"

He laughed cruelly. "You didn't fight very hard. In fact, the yellow beard spared you."

"Stop it!" Shan T'u cried. "You're nothing more than a beast. Go attack the Mongol if you have the heart. Or can you only use your blade on women?"

"Fool!" He pinioned her wrists. His breath was fetid in her nostrils. "You persist, don't you? You forget that here, the power is mine."

She averted her eyes. "Leave me."

"Shan T'u," he urged, "don't be a madwoman. You are made to rule. You should be the first empress of a new China, not an Indian peacock's toy. Come with me now."

She remained silent.

"I'll have to kill you, don't you know that?"

She began to weep.

"At least you will know *that* of me," Kung said in a strangled voice. "I will not possess your body against your will."

"Please . . ."

His knife blade nicked the flesh of her throat. "Let this be a sacrifice," he intoned. "Let this be a message to Khan. The head of the Princess Shan T'u shall be displayed through the cities, and word shall fly from province to province."

Shan T'u twitched spasmodically as Kung slowly drew the knife blade across her neck, making a thin oozing slit. "There is your royal blood," he said. "Feel its warmth? One more cut, Princess, and the veins will open. Will you save your life?"

Shan T'u prayed desperately, murmuring sacred words to fill her mind in the last moment of her life.

"*Bitch,*" he spat. "Then let your head decorate my sword."

Shan T'u shut her eyes, and then she heard the other voice, as if in a dream: "Try it, jackal, and your own head will follow!"

Kung's knife paused on her bleeding throat. Shan T'u dared not draw breath. She heard De Rais's voice again: "Sit up slowly, jackal. Let the knife drop to the ground."

The knife blade left her throat, and Shan T'u turned her head. Kung sat upright. The knife clattered to the earth near him. De Rais stood over the bandit, his sword touching a point between Kung's shoulder blades.

"I think we'll turn the tables," De Rais said. "I think we'll display *your* head as a warning."

Kung hissed and closed his eyes. His hands clasped

together in readiness. Shan T'u whispered, "No— don't kill him."

De Rais's eyes blazed down at her. "What?"

"Please," she said. She struggled to sit up, feeling the warm blood on her throat. "I know he would have killed me, but he should not die like this."

"Then tell me how, Princess."

"In battle," she said. "He should fall in battle."

De Rais made a disgusted noise. "By God, Princess! He was about to slit your throat!"

Shan T'u cried freely now. "Yes. And yet he showed honor. You could not understand, William. Believe me, I have no love for this man—"

"The hell you don't."

"Please." Her sudden passion silenced De Rais. She turned her tear-streaked face up to him. "This man murdered my soldiers, and he would have slain me as well. But he is more than a cutthroat. It is not meant for his death to come now. He may do great deeds for this land."

Kung's eyes fluttered open and looked intensely at Shan T'u. "You are more surprising than I thought."

Shan T'u's eyes turned to frost. "I despise you, Kung. I question your courage. I doubt your plans. But I sentence you to a more honorable death than this, which will ensure *my* place in Heaven."

Kung smiled, not fooled by her icy words. "Will you bid the knight let me rise?"

Shan T'u looked at De Rais and nodded.

"Damn you," De Rais growled. He put up his sword and snarled, "On your feet, jackal. And I beg you—give me a reason to run you through."

Kung got slowly to his feet and kowtowed to the princess. "I hope we meet once more."

"I doubt that," she said haughtily.

He only smiled, then turned to De Rais. "I suppose you overheard me speak of you?"

"I would vomit at compliments from your lips," De Rais said, "so your swinish remarks suited me well."

Kung laughed, not without respect. "You can twist our language cleverly, Frenchman. I hope to meet you again also, to settle our grievance."

De Rais grunted. "Let's leave it at this, bandit. Tell your scum to forget about this caravan. I expect safe passage the rest of the way. If you attack again, I will personally hunt you down and tie your arms and legs to four wild horses."

Kung bowed. "I stand warned." And then, like a silent night wind, the bandit slipped from the tent and was gone.

De Rais looked after him and cursed. Then he turned back to Shan T'u, who sat on the cushions and swayed. De Rais dropped to his knees and curtly tilted her head to see the wound. He took a silk cloth from his waistband and cleansed the blood.

"Pretty little cut," he said. "It will sting like the blazes."

She nodded. Her eyes shone as they watched him.

"Damn you, Shan T'u, why didn't you let me kill him?"

"There's been enough killing," she said. "And there was something about him . . ."

"Pah. You're infatuated."

She smiled at his hangdog look. Her hands cupped his rough cheeks. "William," she murmured, "you still don't understand."

"Understand what?"

Her lips brushed his. She smiled into his astonished

140

eyes. "There can be no more infatuation for me, William. My love is given. It is yours. It has been yours since you first saw me in the bathhouse."

"Then what in hell . . . ?"

"Duty," she said in a breath. "Everything I have been taught, all I have been trained to be. I accepted my duty, William. I accepted my royal destiny. But it never changed what my heart knew."

He sighed deeply and folded his hands on her shoulders. "I *do* understand. I'll just keep saving you for that Indian bastard."

She trembled under his touch and her voice grew intense. "Three times you have preserved my life."

"I'm not counting."

"And more than that." Her finger touched his lips. "You know more of my life than anyone. You know of my secret training. You know that bandit chieftains want me to ride with them."

"I told you," he said huskily, "you're special."

"Am I?" Her hands wound around his neck. "So many things have changed, William. I have known death, and I know love. May I not know just a little more before I am forever imprisoned?"

She could feel his heart beat faster beneath his cotton tunic. "What are you saying?" he said huskily.

Her eyes filled once more. "Just once," she whispered. "Once before my body is given to the Indian prince, once before I am a slave in his lake palace. Oh, William, let me know joy once. Is it right to know death and not life?"

She could not speak. Her cheeks were wet, her fingers begging him. "Shan T'u," he barely breathed. "Are you . . . ?"

"Love me!" she pleaded. "Please love me."

With a sigh of wonder, he embraced her and gathered her up. Her mouth opened and her arms twined around his back. He kissed the bloody wound on her throat, and then carried the blood to her own mouth as his lips parted hers. She pressed hard against him, wanting to mold her every inch to him.

She arched her back, and with charming innocence she said, "I don't know what to do, William. Show me. Show me . . ."

With a huge cry of happiness, he swept her into his arms and gently lowered her to the cushions. Tonight she felt no terror as his strong fingers unsashed her gown. She let her eyes caress his half-lit face. Impatient, she sat up and shrugged off the gown as De Rais pushed it past her porcelain shoulders, down her velvet back, away from her silken legs. And finally, De Rais tossed the richly embroidered gown aside. His eyes burned with a blinding flame as he beheld her nakedness.

As she watched, entranced, he stripped off his soldier's dress, peeling the cotton tunic from his muscled torso, wriggling out of the trousers to bare his narrow loins and bulging thighs. And tonight, Shan T'u did not shrink from his muscle and bone and skin. Tonight, she ached to taste and to touch him.

For a long, pulsing moment, they devoured each other with tempestuous eyes, and then lips and tongues met with vibrant passion. She nipped at his lower lip, bit softly into the flesh and made him gasp. His tongue sought the recesses of her mouth. Her trembling fingers grazed his neck and trailed rivulets of fire down his shoulders and back. Her nostrils flared at his musky scent and her hands played across his matted chest. She pressed her palms against his

142

knotted abdomen and felt him tighten. And then she discovered his burgeoning shaft, hot and hard, pulsing with its own life against her tender skin.

Her breasts were thrust up to his cupped hands as she arched her back. His tongue laced damp rings around her aching nipples, and his teeth nipped her tender buds as she caressed him with forbidden intimacy. Dizzying sensations rocked her, sensations she had felt for the first time when De Rais assaulted her in the cave. But then she had been afraid and guilty. Now she cared nothing for vows. Now there was only his corded body and his mouth, paralyzing her doubts with honeyed venom.

"Please," she whispered. "Now . . ."

His hands twined in her shining hair and he held her face prisoner between his calloused hands. "I will be gentle," he told her. "If this is the first time . . ."

She managed to smile up at him and her hands touched his own roughened cheeks. "There has never been another."

"No lordling?" he teased. "No mannered prince?"

"Manners could not conquer me," she said hoarsely. "You will be my first lover, paladin."

"Me? A boorish, unmannered lout who disgraced his family and despoiled half the wenches in Burgundy?"

She nodded, her body afire. Her inner flesh screamed for him. "Yes," she said urgently. "Yes, yes, yes . . ."

He kissed her lingeringly on her mouth, and then kissed her eyelids and cheekbones and her little pointed chin. He ran his hands down her arms and up her ribs and around to her damp back. He felt her tremulous heartbeat, like the beating of frantic wings.

"I will try not to hurt you."

Tears filled her eyes. "I don't care . . ."

He cried out softly, in wonder and adoration at this innocent child who begged for a woman's fulfillment. He lowered her delicately to the cushions, and his eyes were like the eyes of the cheetah during the fateful hunt. He poised above her, all bunched muscle and knotted sinew. She caressed his muscled chest and began to breathe deeply, in a passionate rhythm. He forced her legs to part and his hard stomach brushed her own tender abdomen. Her fingers tightened on his biceps and now his questing shaft slid deliciously inside. Even as he entered her, he hesitated at the mysterious curtain of her womanhood.

She wanted to urge him on, but her voice caught in her throat. The surging violence of their passion hesitated, as storm clouds part to flood the drenched land with moonlight just before the howling gales come again. At this moment, De Rais was no ruffian knight. He was a master of the brush, entering her with a balance of hesitation and force.

Shan T'u breathed in sharply, biting her lip. Her throat stung with the bite of Kung's knife. De Rais plunged, deep into her core, shredding the fragile curtain as he had crumpled her silken gown. At this instant, pain and rapture merged, as rocks and water merge in a garden. He was past her torn veil, and he struck now as a warrior strikes. Her legs wrapped around his tremendous thighs and her hips undulated. Again and again his silken rod thrust to her core, filling her. She was consumed in flame and the helpless sensations rocked her in wave upon wave, pouring from her body, drenching her flesh. Then she felt De Rais stiffen as if mortally shot, and white fire rifled through her loins. He moaned like a wounded soldier and shuddered under her clutching hands.

For a long time afterward, she lay nestled in his arms, her skin sweetly damp against his. Her spine was pillowed in his chest and he kissed the nape of her neck and her shoulder. She touched her lips reverently to his knuckles and fingers and enfolded his hand in both of hers, as she had cuddled her doll when a child. She listened to the mountain wind and looked past the flap of her tent to the burning stars.

"I have never known such ecstasy, William."

"I'm glad."

"It didn't hurt. Or if it did, I hardly knew."

She could feel him smile. "I have been told 'tis a sweet pain."

"Very sweet." She kissed his hand again and her eyes glistened. "I love you."

He sighed. "Do not speak idly of love, Shan T'u. You have foretold the swift end of this fulfillment."

"I know," she sobbed.

She felt his weight shift. "And I must be gone."

"*No.*" She turned, her body whispering against the cushions, and she hugged him urgently. She caught his eyes and saw the dawn rising in them. "Stay with me."

"And let your ladies in waiting find us? Or your soldiers?"

Her heart ached. Her fingers trailed along his shoulders and arms, and reluctantly dropped away. Her loins throbbed with the memory of his beautiful invasion. "Yes, of course."

She curled up in a despondent ball as he arose and found his raiment. She watched as he dressed, drinking in a last glimpse of his soldier's legs, of the powerful manhood that had claimed her, of his belly and ribs and chest, his arms and shoulders. Finally he was clothed, still lithe and magical, and lodged in the innermost chambers of her heart. He looked down and said, "I will always remember this night."

"And I, too."

Now the first blue fringe of dawn showed in the sky, and he exited from her tent with a crunch of his boots on the earth. She was alone, the morning wind tracing fingers across her spine. Her skin glowed like the last embers of a fire. She wept bitterly at her sin, and at her love, which lived though it could never be nurtured.

Chapter Ten

THE NEXT MORNING, DE RAIS RODE AT THE HEAD OF THE caravan, resplendent in his warrior's dress, with his sword at his side. He whistled happily as he rode, and failed to see or hear two of the princess's soldiers whispering behind him.

Shan T'u rode in her cart, her hair freshly coiffed, her body washed and dressed. She smiled a rather complacent smile as her eyes drooped. Shan T'u's personal guards rode on horseback and nursed their aching heads. There had been much consternation about the attack on the soldiers last night, and about Shan T'u's wounded throat. Shan T'u had faced her concerned questioners with a puzzled air. She'd slept well, she insisted, and nothing of value was missing. Perhaps the soldiers tossed in their sleep and struck their heads. As for her neck, she may have cut herself on a loose hairpin.

She laughed at the deception, which also served well to account for the stains of her lost virginity.

She sighed and leaned back against the cushions. Her fingers idly toyed with a hairclip, and then returned to the welt on her throat. Yes, her skin had been sliced by Kung's knife, and kissed by De Rais's lips. And she felt no remorse. Only a love that spread like the sun's rays through her body. She shut her eyes and her lips traced his name. Her eyes filled. To know this love only once, and never more . . .

And would Master Po ever forgive her for what she dared to dream now?

Slowly, with the wakening day, the caravan descended from the topmost crags. They rode through banks of heavy mist that at times obscured all vision and soaked their skin. Sometimes they could see mossy rock, and vegetation that luxuriated as they went lower.

And finally, De Rais guided his horse through a great, drifting white cloud, and there before him lay a vista of forested mountains, broken cliffs plunging ten thousand feet, granite faces wreathed in mist, great rock teeth soaring to the sky. Towering and majestic, the panorama burst upon his eyes; far below, golden and serpentine in the sunlight, wound the Great River, and even at this height, he could hear the dull thunder of its current.

De Rais shouted, *"Victoire! Victoire! Mes amis, allons, allons!"*

Soldiers galloped up to him. De Rais pointed and the soldiers burst into cheers. They slapped each other's backs, and nearly stumbled while pivoting to ride back and pass the word.

De Rais remained, gazing at the heart-stopping beauty and thinking of Kung. A tremor of foreboding rippled through him. He no more trusted Kung than he'd trust a bandit of his own country. Could the chieftain have held back, waiting for an unguarded moment? Or had he indeed been purified by the forgiveness of Shan T'u?

De Rais grunted his opinion of *that* idea. He determined to remain on the *qui vive,* but a little celebration was in order.

Shan T'u ran like a golden deer through the waving grass of the mountainside, her silk gown whipping against her skin. She unpinned the last of her ivory hairclips as she ran.

De Rais pursued her at a loping gait, his tunic open to bare his golden chest. A grin split his face, and his warm blue eyes laughed at Shan T'u's delight. Around them, pine trees hummed in the wind. The valley dipped, in a series of plateaus, down to a gorge where the crags receded into blue mist.

Far behind them was the caravan. The feasting had begun, with fresh game courtesy of the huntsmen and their falcons. Music played and girls danced. Clever servants performed magic tricks or juggled. Horses, camels, and oxen were groomed. Priests offered sacrifices to Buddha in thanks for their deliverance from the cruel mountains.

Shan T'u put out her arms as she ran, to embrace the wind. Her bare feet slipped in the dew-soaked grass and she fell. Laughing, she stretched out in the fragrant growth, her hair festooned around her face. De Rais dropped to his knees beside her. He tried to catch his breath.

"Maybe they *should* have bound your feet," he said. "Then I could catch you."

She smiled up at him, her dark eyes filled with sunlight. Her fingers toyed with his flaxen locks. "Another sin, William. Another heresy, as you call it."

"You're hopeless, Shan T'u. You'll have to burn at the stake."

"Let me see *you* as the flames reach higher," she whispered. "I want you to be my last earthly sight."

"I'll return to India when I am ancient," he chided, "and appear at your deathbed."

"Ugh," she said. She thrust up both arms and brought down his head. He kissed her mouth thoroughly, and still she begged for more.

"There is so much love in you," he said feelingly.

"For you, William."

He looked beyond her at the tumbling valleys. "What would Confucius, or Tao, or Buddha say of our destinies, Shan T'u?"

"How so?"

"You are a royal princess, raised to be obedient and submissive. I am a knight of Burgundy, raised to be devout and chivalrous. Yet we've both defied our heritage."

"Ah, but only one of us is beautiful and sweet and . . ."

He grinned. "Oh, be still. This will swell my head."

"Ah! *More* of you to behold! Then swell, oh head . . ."

She collapsed into laughter, and he pinned her shoulders and kissed her. She lay stretched on her back in the cool grass, adoring him with her eyes. He said, "Think of it, Shan T'u. I left my home, trailing wicked deeds and unholy thoughts, while you remained, prepared to wed your prince."

"I *almost* bolted," she reminded him.

"True. But you fought your wildness, while I gave in to mine."

She took his hand and lingeringly kissed each finger and joint. She rested her cheek on his wrist. "And you found the wildness inside me. You made me betray my duty."

"And you made *me* remember *mine*," he said. "You made me behave like a knight for the first time in my life." He laughed. "Dear princess. Will you be my lady?"

The sun irradiated her face, framed against the grass. "If you are a knight, then I will be your lady. If you are a hunter, then I will be the falcon who sits on your wrist. If you are a priest, then I will be your holy book. Whatever you be, William, I will be part of you."

"My God," he breathed. "My God."

Her eyes darkened with need. Her breasts moved smoothly with her aspiration beneath the plum-colored silk. "Love me, William."

"Ah! I thought it was to be *one* night of sin."

Tears sprang to her eyes. "No. Each night. Each day. I need you so."

He stopped her lips with his finger. With tormenting gentleness, he kissed each eyelid, then each ridge of her delicate nose, then her lips. He kissed her high-boned cheeks and her forehead. He guided her head back to its pillow of green, then stood, his virile form framed by pine trees and blue sky. As she watched, he doffed the tunic, revealing once more the vee of his chest and the brawn of his arms. He unclasped the sword and let it drop with a clatter. He stripped off the riding boots and the billowing trousers.

He stood for a moment in tawny nakedness and she worshiped his lean strength. He knelt beside her and her hands rubbed his chest and belly. He undid her gown and bared her breasts.

She touched his scars. "How did you get these?"

He glanced at where her fingernail traced the shining skin. "Well, that one was dealt me by Sir Giles D'Aubert, an incredibly ugly duke of a neighboring manor. It was a matter of great honor. Sir Giles resented my midnight forays against his livestock. I liked fresh eggs, you see."

"He attacked you for stealing chickens?"

"*And* his daughter. One summer she bloomed"— he indicated swelling pregnancy with his hands—"and tearfully told Papa that I had ravished her in the pig barn the winter past."

"Did you?"

"To be sure. So had eighteen of the other local lads, sometimes two or three of an evening. So it was truly a coin toss as to whose progeny this was. But I had the seediest reputation, so Sir Giles rode up on his horse one morning—in full armor—and challenged me to a duel. My father the duke rousted me out of bed and made me fight."

"How terrible!"

"Oh, it *was*. I had a great whacking headache. I stood there in my hot armor and faced Sir Giles. He got off his horse and cursed me. He cursed me for quite a long time. That was his mistake. I grew ill standing there inhaling his foul breath. And I . . . overflowed."

"You . . ."

". . . heaved up the last evening's food and drink, right in front of him. Some, I believe, got *on* him."

Shan T'u clapped a hand over her mouth to stifle her laughter. "What a terrible thing to do."

De Rais nodded. "Indeed. Well, Sir Giles started swinging. He caught me under my breastplate and laid open my side. I saw my blood running freely and got ill all over again. Wisely, I fell down to avoid further injury."

Shan T'u kissed his hand. "And how did this legendary combat end?"

"Sir Giles got disgusted and called me a coward, and my father a bastard, and the whole family the children of whores. Then he rode away. The duke, my father, had me bandaged, and then he had me whipped, and then he killed Sir Giles in combat."

Shan T'u's mouth popped open. "He *killed* him?"

"Started a hell of a feud between our families.

Went on for years until the bishop put a stop to it. As it turned out, the wench's infant had red hair and so did a drooling cretin of a farmer's son who lived on Sir Giles's manor!"

Shan T'u pursed her lips in mock reproval. "Is this the brave paladin I've fallen in love with?"

"I told you I was no legend."

"You are legend enough for me."

He stretched out beside her. His hand teased her breasts into shuddering readiness. "How small and perfect they are," he said wonderingly. "And how sweetly they fill my hand."

"How sweet your hand feels," she murmured.

"I want to see you in the light of the sun."

Shan T'u sat up and unwrapped the gown, letting it whisper from her body. As she lay back, she arched like a bow; the grass tickled her back and the wind fluttered her stomach. De Rais lay on his back near her, one arm stretched languorously over his head. His eyes beckoned her.

"Touch me," he said.

She moved closer and knelt by him, with eyes downcast. She saw the breeze ruffle his hair and beard like wheat in a summer field. His eyes flicked from her face to her throat to her breasts. Shan T'u shivered with delicious sinfulness at his frank examination. She massaged his deep chest with her fingertips, liking the curled mat of his golden hair.

"Does this excite you as well?" she asked, as she rubbed a fingertip over his nipples.

"Everything you do excites me."

"Ah, that's the idle flattery of a nobleman."

"And this is the idle adultery of a princess."

She laughed and lightly cuffed his face. He seized her hand and bit the fleshy mound near her thumb. She cried out at the pain. Then she resumed her exploration of him, moving her hands down his ribs, swirling her fingers across his taut belly, and then working into his inner thighs. "Such a big, powerful body," she said. "Our men are not as big as you Europeans."

"Nor are our women as tiny as you."

"Do you like that?"

"You are an exquisite mannequin, Shan T'u. You are a perfect porcelain miniature."

"Then do not break me," she said. With her lips parted, she moved her fingers timorously to his manhood, awed to know that wondrous secret part of him that gave her so much pleasure. She exhaled in ardent delight as he came to life at her touch.

His eyes caressed her face with smoky passion. His hands cupped her breasts more urgently, and his palms made fiery arabesques. Shan T'u sighed with pleasure. "Oh, my love . . ." she breathed.

She dipped her head and her lips grazed him where her hands had awakened his love. Her hair fell in cascades about her shoulders. She heard him gasp and she exulted in her power to subdue this mighty knight who could rout bandits and conquer storms.

"Shan T'u . . ." he begged her.

She looked up and shook back her hair. His head was arched back, his lips curved away from his teeth. Her blood sang in her temples. Gracefully, she bestrode him and poised above his throbbing manhood. Her own inner flesh ached for him and her throat was dry. With a sob, Shan T'u lowered her body and filled herself with him. Her eyes caught a glimpse of sweeping valleys and distant violet hills as she swirled her hips in a slow, maddening rhythm.

He brought her face down to his. She attacked his mouth hungrily, deeply thrusting with her tongue. He was a torch within her, spinning at her core, turning her insides white hot. She rubbed her body urgently against him, her skin seeking his everywhere. Her lungs felt ready to burst.

She felt a completion at hand, an unbearably sweet togetherness, as she intensified her motions. He moved with her, his body intertwined with hers like the very symbol for yin and yang. It seemed to her that they were shooting across the valley, riding the winds, escaping from princes and bandits and everything that chained them down.

Then her release came in wave upon wave of red ocean crashing on indigo beach, and she clutched him spasmodically, fearing that she would drown in this sea. His arms enwrapped her like steel chains and she could feel his own heat, like flaming arrows, coursing deep inside her. The red ocean at length became the pounding of her heart and the indigo beach became the cool, waving grass. She was panting for breath, her head on his heaving chest. Still she could feel him within her, and when she writhed, tiny fires sprang up.

His hand stroked her hair and his eyes fluttered open, the golden lashes catching the sun. In his eyes, the clouds drifted majestically. His beard blew stiffly in the wind and his lips glistened, dark and sensuous.

"My God, Shan T'u," he husked. "Surely you were not *taught* these arts . . ."

She smiled into his chest. "I spent much time with Father's concubines."

"Devil!"

Finally, they parted, and she lay on her back. He raised himself slightly to look down at her. He plucked a green blade of grass and tickled her chest and stomach. "No woman has ever made me feel as I do now."

"Is that what you tell the other wenches?"

He grinned. "Yes. But I lie to them. I can't lie to you. What little good there was in me transmutes into sainthood when you touch me."

"Simple alchemy," she said. "You find all that is sinful in *me* and it conquers my soul."

Abruptly, he sat up. "Your body speaks with your heart and soul, Shan T'u. Like a poem."

"Yes. It's very much like poetry, or painting, or a garden. I'll always cherish these sins, William."

He looked sadly at her. "You had to bring that up, didn't you?" He chewed on the blade of grass solemnly. "We'd best return to the caravan before they search for us. Looks like the worst part of the trip is over."

She nodded, eyes brimming. "And the best as well, my paladin."

He sprang to his feet. "Get dressed, Princess. Don't tempt me further."

Lazily, drinking in his wondrous beauty, Shan T'u stood. De Rais's eyes ravished her as she stood poised in the meadow like a splendid wild deer, her flanks satiny and glowing with the sun. She put on her gown and shoes. De Rais dressed in his soldier's garb. The two figures stood windblown against valleys and crags.

"I love you, Shan T'u," he said.

"I love you, William."

He took a deep breath and strode away from her. She followed mournfully. The laughing nymph of before was gone now, transformed into a grieving princess.

As the sky glowed ochre with evening, and the saw-toothed peaks paled to misted green, the evening meal was prepared. Shan T'u stood outside her cart, shivering in the cold wind. So many tempests whirled in her brain. Dark, forbidden thoughts raised their demonic heads. She had already given her body to William, and her heart. Only the most tenuous thread of tradition connected her to what she was. And that thread was unraveling.

Shan T'u turned from the sunset and walked sadly around the encampment, glancing at soldiers and servants who talked or played cards. Two soldiers, who sat by a cart, stopped talking very suddenly as Shan T'u approached. She looked at them, and they averted their eyes.

Then one of the soldiers took up a stick and began to write in the dirt. Shan T'u's curiosity made her stop and watch as the glow of the setting sun flooded the camp.

The soldier, a high-ranking officer named Hui Cha, was writing characters. Shan T'u smiled. Obviously, he and Li Yiu, his companion, had been gossiping about matters she was not supposed to hear. So they would now write the gossip. Writing, of course, was a skill that most Chinese warriors did not bother to learn, nor did the snobbish scholar elite encourage soldiers to be literate. But in the palace of Chang Hu, all men were taught these arts.

And no women. So Shan T'u enjoyed her secret ability to read what was being drawn in the sand. She saw the character for *shoot* and the character for *this night*. Idly, she wondered what Hui Cha was writing. What court gossip could they possibly know?

But now Hui Cha was writing the character for *warrior* and the character for *yellow* and the character for *hair*. Shan T'u edged back into the shadows and her eyes widened in growing horror as the characters were crudely drawn. Soon the message became clear, and her breath had stopped.

No! It was not possible! Not such treachery . . .

Her reason fled. Her heart overflowed with terror for her beloved. Who else was involved? Might they be doing this deed even now . . . ?

Shan T'u backed away from the soldiers as her heartbeat drummed. Then she began to run through the encampment, crying out William's name. Soldiers and huntsmen sprang to their feet, alarmed.

De Rais was grooming his horse near a campfire. He heard Shan T'u's cries and turned, gripping the reins.

She ran up to him and clutched at his sleeve. "They're going to kill you!" she blurted. "Tonight— the two soldiers Hui Cha and Li Yiu, while you sleep—"

"Shan T'u, slow down," De Rais said. He gripped her hands tightly and looked with astonishment at her trembling body and wide eyes. "What are you talking about?"

By now, others had gathered. The glow of the dying

sun lit the scene. A cold wind gusted around them. Shan T'u said, "There is a plot. The soldiers Hui Cha and Li Yiu have been ordered by my father to kill you. They were to wait until the minions of the Indian prince met us. But they are frightened. The bandits . . ."

There was astounded murmuring. De Rais's eyes flickered with suspicion. A soldier stepped forward, his face set grimly. "I am Hui Cha," he said. "How does the princess defend this accusation against me?"

Shan T'u whirled, her eyes ablaze. "Traitor! I discovered the plot just now."

Hui Cha smiled, confident. "From whom? Let the accuser stand forth."

De Rais lightly brushed his sword hilt with his fingers. "Princess, how *did* you find out about this plot?"

Shan T'u blushed. Many pairs of eyes looked at her in the dusky light. Around them, campfires sputtered and animals brayed. The caravan had suffered grievous losses. The princess had already led them into ambush. Nobody trusted her now.

Nasty laughter was heard in the outer darkness. Hui Cha grinned openly. De Rais drew Shan T'u close to him.

Shan T'u said, "I know of this plot because the two soldiers wrote it in the ground."

This brought a stunned silence, followed by great whoops of laughter. Hui Cha spread open his hands in supplication to the crowd. "Wrote it in the *ground!* And does the princess *read?*"

The jeers grew in volume. De Rais whispered, "What in hell are you trying to do, Princess?"

Shan T'u said nothing. She stood with her lips thinly drawn. Her destiny had somehow brought her to this, and a decision had to be made. Aware that her life was about to change forever, she seized a stick from a teamster at his bullock cart. For the second time, the spectators became quiet. Hui Cha's eyes narrowed. Shan T'u walked to the center of the semicircle that had formed around her. With sure, artistic strokes of the stick, she wrote in the dirt: *"Tonight we fulfill Chang's command and kill the yellow-haired knight. Let us not wait for the arrival of the Indian prince. The knight is not to be trusted. Already we have been betrayed."*

There were low, terrified mutterings. Servants edged backward, away from this sorceress. They, of course, could not read what she had written, but they knew that these were characters. The soldiers *could* read, and De Rais could make out the ideas as well.

Hui Cha attempted a fresh laugh, but his eyes shifted. "This is a pretty trick the princess has learned, but surely you don't believe—"

"It is true!" another voice shouted. A soldier burst from the crowd, his eyes rolling. "I just saw—they tried to brush the earth over the writing, but some of the characters remained. The princess tells the truth!"

De Rais lost no time. His sword was out in a breath, and he lunged across the semicircle. His arm snaked around Hui Cha's throat and he held the soldier in a relentless grip, cutting off his windpipe. De Rais stuck the tip of his sword under the soldier's chin.

"Now, let's have the truth or this sword will carve out your tongue."

Hui Cha trembled, eyes rolling back. De Rais let up

the pressure enough to permit the soldier to speak. The words came as a strangled rasp. "It was the order of Prince Chang Hu . . ."

"Why?" De Rais demanded.

A third soldier moved into the makeshift arena, and his face was ashen. "I am Li Yiu," he said. "Hui Cha does not lie. Prince Chang told us that you were no friar, that you intended to kidnap the princess and hold her for ransom."

There was a great reaction from the others. "It is so!" a voice cried. Another shouted, "He *is* no friar! Prince Chang was right!" And still another: "But he saved us from the bandits!"

De Rais pricked Hui Cha's skin. "Tell them to be still."

Li Yiu raised his hands, terrified. "Please!" he cried. "Please listen!"

De Rais's eyes circled the group. "Hear me. It is true I am no friar. I needed to dress as a friar to avoid the Mongol warriors in my journey across Cathay. But I am a knight in my own land, a warrior like these warriors. If I wanted to carry off your princess, would I have fought the red masks?"

"She's worth more alive than dead," a huntsman sneered.

"And so am I," De Rais countered. "I could have carried her off *any* night, while you all slept. But I did not. And I *will* not. Prince Chang was lied to. We will learn who told the lie. Until then, who will be your guide? And who will you give to the prince if I die? For I now keep the princess as my hostage, and if you attack me, *she* will die."

Li Yiu blanched and there were shouts and threats from the others. But De Rais maintained his bluff. He flung Hui Cha from him, and the soldier sprawled on the ground, clutching his throat. De Rais brandished the sword. "We are but two days from the river crossing and our meeting with the Indian prince. When the princess is taken on the royal barge, I will ride away. You may find your own way back."

Hui Cha was helped to his feet. Shan T'u stood at De Rais's side and held his arm with both of her hands. "This knight has offered his life for me," she said. "He has proven himself true and worthy. I think I know who whispered lies into my father's ear. I stay willingly with this knight, and he who harms the paladin will be executed on my command."

This brought a grudging, tense silence. Hui Cha and Li Yiu managed to blend into the crowd. Slowly, the soldiers wandered off, followed by the huntsmen and servants. Shan T'u stood with De Rais, who still held his sword at the ready. Night closed in.

De Rais exhaled. "What *other* arts do you possess, my lady?"

She clung tightly to his arm. "For a woman to read and write is sacrilege. It is unheard of."

"Did Master Po slip you *this* bit of learning also?"

She nodded.

"Remind me to thank him." He slipped an arm around her trembling shoulders. "Shan T'u, this is not a good situation."

"I know. The soldiers will try to kill us both rather than face my father's wrath."

"We must make a decision."

She looked up at him. "I will follow you."

His eyes scanned the darkening camp. "Let's talk about it over some rabbit stew. I'm hungry."

Shan T'u leaned on De Rais, seeking the warmth of his body against the cold night. "I'm not frightened with you, paladin."

"Good," he said dryly. "That makes one of us."

Chapter Eleven

CRADLED IN THE SWEET FRAGRANCE OF NIGHT, SHAN T'U and De Rais sat on the ground and ate cooked rabbit. Shan T'u chewed delicately, and looked at her lover's face in the leaping firelight.

"Kung wished me to live with him in the hills," she said with wonder.

De Rais grunted. "I used to promise country wenches they could live in my castle."

"He wanted me to help him overthrow Kublai Khan."

"An extravagant man, this bandit. Were you tempted?"

She drank tea. "You know me well, beloved."

"There is a wildness in you," De Rais said. "You are as comfortable eating rabbit on a mountaintop as you are eating snails in a banquet hall."

She smiled at his words. "I was often beaten for that wildness. Master Po tried to bend me to the ways of obedience."

"And yet he taught you to shoot a bow and to read and write!"

Shan T'u's heart ached with thoughts of home. "Master Po hoped that I might preserve some of our heritage. He said nobody would suspect a princess of carrying this knowledge."

"A clever man," De Rais said. "But you revealed your secrets too soon."

Shan T'u bowed her head. "I was always impulsive. Even Master Po said it would hurt me. I am more the foolish girl than the wise princess."

De Rais laughed sardonically. "To be among men is to be among folly, and to admit your folly is to be wise."

Shan T'u looked at him with admiration. "That sounded almost Chinese."

He made a mock bow. "Thank you, Princess. Even a barbarian may learn." His eyes danced in the firelight, but now his face became serious. "All of this philosophy is stimulating, but we still have a problem."

"What can we do, William?"

He looked around, sniffing. "Well, as long as we sit by this fire, they probably won't put an arrow into our backs. But I think you're right. Those soldiers would rather say you were slaughtered by bandits than risk the truth getting to Chang."

"I'm sorry," she murmured. "I shouldn't have been so rash."

"True enough," he agreed sternly. "But it's done.

If I learned one thing, it's to play the cards you're dealt. We have worried soldiers out there, a bandit chief I still don't trust, and an Indian potentate waiting upriver. Not to mention your father back in his palace."

"With your trade routes," she quipped.

He tossed a gnawed bone into the fire and wiped grease from his lips. "Well, I made a poor knight, so it's fitting that I make a poor trader. Right now, I've got to get you to your husband. Then I can return to Chang."

"You'll be killed . . ." Shan T'u said.

"I've been in tight spots before."

Shan T'u tried valiantly to finish her food, but her appetite fled. She washed down the half-chewed rabbit and scrambled to her feet. With her fists clenched, she walked to a nearby pine tree and looked miserably out into the night-shrouded valley.

De Rais came after her, his boots softly squeaking in the grass. She felt his warm breath at her neck. "Don't worry, Princess. I'll survive."

She shook her head, heartbroken. "It's not that," she said. "The thought of you riding away, forever . . ."

"Aye, it eats at my innards, too." His hand strayed to her glossy hair. "I will never know a love like this again."

"Nor I."

"But it's useless to cry over it, Shan T'u. We have no choice."

She turned, and her heart raced. The fire cast a scarlet corona around him, and his face was all in shadow. She touched his chest with her fingertips, and his skin was hot from the flames.

"Do we *not* have a choice?" she whispered.

"What do you mean?"

"William . . . this is no longer the wedding journey that began at my father's palace. We have seen treachery and slaughter. I have unmasked my soul. I have merged my body with yours. Can't we now risk everything . . . ?"

His hands gripped her shoulders. "Have you changed your mind, then, since that night I begged you in the cave?"

The forbidden words spilled from her now, unleashed. "Oh, William, what else matters now? I was never meant to be a princess. My feet were not bound. Master Po was rescued to teach me forbidden arts. And then you rode over the hill. How can I ignore the portents any longer? *This* is my destiny—to be with you."

She slipped into his arms and pressed urgently against him. She could feel his brave heart beating. He gathered her close. "Shan T'u," he murmured, "how I've ached to hear you say these words."

"Then you will take me?"

He exhaled. "What bitter irony! Now that you agree, *I* must say no. I was the fool to broach it. Where could we go, Princess? Hunted by your father, by the Indian potentate, by these soldiers. We would be fugitives. For a moment of freedom, we would spend our lives stealing chickens and sleeping on straw."

"Your love made you ask me. My love now agrees."

He smiled. "We are both of noble blood, Shan T'u. In time, we'd grow weary of martyrdom."

"We could go back to your land, William."

"Where no priest would recognize our love, and where my enemies would drive us away. We would be beggars or thieves, and freeze in the wintertime. Shan T'u, my heart begs me to ride with you until even the sun can't find us. But my wits tell me that we *can't* run."

She disengaged from his embrace and held his hands. "Then we part forever. And soon after wedding my prince, I will redeem my honor."

"Now damn it, Shan T'u!" De Rais flung away her hands. "There'll be no suicides!"

Shan T'u smiled serenely. "It is no shame in our land. Rather, it is a way to *cleanse* one's shame. Each life is illusion and nothing more. Only the one life in the light of Buddha is reality." She went to him and touched his cheeks with cool hands. "William, if this life is life without you, I have no use for it. Because of your love, this life has already been beautiful and holy. Far more than I had ever hoped."

She stood on tiptoe and kissed his lips tenderly. De Rais gazed into her glistening eyes and his lips trembled as he tried to find words. "I have not known anything like you . . ."

"I'm glad," she said. "My whole being is filled with gladness. I look forward now to my royal wedding and to a sleep blessed with dreams of you."

De Rais seemed to crumble as he stood in the darkness before her. Then, suddenly, he spun and smacked his fist against the tree trunk. *"No!"* he cried. "You won't stick a knife into your belly! Then what in hell am *I* to do? Kill myself as well? I'm already damned to hellfire, so what must *I* look forward to? There must be another way."

"What?" she asked, her heart afire.

De Rais gestured in frustration. "Damn, I don't know. What about this prince of yours? What if we told him the truth? What if we petitioned him to surrender his contract and free you?"

She shook her head. "It would be a grave and deadly insult. This was a contract between the prince and my father. I have no power over it."

De Rais thought furiously. "What if this Indian fellow learned that you had been lying with *me?* Wouldn't he want to be rid of you?"

Shan T'u laughed. "Oh, most assuredly. He would have me tortured and publicly executed as a warning to all wives and concubines."

De Rais collapsed into brooding. In the distance, the other campfires were bright wavering lights on the dark hillside. Horses whinnied. There was an eerie, wind-tossed melody of chimes and bells. *"Look* at you," De Rais said peevishly. "You don't even *look* like a proper princess. You're sunburnt, you're blood-stained, you're filthy."

She smiled. "Then perhaps he won't recognize me."

De Rais slammed the tree trunk a second time. "Damn you, that's it! You're half-disguised already. We'll tell the prince about the bandit attack, but we'll tell him the bandits carried you off. You can be one of the servingwomen."

"A good plan," Shan T'u agreed. "But how do we get all my soldiers and huntsmen and servants to agree?"

"How should I know?" he bellowed. He paced up and down, waving his arms. "Pay 'em off. Cut off their heads. Shan T'u, we're going to be together—I swear it!"

She nodded happily and rushed to his arms. She kissed his mouth and throat and murmured, "I know we will, my love. It can be no other way. It must—"

The first scream brought up De Rais's head sharply. Shan T'u paused, not breathing. A second scream came from the caravan, a scream of mortal agony.

"William!" Shan T'u cried.

"Damn his eyes!" De Rais growled. "The treacherous bastard!"

And suddenly, the night erupted into horror. The cries of attacking bandits shattered the silent mountain air, and the drumming of hoofbeats made the earth tremble. Shan T'u stood next to De Rais and saw the fiery silhouettes of horses and men. She heard the *thwack* of arrows and the clash of sword on sword. Screams punctuated the battle.

"How could it be?" Shan T'u asked brokenly. "We came through the mountains."

"He followed us," De Rais said grimly. "He waited until we felt safe."

"They'll fight bravely," Shan T'u said. "As they did before . . ."

"They won't have a chance."

Shan T'u tore away from him and ran toward the caravan. A man, outlined in flame, flung himself from the black hillside and burned in the night sky like a shooting star. Horses reared in the lurid glow. Great funnels of flame whooshed upward, illuminating the carnage.

Shan T'u could see the horsemen now, coming rank

171

on rank from the velvet hills. She stopped and turned to De Rais, who had followed her. "Help them!" she begged. "Save my caravan!"

"There's nothing I can do," he said dully. "It's too late."

She grasped at his tunic. *"No.* You are a paladin, William. Your sword is magic."

"Listen to me!" He pinioned her wrists. She felt her own body shudder with sobs. "Shan T'u, in less than an hour there won't be a man or woman left alive. If I went in there now, I'd be cut down. I can't counterattack as I did last time. There are too many of them, and it's too dark. Do you understand?"

A dull pain crushed her chest. "No. I don't understand how you can stay here like a coward."

He gathered her body close and wrapped his arms around her. "Princess, stop believing in fairy tales. I was lucky the first time. Don't you see, Shan T'u? They *want* me to fight. They're waiting for me to ride into that inferno. And then Kung will take you."

She looked up at him, startled.

"Yes, Shan T'u, it's a trap. He wants you for his bride and he's willing to murder everyone to get you."

"No . . ."

"It's all over, Princess. The wedding journey is done. We will be fugitives after all, for we must ride away now."

Tears streamed down her cheeks. "No. They are my soldiers, they are my servants . . ."

"They are *dead!*" He yanked up her head with his strong fingers. "We may only have minutes. I'm going to summon my horse. Then we're going to find a second horse, and we're going to ride like the hounds of hell are at our heels."

"Ride where?"

"If we can reach the river and follow it, there'll be places to hide."

She shut her eyes and swayed. "What is happening to my life?"

"It's turning upside down, Princess. And now it's time to save it."

De Rais placed his fingers between his lips and emitted a shrill whistle. A moment later, hoofbeats drummed and De Rais's horse galloped out of the darkness.

At the same moment, two masked bandits burst from the brush, swords whistling over their heads. Shan T'u screamed. De Rais drew his weapon and shielded Shan T'u with his body. His horse pranced beside him, snorting. De Rais parried a vicious downward cut from one bandit and shouted to the princess, "Mount up and ride! Find another horse!"

"I won't leave you . . ."

"Damn it, Shan T'u, you'll get me killed! *Ride!*"

The bandit lunged and De Rais just managed to deflect the blow. The second bandit had reached him. Shan T'u slipped one foot into the stirrup and swung up into the saddle. She looked down at the nightmarish scene of her beloved holding off two swordsmen. Then she forced her eyes to look away, and, leaning low over the horse's neck, she plunged into the night.

Shan T'u felt the wind sting her face. The heat of the burning caravan was at her back. She ducked the branches that swung out of nowhere. Sobbing, she slowed the horse to a stop and sat, gasping for breath.

She saw the tremendous wall of flame licking at the starry sky. A towering fury filled her, and impulsively, she pivoted the horse and galloped in the direction

173

of the caravan. In moments, she was upon the destruction. The brightness of the flames blinded her and the heat seared her lungs. She shielded her eyes with one hand as she controlled the terrified horse. Animals stampeded. One camel had collapsed to the ground, coated with flames. The stench of burning flesh made her feel faint.

Shan T'u tried to guess how the fight was going, but there was only a confusion of bodies. Bowmen, behind carts and wagons, loosed arrows into the dark perimeter of the fire. Mounted bandits leaped over flaming carts and swung swords. There was the shivering thud of steel hitting flesh and the bone-chilling shrieks of wounded men.

Shan T'u was paralyzed with horror. William was right; there was no chance for her people. Her desperate eyes spotted a dead soldier slumped over a bullock cart, his bow and quiver of arrows nearby. She spurred William's horse and reached the cart. She recognized the dead soldier as Hui Cha. For a moment, she averted her eyes and tears flooded her face. Fools. All of them. Especially her fool of a father.

Anger gave her cold courage. She dismounted and swept the quiver of arrows over her shoulder. Grimacing at the heavy weight, she picked up the bow. But a shadow passed over her, blotting out the fire's illumination.

Shan T'u looked up into the masked face of a bandit. He reared on his white steed and swung a sword over his head. Around and around the sword whistled, hypnotizing Shan T'u, who cringed by the wagon.

The bandit laughed and Shan T'u bowed her head for the death blow. But instead there was a swish of air and a piercing scream. Shan T'u looked up and saw the bandit's hand pressed tightly over his arm. Between his fingers, blood spumed. The bandit reeled in the saddle and toppled.

De Rais loomed over her, astride a coal-black horse. "You fool!" he snapped. "You had to come back."

Shaking, she held up the bow. "I have a weapon."

"Much good it did you! Get on this horse—*now!*"

De Rais grabbed the reins of his own horse and smoothly changed mounts, settling into his own saddle. Shan T'u handed up the bow to De Rais, then swung her leg over the back of the black horse. De Rais handed back the bow. "Can you shoot while you ride?"

She nodded.

"Well aim sharply, Princess. I won't look back for you."

The furnace heat of the flames seemed to ignite her soul. "I love you, William."

"Touching," he said dryly. "Let's go."

He swung his horse and rode off, and Shan T'u urged her own mount after him. She held the bow in one hand and the reins in the other. Her thighs pressed tightly against the horse's flanks and the earth surged beneath the flying hooves. She was free and unfettered, as she had dreamed of being. She remembered her riding lessons in secret groves, clip-clopping round and round until her backside screamed, mounting and dismounting a thousand times until she cried for mercy.

And now, through the twists and turns of destiny, she careened down a dark mountain with a foreign knight. Not what her father had planned, and not what Master Po had foreseen. Or was she wrong about that?

It didn't matter now. Shan T'u heard the horses behind her and she glanced back. There seemed to be scores of them, illuminated by the scudding moon. The flaming caravan was far up the hillside, a flickering beacon.

Shan T'u let the reins drop. As the hillside flew past and the wind whipped her face, she reached back and yanked an arrow from the quiver. In one liquid motion, she loaded the bow, twisted her slender body in the saddle, aimed at a dimly seen bandit, and let the bowstring snap. The bandit fell from his horse. Shan T'u smiled exultantly and picked up the reins again.

Still the bandits pursued, and now the terrain was too steep for Shan T'u to try another shot. Arrows hissed past her head and she ducked low as she rode. She saw William a short distance ahead, riding a zigzag trail. His head turned and he beckoned to her with one hand. She snapped the reins and followed him.

She crashed her mount through hedgerows and brush, and suddenly, there was William, waiting for her. Shan T'u pulled back on the reins and her horse reared up. She quieted the animal and sat, panting, in the saddle.

"Why did we stop?" she gasped.

"Remember the story I told you?" he said. "How I turned and charged my pursuers?" She nodded. "We're going to do that now, Shan T'u. Are you ready?"

"Yes," she breathed.

His eyes flared as he looked at her. "God, I love you, Shan T'u."

"And I, you," she whispered.

With her heart swelling, she turned her horse and loaded her bow. De Rais listened for a moment to the wind and the rumble of hoofbeats. Then he nodded. *"Now."*

Shan T'u slapped the reins, and her horse leaped a hedgerow and grazed a tree trunk as it hustled out of the brush and back onto the open hillside. She glimpsed William as he rode wide and whipped his mount up toward the pursuing bandits.

Abruptly, the red masks came tumbling over the hill like ocean waves. She kneed her horse to make it run faster and glued her eyes to the charging bandits. She drew back her bowstring as the bandits spotted her and shouted in surprise. She loosed the first arrow and saw it pierce the chest of a bandit. She wasted no time in exulting, but drew another arrow and fired it. This one fell short.

Arrows now flew past her, as the startled bandits counterattacked. But the surprise had worked. Shan T'u reloaded and sent an arrow through the neck of a second bandit. Meanwhile, William was in the midst of the bandit horde, rearing up on his horse, his sword a dancer of death. The blade swung again and again, and each time a bandit tumbled from the saddle. Shan T'u continued to shoot arrows, and she hissed with vengeful pleasure each time a red mask was jerked backwards and clutched at the shaft in his body.

And now the remaining bandits were turning, urging their horses back up the hillside! A litter of corpses darkened the grass and riderless mounts stampeded. William careened back to her, barely breathing.

"We've chased them away!" Shan T'u cried.

"Yes," he said, with suspicious eyes. "They certainly turned tail, didn't they?"

"We've won, William . . ."

"Don't celebrate yet, Princess. Let's get out of here first."

Shan T'u nodded, and once again they thundered down the hillside. Now she could see the first band of deep blue on the horizon. She glanced over her shoulder but could no longer see the burning caravan. It was forever a memory, a bitter horror that was emblazoned on her heart. She could not think about the slaughter now. She had to think only of riding until they reached the river. But even as she rode, she wept in despair.

In the gray light of morning, Shan T'u and De Rais rode along the river's edge. Sheer cliffs lined the gorge, and now and then a junk sailed by, laden with provisions.

Shan T'u dozed in the saddle, then roused herself. Every bone ached, and she smelled singed. She petted her horse's neck and looked ahead at De Rais, whose back was straight, though his tunic was torn.

"William . . ." she cried weakly.

He reined up and turned. His face was blackened from smoke. "Yes?"

"I must rest."

He nodded. "We can water our horses here." He dismounted and led his horse to the river's edge. The animal dipped its head and drank deeply. Shan T'u winced in pain as she lifted her leg over the horse and dropped lightly to the ground.

She stood with the damp wind billowing her hair. Her silk gown was savagely tattered. Her shoulder burned with pain from bearing the quiver of arrows. Hunger gnawed at her stomach and thirst parched her throat. Never in her life had she known such discomfort and such anguish.

De Rais looked out over the river, which flowed with ponderous current. Under the dense clouds, the water glowed silver. Shan T'u looked at De Rais and saw a dark stain on his sleeve.

"You're hurt," she said.

"A nick, nothing more. And you?"

She shook her head and bit her lip. "Only the wounds in my soul."

"Poor princess." His healing hands curved over her shoulders and his warm lips brushed her throat. "A knight sees many slaughters. The first always rends the soul. After that, he becomes used to it."

She looked searchingly at him. "And are you used to it, William? Does it mean nothing to you?"

"It means that good men died."

"Protecting *me*."

"It was *their* task to bring *you* safely through the mountains, not *your* task to save *them*."

She made a disgusted gesture. "You toy with words. Fifty of my father's finest warriors are dead. Fifty of his finest huntsmen are corpses on a hillside. Priceless treasures are in the hands of cutthroats."

His eyebrows went up. "Oh? I thought they were going to do great deeds."

"How could he betray me so?" She made a fist and pummeled her thigh. "After I spared his life!"

De Rais wrapped his strong arms around her waist from behind and she leaned gratefully against the protective wall of his chest. "Inside the palace walls, Shan T'u, it is all poetry and philosophy and moral truth. All of your balance is there, in your gardens and your temples. Even your hunts are carefully planned on your father's game preserves.

"But then you left the palace. Out here, life does not follow the precepts of the sages. Kung wanted you badly enough to slay your entourage. He is an outlaw who lives by his wits, has no principles, and has trained an admirable army."

"You admire them?"

"I admire their courage and precision. They cannot afford to be honorable men. Deceit and ruthlessness ensure their survival. Perhaps these are the men who *will* challenge the Mongol overlords. That kind of bloodthirsty commitment is what you need."

Shan T'u felt a great emptiness inside her. She slipped out of De Rais's embrace. Rain misted in her face. "I don't know you, paladin. You declare your love, and you speak of the slaughterers of my people as heroes."

De Rais took up the reins of his horse. "There is still much of the little girl in you, Shan T'u. Kung was romantic and worthy enough as long as he followed the rules. But the rules have not helped. Your sages and scholars knuckled under to the Mongols. Your Tartar conqueror considers each one of his subjects a soldier, prepared to kill or die at a command. Who, then, will rise up to reclaim your land? Bold knights?"

"I had thought so."

"Well, Shan T'u, *I* am a bold knight. And I will tell you that most of us are pretty much like Kung. We swing a sharp sword, we ride a fast horse, and we have very little respect for sentiment."

"And murdering my entourage is *knightly?*"

"These are rough men with brutal ways. That kind of man wins crusades and wars. If China should ever be returned to the Chinese, men like Kung will return it. And promptly they will be executed for offending the public taste."

The wind picked up. Shan T'u's eyes swept the gorges and cliffs. "I am sorry I gave myself to you, William. I regret running from my people. I should have died fighting for them."

He smiled. "No, Princess. You regret that we did not fly over the mountains on a winged horse. You regret that I did not drive off the bandits with a holy sword. You feel guilt, Shan T'u, for saving your skin. You are tired, hungry, and thirsty, and your lovely eyes have seen horrors enough for a lifetime. This is what it is to run away and deny your royalty. It's starvation, sore backsides, rain in your face, and the stink of death. Can your love survive all that, Shan T'u? Can it rise above your broken spirit?"

The truth of what he said penetrated her bleeding soul. She sank to her knees on the riverbank and bowed her head, and her tiny body heaved with convulsions of grief. Like great monsoon waves, they washed up from deep inside. De Rais stood quietly by, his own eyes brimming with tears. Shan T'u wept for a very long time, until at last she collapsed in exhaustion. The rain pelted her shivering form and she curled up tightly like a bruised flower.

De Rais stooped and gathered her up in his arms. He held her like a precious infant, rocking her back and forth. Shan T'u felt her aching eyes close and heard his scratchy voice absurdly crooning a French lullaby. Her arms sneaked around his neck and her head nestled against his collarbone. She let blissful sleep, like ripples on a lotus pond, carry her away.

Later that afternoon, De Rais and Shan T'u rode across a stone bridge of many arches. Shan T'u gazed fondly at her knight as his horse pranced on the echoing stones. They had begged food from a passing junk and Shan T'u felt stronger and lighter of heart. The terrible sense of loss still clung to her, but she was with her beloved.

He let her ride alongside him and asked, "Where shall we go now?"

She looked out at the stippled water, which was the color of the stones. "I want my revenge on the serpent whose venom turned my father against you."

"And who is that?"

Shan T'u's eyes became granite. "It could only have been the Lady Feng. She has always despised me for my wild ways. She has always lusted for more power and riches. Her jealousies and intrigues consume her vitals."

"Well," he said, "she sounds charming. And I'd like a whack or two at her myself if she poisoned Chang's good opinion of me."

"Then that is our quest!"

He grinned. "Of course. Once we explain to your father that you were not wed to your prince, but gave your body to me instead, I suppose he'll allow you to enjoy your vengeance."

Shan T'u sighed in frustration and anger. "I'm sorry, William. My heart clouded my head."

"Naturally."

She glanced up at him. "Where, then, *can* we go?"

He assumed a boyishly innocent expression. "Well,

of course I am no expert on Cathay, but since we are fugitives in the southern lands, perhaps we can go north and seek our fortunes there."

"North?" Her eyes narrowed in suspicion. "To the court of Kublai Khan?"

De Rais shrugged with elaborate casualness. "Perhaps . . ."

Shan T'u glared at him. "William! You still cherish your visions of trade routes!"

He gestured reasonably. "Why not? I've heard that Khan likes foreigners, and you could pass as my concubine . . ."

"Your *concubine!*"

"Well, then, my wife, if we can find a priest to marry us."

Her heart jumped. "Yes! I'd like that very much."

"Good. Then we marry, and seek Kublai Khan, and become rich."

She sighed in exasperation. "Is there no other course for our lives to follow?"

He laughed. "Well, we could go back to Persia, or Arabia, or even Europe."

"I know—to open trade routes!"

"Well, now, Shan T'u, I'm not cut out to be a scholar or a poet. And unless I join somebody's foul-smelling army, I won't be paid to break heads. Swindling is what I do best. We can have our own manor house one day, with children scampering about . . ."

"And will you seduce neighboring wives and fight duels?"

He guffawed. "You paint a vision of paradise."

She smiled, but still her spirit troubled her. She idly noticed a band of travelers approaching at the far end of the bridge. They seemed foreign themselves, huddled together and hunched over their horses as if ducking the rain.

"William," she said boldly. "Surely there must be more to our fates than that."

"More adventure, you mean? More nobility?"

"*Yes!*" she cried. "You won my heart, William, and you made me break my vows to everything I have been taught. I didn't deny my birthright for a swindler."

"Now, Shan T'u, I never promised you more."

"Your *eyes* promised," she insisted. "Your heart promised. Look what we've come through. We have looked into the mouth of Death and escaped. We have passed through water and fire, and trials by combat. You have proved yourself courageous, strong, and honorable despite your worst intentions. Look deep into your soul, William. Our destiny lies beyond swindling. It lies—"

"*Quiet.*"

She skipped a breath at his sharp tone. Her eyes widened. De Rais said, "I think, Shan T'u, that once again our destiny has been decided for us. Look there."

Shan T'u turned her head and gasped in terror. The travelers she had seen now sat erect in their saddles. There was no mistaking their identity now. No mistaking the warriors' hats over swarthy moustached faces, no mistaking the dark robes, the corded leather belts, or the wide boots. No mistaking the huge, powerful bodies astride magnificent horses. No mistaking the bows and arrows at the ready.

"*Mongols!*" she whispered. "So far south . . ."

"I think they're expecting us," De Rais said.

"Let's run . . ."

"You can try."

Shan T'u felt a prickle of terror at his words. Panicked, she turned her skittish horse and saw the second war party of Mongols blocking the other end of the bridge. She spun in the saddle and stared helplessly at De Rais.

"Shall we swim for it?" he joked grimly.

"William, I'm frightened!"

He fingered the hilt of his sword and his eyes narrowed. "If they wanted to kill us, they would have done it already. They want us as prisoners, Shan T'u."

"Why?"

He shrugged. "We'll find out, won't we?"

Shan T'u quieted her nervous mount and moved closer to De Rais. She shut her eyes and prayed that her love would sustain her now.

Chapter Twelve

DE RAIS KNEED HIS HORSE AND GESTURED FOR SHAN
T'u to follow. The princess held up her head bravely;
she would not show fear to these barbarians. She rode
behind De Rais, the hoofbeats echoing on the stones.

As they reached the Mongols, Shan T'u recoiled at
the whiff of unbathed skin. There were five of the
warriors; the three at the other end of the bridge rode
across with a clatter to join the rest. Beneath their
coarse woven robes, the Tartars wore armor of dried
buffalo hide. The leader of the war party smiled,
showing rotted teeth. His tiny black eyes sparkled.

In Mongolian, the leader said to De Rais, "I am
Nayan. You are the Yellow Beard?"

"I can't hide it," De Rais said.

"The Khan of all Khans asks you to be his guest at the grand palace."

"That is a great honor," De Rais said.

Shan T'u's back tingled. Nayan said, "We will take you there."

De Rais gestured at Shan T'u. "This is my bride," he said. "She must come with me."

The Mongols laughed at that, a cruel and unpleasant laugh. "The ride will be long and difficult," Nayan said. "We have no sedan chairs for women."

"She can ride," De Rais said.

This created much merriment among the Mongols. Shan T'u examined their horses, laden with the bare necessities a Mongol warrior carried: cooking utensils and a folded felt tent.

Nayan said, "If the woman falters, we leave her to die."

De Rais turned to Shan T'u. "Can you do it?"

Shan T'u lifted her face against the fine rain. "Yes."

De Rais smiled encouragingly. "Just remember that I love you, Shan T'u. Let that give you strength."

"It will make me immortal," Shan T'u joked weakly.

They had carried on this conversation in Chinese, and the Mongol leader grew impatient. "Enough," he growled. "We ride."

Nayan turned his horse with a clatter of utensils and a flap of his robe. He whipped his mount into a canter. De Rais and Shan T'u followed and the other Mongols surrounded them. Soon, they were galloping across the muddy countryside in the slate shadow of the mountains. Shan T'u squeezed her thighs tightly to her horse's flanks and tried to ignore the shooting pains in her legs and the dizziness that threatened to topple her.

The rain became a hissing summer storm and Shan T'u blinked away the water as she rode. They had turned north and east, heading for the Tartar capital, which her father had always called Yenjing, but which the Mongols called Kanbaliq. Shan T'u could not help thinking that behind her, in those forbidding, rain-glistening mountains, lay the ashes of her wedding caravan.

And she could not help thinking that it was no accident for these Mongol warriors to be here.

Still they rode, across great swampy fields and through little villages, along canals where junks folded their sails and rocked at moorings. As the sky turned to violet, a raving hunger flayed Shan T'u's vitals. Only her riding skill kept her astride the horse. She tossed her head and wiped at the rain with her hand. The Mongols rode with arrogant ease.

But now Shan T'u felt a suffocating panic at the back of her throat. She urged her horse alongside that of De Rais. "William . . ." she gasped.

He glanced at her. "Keep riding, Shan T'u."

". . . can't . . ." she whispered.

"Listen to me," he said. "These Mongols can ride ten days without lighting a fire or taking a meal. If we stop, they'll kill us."

She shook her head, her tears mingling with the rain. "I *can't*, William."

The slurried earth suddenly rose up like a slimy wall and spun before her. Her hands went numb and she could not feel the reins. Her legs could not sense the horse. She was floating in the sky. Dimly, she heard a shout, but it became a drawn-out, echoing cry of a ghost.

Moments later—or perhaps years later, for time was not clear—Shan T'u felt the wet hands of De Rais on her face. She opened her eyes and saw him. The rain streamed down his cheeks and pasted his hair to his forehead. He pushed her own soaked hair out of her eyes.

"Shan T'u," he whispered.

Now she realized that she lay on the drenched earth, supported only by De Rais. She felt her heart beat weakly. "William," she managed to say.

Now her eyes could make out the Mongol warriors, still on horseback. They loomed like spectres of death in the lurid daylight. De Rais said, "You fell from your horse. Can you get up?"

"No . . ."

"Please, Shan T'u. You must."

She shook her head. "Let me die here, beloved. I will not debase myself for these animals."

Nayan said, "Enough! Back on your horse, Yellow Beard."

De Rais held Shan T'u, his face drawn and desperate. "I won't leave you."

"Don't be foolish," she murmured. "Go on . . . you will do well in the court of the Khan."

"Get it through your head," he snapped. "You're my lady now. And a knight does not desert his lady."

She managed a game smile. "What a poor time for the scoundrel to become a knight . . ."

The Mongol leader trained an arrow on De Rais's back. The other warriors whipped out their own weapons and followed suit. Shan T'u drew a harsh breath. The wicked steel points glistened in the rain.

"On your horse," Nayan ordered. "Now."

De Rais sighed. He gently lowered Shan T'u, bunching the back of her tattered silk gown to make a pillow. He stood, licking rain from his lips. "Sorry," he said. "This is my bride. You Tartars understand a man's loyalty to his wife. If your emperor wants me, he'll have to wait a day longer. If he wishes me dead, so be it. I only ask to draw my sword and fight you like a man."

Shan T'u held her breath. The rain drummed in her ears. If they allowed De Rais to fight . . .

The arrows remained poised in the drawn bows. The Mongol leader hesitated, then relaxed his bow-string. A smile twisted his face. "A good bluff," he said. "But we will simply kill your bride and lash you to your horse."

"You'll die first," De Rais threatened.

The Mongol leader laughed again. "Let the woman die."

Shan T'u shuddered at the words. She shut her eyes and prayed softly. She heard a blur of movement and then De Rais was on top of her, his powerful body spread-eagled. She could not draw breath, for he crushed her to the sucking earth by digging in his fingers and the toes of his boots. He turned up his face to see the Mongols.

"The arrows will have to pass through me," he said, "and you will not have a guest for the emperor."

"Drag him off!" Nayan cried. "End this!"

The leader was nearly hysterical with rage. But now another warrior walked his horse over to the leader. With some urgency, his whispered in Nayan's ear. Nayan's face remained distorted with fury, but he nodded and hissed in reply.

Nayan drew in several deep breaths. When he spoke, his voice was strained. "Get up," he said to De Rais. "We will stop and eat, then go on. *Get up!*"

De Rais's chest rose and fell atop Shan T'u's body and she was intensely aware of her breasts crowded by his torso and her trembling thighs crushed against his loins. They lay in a grotesque mockery of lovemaking. De Rais whispered to her, "Should I trust the bastard?"

Shan T'u said, "They are known to be loyal to their Khan. Perhaps the other one reminded Nayan that the emperor wants you alive."

De Rais nodded. "That's my guess, too."

De Rais rolled away from Shan T'u and hurried to his feet. Moving with deliberate swagger, he reached down and hauled the princess to her feet. She stumbled into his arms, weeping. De Rais held her tightly, his wet fingers stroking her face and hair, his lips kissing her throat. She clung to him, her hands tightly tangled in his hair.

The Mongol warriors dismounted and set up their utensils. They made no attempt at a campfire. As the horses champed and shivered nearby, the warriors produced leathern bottles and from these bottles poured a thick white porridge into bowls. De Rais and Shan T'u were each handed a bowl of this mush.

Shan T'u was too hungry and tired to be put off by the texture and sour odor of the victuals. She sipped at it and then greedily swallowed it all. It left a thick curdled flavor in her mouth. De Rais drained all of his ration as well. "Sour milk," he said, "made into some kind of paste."

Nayan had already packed up his utensils. "Have you fed long enough?" he asked.

De Rais looked coldly at him. "The rain is blinding, and night is upon us. Might we not make camp?"

The Mongol snickered. "We will come to an encampment tomorrow."

De Rais firmly held Shan T'u's shoulders. "Can you ride through the night?"

She nodded. "I think so. But our horses . . ."

De Rais scanned the lightning-streaked sky. "I don't doubt that provision will be made for that. Come."

Shan T'u kissed his mouth. She returned to her horse and climbed into the saddle. Mercifully, the rain diminished and a ghastly yellow glow suffused the night sky. Shan T'u had never felt so lonely as she did in this endless wilderness on this stormy night. How she longed now for her bed!

But the Mongols spurred their mounts and Shan T'u kneed her horse into a run. She was determined to survive.

De Rais proved right about the horses; during the long, sodden night, horsemen rode out of the blackness to meet the Mongol war party. The new warriors led fresh horses, already saddled and laden with supplies. Nayan told De Rais, "Change mounts, quickly."

Shan T'u looked sharply at De Rais. "Must we leave our own horses?"

De Rais said, "I don't like the idea, but we have no choice. We'd only kill our beasts to make them run more."

He climbed off his horse and took a moment to touch his forehead to the animal's lathered neck. The beast whickered piteously and De Rais petted him.

He looked up at the Mongol leader. "Will I see my horse again?"

"The beast will be attached to the emperor's stables."

De Rais bit back his rage. He slapped his horse on the rump and mounted the fresh animal. Shan T'u left her black mare with a quick pat and mounted a white steed. The Mongol warriors changed mounts as well, within seconds. "Let's go," Nayan said.

Shan T'u threw back her head and took in a deep breath of wet, fragrant air. Then she narrowed her eyes and kicked the horse into motion.

They rode for the rest of the night and for much of the morning. After a time, Shan T'u began to accept the agony in her legs and spine. She even dozed while riding. This, she noticed, the Mongol warriors were able to do quite adeptly. They maintained a steady pace, galloping over endless miles of farmland, and then ascending gently into the hills. For a while, they rode alongside a small river. The smells of earth and wild flowers sustained the princess.

She felt a dim joy when the sky lightened and the land became visible once again. She felt as if she had passed through the kingdom of Death. The sun rose pale and pink, and the heat of the summer day evaporated the dampness from the earth. As the day brightened and the sun cast a bleached haze over the green land, Shan T'u enjoyed seeing peasants gathering sheaves on a terraced hillside, and farmers hoeing the rich loess. Once, they rode a high plateau and she could see range upon range of distant blue peaks.

Shan T'u recalled the words of Kung, the bandit

chief. All of these sweating, toiling peasants were working for the Mongol emperor now, to finance wars in foreign lands. Soon Kublai Khan would rule the world and every peasant and farmer on earth would raise tribute to him. Shan T'u swallowed a lump of blind fury.

The day's heat took its toll on Shan T'u. She could no longer feel the reins in her swollen hands, and her thighs were like thick puddings. She dreaded falling from her mount again and having to face the sneering wrath of Nayan.

But as a wave of dizziness swept over her, she heard the Mongol leader cry out. There, on a verdant hillside, were hundreds of rounded huts and tents. Mongol women and children swarmed over the encampment, and as far as she could see, there were cattle, camels, and horses. The women closest to the war party were on their feet, grinning with toothless mouths. A huge stench of filth and animals arose from the camp. But Shan T'u was filled with gratitude and joy.

Shan T'u was helped from her horse by the women, as she was too stiff and swollen to dismount on her own. Chattering and giggling, the women led her to one of the felt-covered huts, where a cooking pot boiled over a wood fire. Shan T'u was invited to sit. She hugged herself and shivered from exhaustion. The women, chattering and stinking to high Heaven, piled cooked meat on a plate and handed it to her with a cup of whitish liquid.

Shan T'u first downed the liquid, which was warm and sourish but with an odd hint of white wine. It brought her parched mouth to life. Then she wolfed the hunks of cooked meat with her fingers, sucking the grease. Her starvation and her physical torment had stripped her of all royal manners. The women seemed not to mind her vulgar behavior.

After the meal, Shan T'u was offered new clothing: a white belted robe woven of camel and goat hair, with a darker vest and leather boots. Shan T'u shrank from the garment even though she had already retied the tatters of her silk gown a score of times and her slippers were so badly shredded they were no longer wearable.

De Rais found Shan T'u as she was protesting to the women. "How do you feel?" he asked.

She turned to him. "William . . . Have you eaten?"

He nodded. "Pretty good stuff. Roast dog and mare's milk."

Shan T'u felt her stomach heave. "You joke . . ."

He smiled. His skin was burnt brown, his hair burred and filthy. "These nomads live on the stuff. Their whole life is hunting and letting their cattle feed. And when the cattle eat up all the grass on this hillside, they fold up everything and wheel it up the mountain."

Shan T'u touched her fingers to his face. "Will we ever be together again, my love?"

He kissed her fingertips. "Perhaps the emperor will give us an apartment in the grand palace."

Her eyes blurred. "I cannot laugh, William."

"Well, they haven't killed us yet, so the Khan must want me for something. We'll get some sleep here before we go on. I see you've been offered a change of clothes."

"No! I don't want to wear their horrid robe. I am a princess."

"Well—Princess—your royal gown is somewhat shoddy. Are you sure you can make it to Kanbaliq before you're naked?"

She bristled. "Must I wear it, then? It stinks of goat!"

He gestured at the Tartar women. "True, these dames do not reek of perfume, but they weave their clothing to last. We've a long way to go."

She felt a wrench of pure misery. "I think you are beginning to *enjoy* this trek."

"Well, I'm more accustomed to long marches, Shan T'u."

"And to the company of barbarians."

He stiffened. "I didn't say I *enjoyed* their company."

"Oh, I think you do. I think you *like* drinking horse's milk and eating dogs and riding all night to prove your strength . . ."

Tears overwhelmed her and her lips trembled. He sighed. "And you must suppose I can't wait to arrive at Kanbaliq and start swindling."

She averted her eyes. "It's what you *said* you wanted."

He slipped his hands over hers and kissed her bruised knuckles. "So the princess feels insulted."

"Don't patronize me!" Her eyes blazed. "You have reveled in all the blood and slaughter. Oh yes, you *saved* my life, but you don't *ease* my life."

"What do you expect me to do, Shan T'u? Build a litter and carry you about?"

"Yes! Or have *them* do it!" She gestured angrily at the Mongol camp. "You might *suggest* that I be carried. Or do you truly love me anymore, William?

Once you deflowered the virgin, did you grow bored?"

De Rais exhaled with annoyance. "Shan T'u, it's a hot afternoon and we're prisoners in a Tartar camp. I am not in a mood for your girlish whims—"

"Whims? My whim is to be treated as a woman!"

"A woman who can bring down a bandit at fifty yards on horseback!"

"Ah, so there we have it!" She thrust her arms into the air and strode away from him. "You think me grotesque for knowing those arts. You no longer consider me a desirable woman, but only another knight to whack about with."

"Don't be asinine—"

"I, asinine? I think you're being pompous and obnoxious."

"Do you?"

"Yes I do. And I'm really rather tired of being prodded at arrow point to exhaust and injure my body. I don't intend to wear foul-smelling buffalo robes, or change horses in the middle of the night, or eat dog meat. You are my knight and protector. Your task is to find me proper accommodations and to accord me proper treatment."

De Rais fumed. "What you want is a eunuch! What ever happened to the obedient reverential Chinese woman? You knew what I was."

"Oh yes, you were accurate about *that.*"

"Well, then, if you thought to change me, you're a jackass."

Her mouth dropped open. *"Jackass?* You . . . barbarian . . . you *Mongol* . . ."

He shook a finger at her. "At least the Mongol women keep their mouths shut before their masters!"

Shan T'u was speechless. She gestured in exasperation and turned away, her arms crossed.

De Rais followed her, his lip thrust out defiantly. "Now you give me silence, eh? Well, talk to the camels for all I care. I've got my hide to save, and I'm damned well going to save it. All I ever wanted was to make my fortune in this Godforsaken land."

"Then do so," Shan T'u whispered fiercely. "And leave."

"Oh, with pleasure," he taunted. "I'll go back to my own country, where women know their place."

"Yes," she retorted, "flat on their backs in a barn!"

"It suited *you* pretty well!"

Shan T'u whirled, her face a mask of rage. She flung herself at De Rais and her hands were a flurry of tiny fists, pounding impotently at his massive chest. De Rais stood in stunned astonishment for a moment, grunting at the blows that rained down on him. Then he seized her wrists and held them fast as she wriggled. A smile overspread his face.

"No!" she squealed. "Let go of me . . ."

"Shan T'u . . ." he murmured. "Princess . . ."

Abruptly, her temper calmed. Tears streamed down her cheeks and her lip quavered. "William . . ." she sobbed. "Oh, William, I didn't mean . . ."

He hushed her with his lips. She wrapped her arms desperately around his neck and pressed her body urgently against his. Her damp cheek rested against his throat and she sniffled back her crying.

"How could we fight that way?" she moaned. "How *could* we?"

"Lovers have spats," De Rais said with a sense of wonder.

She looked up at him with glistening eyes. "I don't want to have spats, William. I want to be with you."

"Yes, yes, I know," he soothed. "And you will. But right now, we must survive the ride to Kanbaliq. You must wear a practical costume, and you must eat and drink what our captors give us."

She nodded. "I was not ready to be a . . . rapscallion."

He laughed. "Well, you *are* one. What a nasty temper."

"And how crude you can be."

He kissed her forehead. "You're right, Shan T'u. The Mongols bring out the worst in people. They *should* be conquered. I for one pray that China is liberated from their empire."

She smiled radiantly. "You do? Oh, William, I knew you would see your destiny!"

Puzzlement flecked his eyes. "Now wait a minute, Princess . . ."

She hugged him and kissed his mouth richly. Then she pulled away from him, her eyes dancing. "I *will* change my clothes, paladin. I will follow you to Kanbaliq, and I will be your page and armor-bearer when you battle the Robber Knight."

"The *what?*"

Her laugh was like a skipping roe. "Kublai Khan, of course! I have strength now, William, for anything."

She clenched her fists with intense happiness and gave him a last, wonderful smile before returning to the hut of the women. De Rais stared after her, wondering what he had promised, and how the little minx had tricked him.

Chapter Thirteen

AT LAST THEY REACHED THE CITY OF KANBALIQ. FOR much of the trek, they rode along the Grand Canal that wound through Cathay. Junks and barges crowded the brackish water under a steaming sun. They rode past ramshackle villages and cultivated fields, and within view of distant green mountains.

The city of Kanbaliq was vast and sprawling, a series of great walled towns. The suburbs stretched for hundreds of miles, their boulevards dotted with hotels and caravanserais, and with ornate buildings housing peoples of all lands and races. De Rais dryly noted the vast numbers of prostitutes who infested the towns, working under the command of captain-generals. Nayan told De Rais, "Every ambassador to the Khan is provided with entertainment." De Rais laughed in admiration but Shan T'u scowled with disapproval.

Once they reached the walls of the main city, Shan T'u's eyes darted from side to side, fascinated with the gigantic dimensions of the Mongol stronghold. The white battlements, the straight boulevards enabling her to see from one gate of the city to the other, the fabulous courts and gardens laid out in chessboard squares, all were accomplished with such astonishing precision and beauty that she was overwhelmed. Equally as impressive, but far less beautiful, was the garrison of thousands of armed, fierce warriors.

The multitudes of people in the city presented a kaleidoscopic show. There were Mongols in traditional robes and boots, Indian Moghuls in jeweled turbans, Afghans in white tunics and trousers, Persian princes in pleated caps and Median robes, Arab merchants in coats and Phrygian caps, and so many more, impossible to count or even embrace with one pair of eyes. Shan T'u felt like a small girl being taken to market for the first time.

She had come to appreciate the comfort of her bedouin garb; the white handwoven cotton repelled the rays of the sun better than silk. Her striped headdress shielded her eyes from the burning rays. De Rais, too, had surrendered the torn raiment of a Chinese soldier for the dark robe and wide boots of a Mongol warrior. Shan T'u felt her blood sing at his dashing figure. If her father could see her now—or Lady Feng!

Nayan raised a cry and lifted his bow high in the blue air. Shan T'u looked up, and got her first glimpse of the palace of Kublai Khan. A strangling chill crushed her ribs like skeletal fingers of ice. All she could see from here was a great wall built along a deep gorge, but *knowing* that somewhere behind that wall was the emperor of all China, the subjugator of her people and the butcher of her race . . . She took deep breaths to calm her nerves.

The wall seemed to go on forever as they approached the forbidding fortress. They rode up to a gargantuan entrance gate hewed out of the wall. Under its looming arch passed soldiers and traders. The Mongol warriors herded Shan T'u and De Rais to the gate, where Nayan spoke brusquely to the heavily armored guard. Shan T'u guided her horse next to De Rais and spoke to him in Chinese.

"Are you frightened?"

"Well, I'm watchful."

"I think my heart is going to burst from my body."

"Don't let them see your fear."

She exhaled, trying to still her bounding pulse. "What will they do to us?"

"I don't know. Let's keep our ears open."

Nayan barked a command and the party continued through the gate. They emerged into a broad, open field as vast as a great farmland, and here were housed the Khan's military barracks. Shan T'u felt the earth shake with the hoofbeats of thousands of horses, and saw the meadow blackened with the bodies of thousands of warriors. Her muscles tightened in fear; it was as if the hordes of the Khan were massed for invasion, striking despair into the heart of the enemy. One battalion practiced riding perhaps half a mile away. Bowmen in ranks of a hundred knelt as one and loosed swarms of arrows at targets. The very air shook with the twang of loosed bowstrings. To her right were the stables, buildings enough to make a city, where an army of grooms watered and exercised an army of steeds. Shan T'u felt strangled by the sheer numbers of men and by the crushing stench.

De Rais asked Nayan, "Is this the Khan's army?"

The leader looked at De Rais and laughed uproariously. "Ha ha! Yellow Beard, the armies of the Khan cover half the earth. Here you see part of the emperor's *Kasitan.*"

"*Kasitan?*"

"His personal guard. Not that the emperor fears a personal attack, mind you. This is purely a matter of state."

"Purely," De Rais said.

Nayan gestured toward the immense encampment. "There are twelve thousand warriors here, every three thousand commanded by a superior officer. There are no less than three thousand guards on duty within the palace at any time."

"Rotating shifts," De Rais noted. "And where are the nine thousand who aren't on duty? Getting drunk?"

The Mongol leader's eyes narrowed. "They do not leave the palace, Yellow Beard, unless in the service of His Majesty."

De Rais whispered to Shan T'u, "I wish Kung could see this. It might humble him a bit."

"Yes," Shan T'u agreed fiercely.

Now the party approached a second great wall, nearly as long as the first but with three gates. The middle gate, the most ornate, was shut. Traffic flowed in and out of the two other gates. Nayan explained, "Only when the emperor enters or departs does the center gate open."

De Rais pointed to several spacious wooden buildings, ornamented with carvings and gilt. "What's in there?"

"Military stores," Nayan said. "Bridles, saddles, stirrups in one building; bows, strings, quivers, arrows in another; armor in a third; and so on."

De Rais uttered a low whistle. "The organization is incredible," he said to Shan T'u. "These nomads can outfit a battalion in ten minutes!"

Shan T'u felt her heart sink. "You sound afraid of them, paladin."

"Respectful," De Rais corrected. "I begin to understand how these barbarians were able to gobble up half the world. If we could organize our knights this way . . . Hell and damnation, *we* could own Cathay."

Shan T'u sighed as Nayan spoke with the guard at the second gate. "Then truly, all is lost, William. If *you* cannot see how to escape . . ."

"*Escape?* Shan T'u, I never entertained thoughts of escaping from this citadel. Our only hope is to fall into the emperor's favor and trick our way out."

"Swindling."

He nodded. To the Mongol leader, he said, "I am a knight in my own land, Nayan, but I am moved by the brilliance of what I see."

The Mongol leader puffed out his chest and grinned. "No surprise, Yellow Beard."

Now they rode beneath the vaulting shadows of the second wall and came upon still a third, some twenty-five feet high. This wall, with its notched parapets, was blinding white and stretched for a mile in each direction. Shan T'u counted eight gates and three of the storage buildings. Nayan said, "The emperor's wardrobe."

De Rais threw back his head and laughed. "His wardrobe! Dear *God*, I must live to tell of it in France!"

Shan T'u's terror mounted with each new wall, and each new evidence of the Khan's limitless might. At least here, between the two inner walls, there were green meadows and fragrant trees. Her eyes caught the flicker of a roebuck in a small grove. She thought inevitably of home, and of her father's palace, and of Master Po.

Now, at last, they walked their horses through the final gate, and Shan T'u gazed upon the palace of Kublai Khan. Her eyes filled with helpless tears and her blood thundered in her veins. Yes, it was all she imagined it would be, all she dreaded that it would be. It shone with the splendor and ferocity of a million suns and bestrode the earth like a sneering colossus. *Crawl on your belly*, it thundered to the masses of the teeming earth, *for I am Khan, and thou art dust.*

Between the wall and the palace itself was a courtyard, bustling with military guards and men of great rank from many lands. There were Chinese magistrates with silk robes and peacock feather hats, Japanese ambassadors in full court dress, Hebrew merchants in fringed caftans and felt hats, Kurdish horsemen in black silk *djubbahs* with silver embroidery, and more. These were the honored guests and the civil servants of the Khan.

But all were dwarfed by the portentous shadow of

the grand palace itself. Shan T'u craned her neck to look up, up, up, past the soaring foundation, to a snowy cliff of marble, afire with the sun. She could see miniature men, halfway up to Heaven, walking about on a terrace with an ornate balustrade and titanic carved pillars. To her left and right were sweeping marble staircases, and high above all the rest, burning like an unholy molten flame, the colossal gilded roof swept outward to mask the sky.

A greeting party descended a marble staircase with much pomp, accompanied by musicians. The emperor's officers dressed like the warrior horsemen, save that their robes and hats were trimmed in rich fur and velvet. Nayan saluted with his bow and said, "I have brought the Yellow Beard to the Khan."

The officers bowed perfunctorily and the older and portlier of the officers said to De Rais, "Dismount, Yellow Beard, and follow us. The Khan awaits you."

De Rais glanced at Shan T'u. "A royal reception."

She swallowed. "My limbs do not want to obey."

"Come on. Maybe the old Tartar isn't so fearsome after all."

De Rais dismounted and Nayan took the reins of his horse. De Rais lifted Shan T'u from her horse, much as he had lifted her that night so long ago when she tried to flee her father's palace. She welcomed his firm hands on her waist and she grasped his arms, even when her booted feet touched the ground.

"Stay with me," she whispered.

He squeezed her hands and winked. "Stout heart, Princess."

Shan T'u felt a rush of affection for him, but could not display it here. She worked up a thin, brave smile and humbly bowed her head as she followed De Rais and the officers up the marble steps.

Many steps later, they emerged onto the dizzying terrace and were regarded with odd stares by the ornately dressed palace visitors. Shan T'u walked with small, deprecating steps as her eyes drank in the beautiful carvings of warriors and animals, done in gleaming gold. There was a scent of exotic spices and perfumes. As they wended their way through the chambers of the palace, Shan T'u drew breath at the radiant sunlight pouring through windows glazed to look like purest crystal.

Abruptly, she and De Rais were stopped at a curving flight of carpeted steps. She could hear a great hubbub of talking and music. An officer in a deep blue robe turned to De Rais and said, "When you enter the Great Hall, you will approach the emperor and prostrate yourself. You will then be seated in your proper place. Now—do you observe the officers who guard this door?"

He gestured with one berobed sleeve. On either side of an arched entryway stood a Mongol warrior gripping a long staff. The men were enormous and foul smelling. The officer said, "When you enter the hall, you must not touch the threshold with your feet. If you do, these guards will beat you."

De Rais glanced at Shan T'u. "Superstitious bunch."

Shan T'u only nodded, but didn't trust her eyes to look at him. She ached to embrace her knight, to kiss his mouth and to be enfolded within his arms. She longed to lie naked with him by a purling river, to feel his throbbing manhood deep within her, to know his hands on her pouting breasts, his lips draining honey from her tongue.

But now De Rais was ascending the steps and she followed him. De Rais glanced at the two towering guards and carefully lifted each booted foot over the threshold. Shan T'u, her eyes modestly lowered, did the same.

She kept her eyes lowered even as she entered the Great Hall, and the noise crashed down upon her. She cautiously looked up, but had to blink hard to avoid fainting. She and De Rais stood on a marble floor as vast as a desert and laid with intricately beautiful cashmere carpets. She glimpsed walls that towered like golden cliffs, hung with tapestries as mighty as waterfalls. So immense was the room that a haze of clouds floated near the exquisitely carved ceiling.

She followed De Rais across the hallways, past tables crowded with thousands of men and women. The sheer volume of their chatter vibrated through the floor like ocean waves beating upon a beach. Even the massive tables could not accommodate all the teeming humanity; hundreds of richly dressed nobles sat upon carpets to eat and drink. Women occupied their own tables, giggling and pointing. These were probably the wives of the nobles and military officers.

And now Shan T'u and De Rais began their ascent, by way of marble stairs, to the veiled summit of the room. On each level were more tables, peopled with Mongols and visitors of higher rank and degree. As nomads climbed ever upward on the windy steppes, Shan T'u and De Rais mounted each plateau in this soaring range of marble peaks.

And there on the highest peak sat the Great Khan,

high on an elevated throne, high above every other table, high above his minions. He benignly presided over the Mongol princes who drank and laughed at his feet. In the middle of the hall, within sight of the Khan, a magnificently carved and immense wooden coffer held a golden vase. Four golden vessels stood on each of the four sides of the coffer, with cups and flagons of gold plate. As the Khan watched, servants in red robes and high-crowned hats continually filled these cups from the four vessels and brought them, brimming, to the tables.

Shan T'u's head whirled from the noise and confusion. She thought she glimpsed gaily caparisoned elephants, and peacocks, and musicians and tumblers. Her senses shrieked with pain at the assault of color, din, and stink.

But somehow she had reached the summit where the emperor sat on his coruscating throne. She fell to her knees, as much in exhaustion as in respect, and she bumped her head softly against the woven carpet.

"Get up," Kublai Khan said.

Shan T'u dared to raise her eyes. She looked up past thick table legs, carved with fierce animal shapes, to a medium-sized man in a billowing ivory robe. A puffy pink face floated like a bloated sun above the robe, with a well-groomed moustache and goatee. The Khan's headdress was a richer, more embroidered version of the traditional hat of his warriors. He seemed amused, almost fatherly.

"All the way up," Khan said, beckoning with his finger.

Shan T'u slowly stood, and felt stripped to her skin as Khan's miniature, glittering eyes raced over her body. A hint of a smile touched his wet lips. Shan T'u heard the Mongol princes at the table to her right snickering and making filthy remarks.

Khan glanced idly at De Rais, who stood beside Shan T'u. She ached to take De Rais's hand but dared not. A swarm of servants darted in and out like honeybees, serving food and drink to the Khan, who hardly seemed to notice. Shan T'u saw that each servant wore a veil of worked silk so as not to breathe upon the Khan's victuals.

"Yellow Beard," Khan said. The name sounded more frightening in Mongolian than it did in Chinese.

"Your Majesty," De Rais said.

"Stories have come to me from the South of a warrior out of the West who cuts down bandits with a mighty sword. Is this true?"

"I've had some scraps," De Rais said.

"*Scraps.*" Khan stared for a moment, then laughed to himself. "I've been in some scraps, too!"

There was a painful pause, and then the emperor rumbled with merriment. In a moment, the leviathan hall thundered with laughter so voluminous it threatened to crack the walls.

Khan regained his regal demeanor and accepted a brimming golden cup from a servant. The page stepped back and knelt down. Suddenly, there was a cacophonous shifting and rumbling in the hall. Incredibly, every guest in the vast room was kneeling! Shan T'u looked around with wide eyes, then quickly went to her knees. De Rais did likewise.

The Khan regarded the huge cup balefully, then tipped it to his lips and drank. A blast of music shattered the silence: a din of bells, chimes, bamboo pipes, drums, and flutes. Khan continued to gulp down the wine, which now streamed down his beard and splashed his gown. His larynx bobbed in his sagging throat and his skin reddened.

Finally, he slammed the cup down on his table and emitted a tremendous, stinking belch. The music ceased as if on a signal, and with another great racket, the guests resumed their seats. Shan T'u found herself shivering. The enormity—and vulgarity—of his power sickened her.

"Yellow Beard," Khan said. "I employ a number of men from the West. The Pope of Rome sent me a friar to convert me to Christianity. I asked for a hundred priests to convince me, but nobody else came." He spread open his hands. "So I didn't convert." He grinned widely. "Can you serve me in any way, Yellow Beard?"

De Rais clasped his hands smartly behind his back. "I can fight, Your Majesty."

Khan made an extremely rude noise. "Don't waste my time. I have ten times ten thousand men to conquer the world for me."

Shan T'u held her breath. Was it going to end here, at the emperor's feet?

De Rais said, "I can see that. But I didn't ask to come here. *You* sent for *me.*"

This brought an audible gasp from the assembled princes. Khan's ears reddened and his eyes became slits. "You have a sharp tongue."

"I mean no disrespect."

"Don't tell me what you *mean!*" Khan thundered. He half rose out of his throne. "You're horsemeat to me. You're a fly. I *squash* flies."

Shan T'u began to compose herself to die as the Khan sat down and huffed. He squinted at De Rais, his beefy cheek on his hand. "You have not yet told me what service you can perform. Your life depends on this."

De Rais spread his hands. "Your Majesty, if your days are dull and you require the murder of one French knight to amuse yourself, then kill me. I'll try very hard to run my sword through your fat guts, but no doubt you and your armies will prevail. Is that why you summoned me on this journey?"

The bold knight had now gained the attention of nearly everyone in the hall. Hundreds of eyes watched him, some from great distances. The clatter of cups and plates quieted. Khan slumped moodily in his throne and stroked his wine-damp beard. "Who is this woman you bring with you?"

De Rais glanced at Shan T'u. "A Chinese girl. I swindled a fat and ignorant merchant out of his gold *and* his daughter. He was glad to have her off his hands. She has big feet and doesn't act like a lady."

Khan raised an eyebrow and his gaze rested on the princess. "Why did such an unpleasant woman interest a valiant knight?"

De Rais chuckled. "A few evenings of pleasure while in China, and then, when I return to Arabia, a quick resale. She'll make a nice addition to a small harem."

This brought salacious laughter from the nearby princes. Shan T'u was grateful that most of the guests couldn't make out the words being spoken. Khan laughed as well, but his eyes showed crafty deception. "You're unscrupulous, Yellow Beard."

"I never pretended otherwise."

"I wouldn't trust you in *my* army."

"When I fight, I play no games."

"Hm." Khan's eyes flicked from Shan T'u to De Rais. "Yellow Beard, you have traveled far, have you not?"

"Halfway across the world, Your Majesty."

"Good. I like hearing of strange places and strange people. You can entertain me with stories of fabled lands."

"Certainly."

Khan leaned forward. "No doubt you have some . . . rousing tales?"

De Rais laughed. "Hair-raising."

Khan boomed with merriment and slapped his table. "Hair-raising! I'd like to hear those tales. *Lots* of tales. All about Persia and Samarkand and Turkestan and Japan . . . ever been to Japan?"

"Not yet, Your Majesty."

"Have to sail there, you know. God damned boats. We're mountain people." He cocked an eye at De Rais. "Can you navigate a boat?"

"I'm a pretty fair hand at it."

"Are you? Then you must tell me some sailing stories, eh? And oh—some stories of France, too. Of your Burgundians, and Franks, and Alsatians."

"I'm a good yarn-spinner," De Rais said.

Khan giggled and chewed absentmindedly on his fingernail. "There you are, Yellow Beard. There's some service to keep your hide tacked on. And I'll feed you well for it. And give you a comfortable bed, and maybe even some baubles to take back home."

De Rais nodded graciously. "I like baubles."

Khan chuckled delightedly. "Good. I'll have you dressed and ready for a big supper tonight. Music and dancing. And *stories*."

"And stories," De Rais promised.

Khan clapped his hands. "Let it be done!" He raised a finger, almost as an afterthought. "Oh yes—the little Chinese girl. I like her looks. I'll take her for my own concubine."

He sat back, his eyes heavy-lidded. Shan T'u looked frenziedly at De Rais. Keeping a jocular tone, he said, "Your Majesty, of course you have many concubines and I have only one bride."

"Bride? Come now, swindler. You *bought* the girl!"

"But I do fancy her, Your Majesty, and she'll bring a good price . . ."

Khan dismissed the protest with a vulgar noise. "Nonsense. I'll load down your horse with enough gold and silk to double what the girl would fetch. And think of it—she'll get to lie with *me*. Take the woman to the concubines' apartments and prepare her. Let her come to me tonight."

Shan T'u cried out, "No! I will not—"

Khan stared at her with bulging eyes. "Would she like a few strokes of the whip to shut her mouth?"

Two guards came up behind Shan T'u and she looked with terror at De Rais. "William . . ."

His face was grim. "Don't worry, Shan T'u. I'll think of something."

"William, please . . . *please* . . ."

But the guards had laid hands on her. De Rais was being escorted away from her, down to one of the tables. He glanced back with hopeless eyes, then

214

turned away. Shan T'u sobbed once, then wept softly. "William, no . . ."

She looked up at the Khan, wild-eyed, but he did not deign to see her. He ordered his cup refilled and looked down with bored savagery at the mammoth feasting that continued below him.

Chapter Fourteen

SHAN T'U WAS BORNE IN A LITTER UP A GREAT HILL covered with evergreen trees. Atop the hill stood a green pavilion with a golden roof. As Shan T'u was carried up the fragrant hillside, she saw a brace of elephants dragging a massive tree, whose roots, like serpents, crawled along the earth. Workmen in straw hats were sweatily digging an excavation for the tree. So *that* was how Kublai Khan forested this verdant mountain, Shan T'u thought; by uprooting beautiful trees and dragging them here. Could *any* army defeat such a tyrant?

Shan T'u folded her hands in her lap, noticing how raw and calloused they were. Hardly the smooth hands of a princess. But they could still grasp a knife.

She would not shed her raiment before that swine, nor would she suffer him to lay a finger on her flesh.

They attained the summit and Shan T'u's litter was set down. Eunuchs with fans bowed as the curtain was pulled aside. A strikingly lovely Tartar woman in a pale aqua gown and dark blue caftan waited with her arms folded. She bowed her head and dropped her eyes as Shan T'u stepped out of the litter. "I am Aya," she said.

"I am Shan T'u," the princess replied.

"Welcome, Shan T'u."

Aya led Shan T'u through a serene courtyard, past a pool of water landscaped with rocks and shrubs. A jade basin rippled with goldfish whose scales caught flares of sunlight. A cool breeze ruffled the treetops. Shan T'u could glance downward and see the white splendor of the grand palace, and the maze of walls and gates that surrounded it.

As Shan T'u passed beneath the curving roof of the pavilion, the green paint shimmered in the sunlight. A porcelain vase held peonies, and within the pavilion, there were myriad flower pots filled with shrubs, vines, and bamboos. Aya led Shan T'u past inner courtyards that teemed with monkeys, peacocks, and birds of magnificent plumage. Shan T'u saw flashes of scarlet, iridescent green, and blue.

Yet Shan T'u had a troubling vision of the storehouses she'd seen on the way in, the buildings that contained the Khan's bridles and saddles and his wardrobe. This serene pavilion was just another storehouse. Despair overwhelmed Shan T'u.

Aya conducted Shan T'u to her apartment, which consisted of a bedroom and a study. The doors and windows opened onto a private courtyard. A *liene-tse* of woven bamboo threads could be rolled over the windows to shut out the sun and the rain. On the walls were white satin hangings painted with flowers and birds.

Aya said, "Soon you will be bathed and given fresh clothing. Tonight, at the banquet, you will sit with the other concubines. Later, you will be honored to service His Majesty in the royal apartment."

"I am *not* honored," Shan T'u said acidly. "I assure you the Khan will not enjoy me for long."

Aya looked at her sharply, her cheekbones flushed. "I would advise you to school your tongue."

Shan T'u averted her eyes and looked at the magnificent bed. Built of precious woods, it was lacquered and gilded, and hung with white taffeta embroidered with gold flowers. "I have been so advised before, Aya, by ladies of my father's court. I have suffered too deeply, and risked too much, to heed a slave."

She heard the infuriated hiss of breath. "You will learn a hard lesson," Aya said thinly.

Aya left the apartment, ruffled. Shan T'u fell upon the bed, unable to control her sobs. The hopelessness of her situation robbed all of her strength. She was only a pampered princess whose impudence had led her to catastrophe. She had lost everything.

No. She sat up, swiping at her tear-streaked face. She had *not* lost everything. Not while De Rais lived. Not so long as her skin remembered the sweetness of his touch or her mouth tasted the honey of his tongue. Not so long as her inner flesh tingled with the ecstasy of his proud invasion.

And never so long as her wounded heart cherished him. She had fulfilled her girlhood fantasy of the dark rider from the hills. That much she had, and not the Khan himself could take it from her.

Shan T'u stood as two ladies-in-waiting appeared to bathe her. Her breasts swelled beneath the rough cotton robe. Her death was imminent, her adventure done, but she had known her paladin's love.

In a better frame of mind, Shan T'u enjoyed her bath. It was good to strip off the dusty Mongol garments and step into perfumed water. The water was cooled by ice and Shan T'u gasped as she lowered her body. Marble beasts sprayed fresh water, and the deep jade pool was decorated with swans and fish painstakingly carved of wood.

Midway through her bath, Shan T'u mounted one of the carved swans. She sat astride the wooden bird, whispering playful commands into its sculptured head. She laughed, and glanced furtively to see the sour frowns of the ladies-in-waiting.

Shan T'u rose up upon the great wooden swan and spread her arms regally. She felt her nipples become taut peaks and her thighs tremble with desire. "William . . ." she whispered despairingly. She dove gracefully into the dark pool, knifing the water and rifling down. Through the cold blur, she saw her own light-dappled fingers as she twisted her supple body and kicked toward the surface.

She burst into fresh air and hugged herself, her arms and breasts covered with goose bumps. The dirt and pain of the punishing ride washed away. She shook her head and wiped water from her eyes.

She clapped her hands sharply and the ladies-in-waiting scurried forward. Shan T'u climbed the marble steps out of the pool. The ladies-in-waiting anointed her body with aromatic oils. Shan T'u breathed deeply of the perfumes that glistened on her skin. She especially liked an oil made from pine moss. Her death was closer now, and her heart beat faster.

Back in her apartment, Shan T'u was left alone to dress. She sat naked on the edge of the great bed and regarded her face and her damp hair in a mirror inlaid with turquoise and amber. The sky outside had turned a pale lemon yellow. Shan T'u could hear the din of music from a hundred instruments, and far down the hillside, she saw the glow of a million silk lanterns. The fresh fragrance of evergreen wafted through the open window.

Shan T'u looked deeply into her own dark eyes. How much more she saw than when she had primped in her father's palace. There was a radiant sunlight in her eyes now, from William's love, and weeping clouds from the deaths she had witnessed.

The music outside made her melancholy. This reverie was not good. She could almost *see* William in her mirror. He wore a white silk robe brocaded in gold and silver thread and belted with a long sash. And he wore silk trousers and golden boots. His flaxen hair was stained red by the sunset. His eyes flamed with a pure blue fire. No, Shan T'u decided, it was not good at all when she began to hallucinate her lover this way. She set the mirror in her lap, the cold metal shocking her bare skin.

"You are a vision of Eden," De Rais said.

Shan T'u gasped and spun around. Her hand flew to her mouth. It had *not* been a mirage! He stood here, in her apartment. A blush climbed from her throat to her ears.

"William . . ." she breathed.

"Don't move," he said softly.

Her breasts burned with an uncontrollable fire. "How did you get in?"

"I'm billeted with a few of the Khan's second cousins. Mongol princes. Most of those monkeys are still in their cups from this afternoon, and with all of them preening for the banquet, it wasn't hard to slip away."

"But the Khan's guards . . ."

William grinned. "You see before you a man who has crept past irate fathers, hunting dogs, and enemy battalions." He came to her bed and knelt next to her. His finger touched her hair and then her cheek. Shan T'u shut her eyes and shivered. "Don't be *too* hopeful," he murmured. "Even *I* can't slip past the Khan's Kasitan. But getting up the hill was child's play, especially since the old Tartar was kind enough to plant a very thick forest."

Shan T'u's eyelashes fluttered as she gazed rapturously at him. Her hands slid up his silken sleeves and curved around his warm throat. "You were a fool. If they catch you here . . ."

"You're my bride," he said. "I wanted a last look."

"But I belong to the Khan. He'll have your throat torn out by dogs."

"Very likely." He brushed her ear with his lips and moved down her cheek with small, adoring kisses. She drew in a shuddering breath and small fires flickered between her legs. "Khan wants me for a reason, though. He didn't drag me to Kanbaliq because I can kill bandits."

"Why, then?"

"Perhaps because I know where the red masks are. Possibly because I can navigate a boat, or because I was a knight in the lands Kublai Khan wishes to conquer."

"He wants you to *spy?*"

De Rais stopped her words with his plundering mouth. She slanted her head, and her starving tongue slithered in to meet his. Her hand cupped his face and she writhed to press her naked body against his torso of silk. She felt her breasts grow hard and full against his tunic. His hands slid down her flanks and up her smooth back, massaging her slim shoulders. The flats of his palms glided lustrously over the film of fragrant oils. She kissed him passionately, caressing his mouth. It was like fresh water following a drought, like sun after a storm.

He stroked the tender flesh of her face and his eyes became liquid pools in which she bathed. "He's got plans," De Rais said huskily. "All is not well in his empire. The Mongols tried to invade Japan but a typhoon wrecked their ships and the *samurai* cut the Tartars to shreds. They never penetrated into Christendom because there was no Khan to order the attack. Now there are bandits in the hills and mutinies in the ranks . . ."

"Truly, William?"

"Nothing to really worry the emperor, of course. But Khan is a fox and his eye is open for intrigue and treachery."

"We have not betrayed him."

"Perhaps not. And perhaps we don't yet know what *he* does. He's up to *something.*" He kissed her throat, then her collarbone, and, as she arched her body for him, the shadowed valley between her breasts. She took his hands and brought them to the pale golden mounds tipped with rosy pink. She moaned deliciously as he teased them into tautness. His lips and tongue made her nipples glisten in the dusk and her fingers dug deep into the yellow wheatfield of his hair. She lay down on the lacquered bed, beckoning him with her arms. He nuzzled her milky stomach as his fingers pressed her inner thigh. She clawed at his knotted back muscles, rubbing the silk in small circles against his veiled skin. "Oh, my love," she murmured. "Take me . . ."

He sat up and sighed. Crimson light poured over his white tunic, making it a deep rose. Birds shrieked and cawed. "I can't," he whispered. "They'll be here to fetch you soon."

She was crying. "William, you cannot torture me so."

"I had to see you," he said. "If we *have* been tricked, if we die tonight—I had to kiss you goodbye."

"I will *not* lie with the Khan," she hissed.

His lips narrowed into a thin line. "And I won't help him conquer."

A smile irradiated her tear-stained face. "My paladin," she breathed.

There were tiny, faltering footsteps in the hallway. De Rais sprang to his feet, eyes darting. "For now, Shan T'u." He bent and kissed her roughly on her mouth. Her hand lingered hopelessly at his cheek, then dropped back as he climbed through the open window and melted into the shadows of the courtyard.

Shan T'u turned her face away and made a tight fist.

The ladies-in-waiting entered the room. "My lady," one of them said. "You are not dressed."

"No," Shan T'u breathed. "I was . . . dreaming."

Shan T'u could not concentrate on the feasting. She sat in a carved chair at a long table with the emperor's other concubines. These women from Ungut, in Tartary, were fair-complected like Aya, and prettier than the other Mongol women she had seen. They were dressed, as Shan T'u was, in richly embroidered caftans worn over silken gowns tied with sashes. Shan T'u's caftan was a luxuriously dark green, her gown a transparent peach. On her feet were pointed golden slippers, and she wore a headdress fastened around her forehead with an *agal*, a cord of hair. A metal necklace adorned her throat.

She barely touched the steaming golden plates of food. The other concubines gobbled the stuff. There were all manner of cooked meats, fowl, and fish. There was salmon and sturgeon, partridge, pheasant and quail, bear and fox and pig. There were grapes, melons, apples, dates, peaches, pears, pomegranates and quinces. Each dish was prepared in a different sauce, and each was accompanied by goblets of wine or mare's milk.

Shan T'u looked up to see Khan, who slumped moodily in his throne high above the revelry. For this feast, the emperor wore a robe woven entirely of cloth of gold, and even in the vast hall, he glittered like a thousand torches. His sons and nobles all wore similar robes, but not as richly decorated. At the emperor's feet slept a tame lion, its tail twitching idly.

At other tables, the emperor's military officers caroused in gold-colored silk robes with girdles of chamois leather. The most elite of the officers sported pearls and gems in their gowns. Shan T'u had never experienced this magnitude of wealth or splendor.

But her eyes only sought her knight. De Rais stood at the feet of the emperor, near the Khan's sons, and near the four empresses who were the Khan's legitimate wives. Aya had explained to Shan T'u that each empress maintained her own court with three hundred female attendants as well as pages and eunuchs and servants. Ten thousand subjects in all.

De Rais was spinning tales, and while Shan T'u could not hear most of his words, she could see that the emperor was at least sometimes amused. His pink-tinged face split in occasional laughter, and the stories were apparently lifting him out of his black mood. William looked youthful and handsome as he made dramatic gestures. Shan T'u smiled to herself. He was a fine storyteller.

She felt her eyes brim. The banquet had lasted for many hours now, through countless toasts to the emperor, through the solemn lighting of incense, through the presentation of snow white Arabian horses by a visiting prince. There had been music, and tumbling acts, and now the knight from France. But soon it would be the hour for Shan T'u to be conducted by elderly ladies of the palace to the private apartments of the Khan.

And she knew, despite William's brave visit, that he could do nothing to prevent this debauchery. He could not rescue her nor escape from Kanbaliq.

Now De Rais finished his story and bowed low to the emperor. Khan clapped his hands with childlike pleasure and the entire hall shook with drunken shouts and applause. The concubine nearest Shan T'u looked at her with wide eyes and said, "Are *you* to serve the Khan tonight?"

Shan T'u only nodded.

"Lucky!" the girl said. "Three days and three nights! To wait on his desires, to fetch him food and drink. It's a *dream*."

Shan T'u looked at her darkly. "Is it a dream to be taken from your family?"

The concubine stared at Shan T'u. "Huh?"

"Didn't you fight? Didn't your father fight? To be torn from your mother, to be degraded . . ."

The concubine laughed. "You're wrong! To be chosen from among all girls as the fairest—that's a *favor*. Every father prays that the stars will give him a beautiful child. Why, even if we fail to please the great Khan, we get to serve other lords in the household. Maybe even *marry* one."

Shan T'u cupped her hands around a golden flagon of wine. "Yes," she said gently. "I suppose it *is* a great honor." She thought fleetingly of her own father and her wedding caravan. Was it so different, then, for any woman in China? Only Shan T'u, the princess whose feet were not bound, dared think differently. Only Shan T'u dreamed of her own lover—and her own life. Only Shan T'u sought the sinful and forbidden. And now she had been punished.

Shan T'u looked again at the throne. Khan was signaling for silence, and staffs were rapped sharply against carpets. Slowly, ponderously, the racket abated. Shan T'u fingered the pin in her hair. Her heart beat faster.

"Hear me!" Kublah Khan cried out now. Abruptly, all shreds of chatter ceased. Ten thousand heads turned toward the throne. De Rais stood obediently at Khan's feet.

"You all know," Khan said drunkenly, "that I am just. You know that I reward loyalty and valor. I give staffs of gold and silver to my commanders who distinguish themselves in the field. I appoint commissioners with authority to give away land, to give away offices, to give away *anything*." He made vague, sweeping gestures.

Khan paused, and even from this distance, Shan T'u could see his ferret's eyes glittering. All at once, a ripple of deadly terror iced her spine. Something was terribly, terribly wrong.

"And you know," Khan continued, "that if I'm betrayed by those I trust, my justice is *swift*." He allowed a small, wicked smile to play over his lips. There was some murmuring now. Shan T'u kept her hands in her lap. She looked around furtively, but saw only the crush of humanity, sweating and drunk and gorgeously attired. The night suffocated her.

Khan let his eyes roam over the assembly. "Maybe you remember what happened to Achmath the Bailo, the Saracen I once loved and trusted like my own son. I let him do whatever he pleased. Remember him? How that snake worked his sorcery on me and poured honey in my ears so I believed what he said and did what he wished?"

There was an ominous tremor in the hall now. Khan cried, "And when I returned from conquest one day, after Achmath had been in power for twenty-two years, I found him *dead!*" The word reverberated on the foul, steaming air. "His head sliced off by the sword of Chenchu. Well, I asked about Chenchu and his treachery and what did I learn? I learned from my captain Cogati that this serpent Achmath, this crawling worm, had used his power to rape all the women he wanted, to execute any man he didn't like, and to grab a vault full of treasure through collecting bribes. All this I learned. And my wrath was *terrible.*"

Khan was bellowing by now, sawing the air with his stubby arms. The lion raised his head. Khan waited until the hall fell silent again. "I caused the corpse of this snake to be dug up and flung to the dogs to chomp on. I had his seven sons lined up and flayed alive." He drew himself up, and with a terrible voice he cried, "I won't have my trust betrayed! I will bring justice on those who cross me!"

Khan raised his flagon. Immediately, the multitudes in the Great Hall stumbled to their knees with a scraping and crashing of chairs. Shan T'u followed their example and trembled as she knelt. Khan drank greedily from a flagon of mare's milk, and the musicians played. He slammed down his cup, and avidly, the guests resumed their chairs.

And now Khan turned his eyes to De Rais. The whitish milk streamed from his beard, stained his golden robe, and soured him with a stink Shan T'u could smell even from where she sat. The emperor's finger pointed dramatically at De Rais.

"This man," Khan said, "presented himself as a knight, which indeed he is. And a slayer of bandits, which indeed he is. But he claimed that the Chinese wench with him was the daughter of a merchant. Well, this knight withheld the truth from me, and the truth stinks of betrayal!"

The hall exploded with amazed reaction. The concubines turned sharply to Shan T'u. She placed her hands on the table and held up her head defiantly. She sensed that her death was moments away.

Khan grinned. "How do I know this? Because I *do* have trusted men in my court. And they're not all military officers, either. Even a *poet* may be trusted. A womanish Chinese aristocrat, real pond scum. But he's arranged for so many of the dancers and jugglers and wild beasts you've enjoyed at my feasts. He's composed poems and songs in my honor. *And* he has informed me of the greed and ambition of certain Chinese princes to the south."

Khan raised a fist and brought it smashing down on the table. "He told me about *this* betrayal. Will you not tell us *all,* poet?"

The emperor turned his head and gestured. Shan T'u half stood at her seat, her pulse racing. Who could possibly know? Who in the court of Khan . . . ?

She cried out, a sharp, horrified scream, as the man in gold-brocaded silk stood up. She had not seen him; he had been well hidden at a table crowded with court nobility. But now, as he got to his feet and kowtowed to the Khan, she recognized his face and her heart sank like a stone in the river.

"Wei Ku!" she sobbed brokenly. "Betrayer . . . betrayer . . ."

Wei Ku smiled, a pale, sickly smile. The emperor raised his hands once more to bring silence. De Rais stood coldly now, staring at Wei Ku.

Resplendent in his green silk robe and scholar's cap, Wei Ku spoke in a tense, constricted voice. "The knight is William De Rais," Wei Ku said. "He came to the palace of Prince Chang Hu disguised as a holy friar. The woman is Princess Shan T'u, the daughter of Prince Chang Hu."

Shan T'u bowed her head and hissed in rage. Around her, the cries and murmurs flew like predatory birds. Wei Ku went on. "The princess was to be delivered to Sultan Akbar of India. The knight convinced Prince Chang to entrust him as guide. But his true motive was to kidnap the princess and sell her for ransom. This he attempted when bandits attacked the wedding caravan . . ."

"No!" Shan T'u cried. "He lies!"

The Khan's eyes flamed with horrified rage. "Silence her!" he screamed.

Mongol warriors shouldered their way through the mobs of guests and seized Shan T'u. She struggled, but a sword tip pricked her lower spine. She tossed her head angrily and looked at De Rais, who watched her but said nothing.

Wei Ku drank wine, and went on. "There was far deeper treachery," he said. "The marriage was supposed to be a favor to the Great Khan, for Sultan Akbar knew the Khan and asked for a bride of royal blood. But in truth, Prince Chang Hu was planning to arrange an alliance with Sultan Akbar *against* the emperor . . ."

Shan T'u whispered, "My father . . . !" She had not known anything of this. And how did this sniveling poet know of it? He was not privy to court affairs.

Wei Ku said, "Chang Hu had already been plotting with other southern princes to challenge Mongol rule. He did not know, however, the true identity of this knight. We have reason to believe that the knight De Rais had met with these bandits on his first trip through the mountains, and that the attack was planned."

Shan T'u's heart froze. *"Liar,"* she whispered. "Liar, liar, liar, liar . . ."

"Shut up!" her Mongol guard barked. The sword dug deeper into her flesh.

Shan T'u wept. Wei Ku was a worm, a horrid beast. To make up such stories, to accuse her knight of . . . . . . of what? she thought with sudden cold horror. Of a plot that was all too plausible? The bandits knew precisely when to attack. Yet William fought and killed them. But might not Kung have agreed to lose a few men? Might it not have been a cruel bargain struck between swindlers? Even Kung's entry into her tent might have been a charade for her benefit.

And how the bandits had turned and run, those ruthless red masks suddenly afraid of a knight and a lady . . .

Shan T'u shook her head, angry at herself. Wei Ku was injecting poison into her mind. He was jealous of the knight, lecherous for her body. She must *not* heed his lies.

Khan spoke once again as Wei Ku sat down. "I announce this treachery tonight to remind you that no betrayal of our throne will go undiscovered and unpunished. The Yellow Beard has much to tell us. He shall be put to torture until the words pour like his own blood. The princess shall be given to the Sultan Akbar. Tonight I will dispatch riders to tell the sultan his bride lives and awaits him. But *I,* not the traitorous Chang Hu, shall take credit for the match." Khan's face darkened. "The snake Chang Hu shall be cruelly punished for this betrayal, and likewise the nobles who plotted with him. And thus we crush all rebellion!"

Once more, his fist pounded the carved table. Then he grinned widely. "And now, let the revels begin!"

He clapped his hands twice and a great racket of music commenced. Once again, the hall rumbled with talk. Wine goblets were refilled. Shan T'u watched with cold terror as guards seized De Rais and led him away at swordpoint. Her heart seethed with rage. She wished only to reach the throat of Wei Ku with her vengeful hands before she died.

Shan T'u felt her wrists being yanked behind her and lashed with cloth. Ashamed and frightened, she walked ahead of the guards, away from the astonished concubines.

They passed a table crowded with noblewomen, all resplendently clothed and gossiping in reedy voices. Shan T'u glanced at the table, downcast and bereft. But in that glance, her eye caught one face that made her stop and lose her breath.

Shan T'u stared with trembling emotion at the woman. She wore her hair elaborately coiffed, aglitter with gemmed clips and golden ornaments. She wore a lavish silk robe of a beautiful cerise color, exquisitely brocaded with gold thread. Her lips were painted crimson, her eyes dark and laughing, her eyebrows meticulously painted. And she smiled now at Shan T'u with a slow, evil smile.

"*Lady Feng* . . ." Shan T'u choked.

"I am so sorry to meet you like this," Lady Feng said. Her tapered fingers cradled a wine goblet.

In a sudden rush, everything made sense to Shan T'u. "It was *you*," she cried softly. "*You* knew of my father's plotting—he plotted with your own husband, Tuan Lei. You monster—to betray your own husband . . ."

Lady Feng chuckled throatily. "Wei Ku and I have long recognized a threat in the hopeless alliances of these jealous men. We put a stop to it."

"And to my life, to my love," Shan T'u said wretchedly. "You hated me always. You told the Khan where to find us . . ."

Lady Feng looked utterly bored. "My sweet child," she yawned. "Your wild ravings were never respectable. They are grotesque in this situation. I warned you that your headstrong, impish ways would bring you to no good end. Well, here you are. You had to defy everyone. You had to throw yourself at a French thief. You had to run about shooting arrows. Now you see the result. Please don't blame *me* for your downfall."

Shan T'u trembled as she looked at the woman who had destroyed her. "Lady Feng, I swear to all the gods that somehow I will have my revenge. I swear . . ."

Lady Feng laughed. "Get her out of here."

She waved imperiously to the guards, who poked Shan T'u with the sword. The ladies at the table set up a tinkling, mocking laugh. Shan T'u felt bitter tears sting her cheeks as she walked in humiliation toward the rear of the hall.

Chapter Fifteen

THEY TOOK SHAN T'U OVER A STONE BRIDGE ACROSS A small lake, to a pavilion on an island near the palace. There the guards threw her into a narrow room with a lacquered bed and a window that looked out on a garden. One guard waited outside the pavilion while the other took a last look at the prisoner. Shan T'u could taste his odor and feel his rough breath.

"The emperor will tear your limbs out," the guard said with an intoxicated grin. "And if you don't please him, he'll give you to us."

The guard uttered a low, revolting laugh, and belched up some of the mare's milk he'd been guzzling. Shan T'u averted her face and curled miserably on the bed. The guard strode out of the cell, laughing.

Shan T'u bit down on her clenched fist and shook

convulsively. She felt as if she'd been trampled by her father's Dragon horses. The image of William being dragged away danced vividly in her brain. Outside, she could hear wildfowl. From a very great distance came the racket of music.

She forced herself to stand. With unsteady feet, she moved across the wooden floor to the window and felt the rank, wet breeze from the lake. She could just glimpse the blazing lights from the grand palace, where the torches and silk lanterns still burned beyond the night.

Shan T'u sighed and found a chair. She sat, feeling foolish in the rich gown and caftan of a concubine. The room was austere, but not barren; there were hangings of silk, and there were flowers in vases. No, she was not being kept in a dungeon but in a pretty little cage. Her sultan would arrive soon to claim her.

Her lips twisted into the ghost of a smile. She would end her odyssey as her father had intended—in the wedding bed of Akbar. She bowed her head, covering her face with her hands. Her father! Oh, she'd known he was a sly fox and a cunning warlord. But she'd never suspected that he'd dared plot against the Khan himself!

Her blurred eyes stared, unseeing, at the room. It made sense that Prince Chang sought to impress the Khan by giving his daughter to the sultan. But the counterplot astonished her. And in cahoots with Tuan Lei! Two hard-bitten old warriors forming doomed alliances with treacherous sultans.

Shan T'u stood once again, restless, and strode to the doorway of the room. The wind struck her full face. Her caftan rustled in the dawn breeze. She shook her head wonderingly. The poet Wei Ku, a spy!

She'd known that he was well connected, an aristocrat whose family kowtowed to the Mongol overlords and bought him a place in the Khan's court. She smiled bitterly. An arranger of puppet shows and trained elephant acts. An unprincipled scribbler of doggerel to tickle the illiterate emperor.

Bah! She turned away in disgust. She felt vindicated for having despised Wei Ku. Master Po had excoriated this man of learning who prostituted his art for position. But Wei Ku had done very well indeed.

Sprawling on the bed, she removed the golden pin from her hair and made futile little stabs in the rolled pillow. She stuck the fabric savagely, wishing it were the throat of Kublai Khan, or even better, the tongue of Wei Ku.

And Lady Feng! The thought made Shan T'u sit upright and throw off her headdress. Her hair fell in glimmering cascades to her shoulders. Of course, she thought, Wei Ku could never get close enough to the princes to know their most intimate business. So he made a liaison with Lady Feng. *She,* naturally, could coax the secrets from her husband.

Shan T'u cursed, an unladylike stream of obscenity clandestinely learned as a girl from her servants. Lady Feng, so stuffy about obedience to one's father and husband. And all the time slithering into Wei Ku's arms, kissing Wei Ku's lips, lying with the poet, plotting with him. What was Lady Feng's reward to be?

Ha! Little question of *that,* Shan T'u thought sullenly. Already, Lady Feng sat with the noblewomen in the Great Hall of Kublai Khan. And soon her dolt of a husband would be killed. Then nothing could stand in the way of her insatiable lust for position. Why, she might even be an empress one day! Yes, *that* would suit Lady Feng. Ten thousand retainers, a court of her very own.

The deep blue glow of morning suffused the room. Shan T'u's heart grew heavy. She had also doubted William tonight. And Heaven forgive her, a tendril of doubt still flickered in her heart. Who *was* this Burgundian who rode from the darkness into her life? He melted her with words of love and lake blue eyes. He defended her with his sword and with his body. He swore eternal fidelity.

But he was a self-confessed swindler, a blackguard who had been disowned by his own father. A ravisher of women. An unscrupulous trader who owed allegiance to no king, to no God. He'd told her as much. Could she believe that he was transformed by her love? Could she *know* that he had not plotted with Kung and that he did *not* intend to ransom her? That this was not his very plan as they rode down the hillside away from the burning caravan? But the Mongols intervened. William, swindler that he was, had been outfoxed by Lady Feng and Wei Ku.

Shan T'u breathed deeply as birds cried. A fine lover *she* was. Doubting her beloved as he was carted off to a dungeon. Feeling sorry for herself, feeling betrayed by everyone . . .

A long, hideous scream pierced the morning air. Shan T'u's heart stopped and her hands turned to ice. She stood and ran to the doorway. She saw nothing but the slowly resolving shapes of willows as the sky was brushed with deep orange.

She was trembling. The scream had ripped through

her like a knife. The cry of a drunkard? A careless servant trampled by a horse?

Or a knight being tortured?

Shan T'u shut her eyes to fight dizziness. She clung to the doorpost, praying with all her heart that it was not De Rais who screamed.

Another cry!

"*No!*" she whispered as her pulse pounded. "*Leave him alone . . .*"

A third cry rent the dawn, this one a twisted shriek of unutterable agony drawn out to a whisper of despair. Shan T'u wept and slowly slid to her knees.

"Get up," a whisper commanded.

Shan T'u's eyes flew open. The whisper came from behind her. The guards? Were they going to take her without the Khan's order? No—this voice had spoken in Chinese, not Mongolian!

She remained on her knees, controlling every muscle. Her eyes beheld the first light of day glowing softly on the misted lake and the stone bridge. "Who is it?" she asked.

"Turn around," the whisper said. "And make no sound or your throat will be cut."

Shan T'u stood with great care. Her body pulsated beneath her gown. Grimly, she realized that she had left the golden hairpin on the bed.

She turned slowly. Her eyes went wide and the breath surged from her lungs as she saw the intruder.

"*Kung!*" she breathed.

The bandit chieftain stood half in shadow. He wore the same costume he'd worn that night in the tent: belted cotton tunic and trousers, boots, peasant hat, and red mask covering his entire face. Shan T'u tried to sort out her emotions. She was frightened, and yet, insanely, she felt relief.

"One day," he said, "we will meet less dramatically." He held his knife at the ready.

"What do you want?"

"Your attention."

"How did you get here? Surely you didn't ride halfway across China—"

"Clearly, I *did,*" he said. "I told you, Shan T'u, you affect me deeply."

She moved away from the door. He followed her with his masked eyes as she sat on the bed. "You are certainly persistent."

He bowed slightly.

Her eyes filled and her heart darkened as she looked at him. "I should not speak to you. I still carry in my heart the memory of my caravan in flames, my soldiers and huntsmen and servants all slain. Are you proud of your victory?"

Kung twirled the knife idly. "I lost a great many of *my* men that night," he said. "And you think ill of your soldiers and huntsmen if you suppose they all perished. Many escaped into the hills." He laughed ruefully. "I imagine they are still searching for you."

Her throat tightened. "Not all dead . . ."

"Foolish girl. Our aim was to take *you,* and to begin a small legend that would attract other rogues to our side. This we did. We have already swelled our ranks. But to butcher all of your people . . ." He waved the knife airily. "No, Shan T'u. There was much death and much blood, but many went free." He looked intently at her. "Including your servants."

She had fingered the hairpin, but now she let it go and stood, trembling. "You did not kill them?"

"No need. Doubtless they huddled there terrified for several days and nights, but they were unharmed."

She felt as if wine bubbles ran through her bloodstream. "I don't understand. William said it was useless to fight, that it was a trap . . ."

Kung laughed. "The bastard was right. Of course it was a trap. We wanted to lure him into battling us so that we could carry you off. I needed time to convince you to join us, to . . ." His voice dropped. "To love me."

Shan T'u looked at him with curiosity and deep emotion. "I was wrong, about everything . . ."

Kung went to the chair and put up a booted foot. He sheathed the knife in the boot. "You jump to extremes. The attack on your caravan was not a slaughter, nor was it a game. Men died. You must understand this. It is not a make-believe hunt on your father's preserve. I don't stock the countryside with paper enemies, nor do I have a revolving couch to shoot from."

Shan T'u's pulse seemed to pause at his words. "How do you know of my father's revolving couch?"

Kung smiled. "Prince Chang's hunting preserve is renowned far and wide."

"Not his revolving couch . . . only to other nobles who have hunted with him."

"We have robbed many nobles."

"And asked about my father's hunting parties? Who are you, Kung?"

Her heart threatened to burst through her gown. Kung stood in thoughtful silence, considering. He sighed softly. He glanced at the doorway, now filled with blue morning light. The clatter and honking of water birds filled the air. "I cannot stay long," he mused. "And I have much to say. Maybe it *is* better if you know. There may not be any time afterwards."

"Kung, what—"

"Princess, I ask you not to cry out, only to pay heed. Our situation is desperate, and every moment is a priceless jewel."

"Yes . . ."

Shan T'u clasped her hands together as her flimsy gown grazed the skin of her body. Kung removed his hat with a flourish, revealing dark, glistening hair in a nobleman's topknot. With a swift, brutal motion of his hand, he reached up and tore away the silk mask.

"Behold, Shan T'u. Judge not by appearance."

Her hands clapped over her mouth and she gasped in astonishment. She sat slowly on the bed as all strength drained from her. When the words came, they were wisps of breath.

"Wei Ku . . . you are the bandit chieftain?"

Wei Ku smiled without mirth. Suddenly, his patrician face did not sneer. Shan T'u saw now a countenance of smooth handsomeness, with intelligent eyes and a cruel mouth. "Can you hear what I say?" he inquired. "Or are you too amazed?"

She nodded, gulping for air. "Yes," she whispered. "I can hear."

"Listen, then." He moved his chair close to the bed and leaned toward her. His breath smelled of the wine he'd drunk. "I have no time for long tales. Briefly, then: I was born an aristocrat, trained as a scholar. But I was kidnapped by the red masks when I was a child. As it turned out, a family servant, an ox driver, was in league with them and hoped to raise money from my ransom. But I was enthralled with these bold men. A world opened for me. I begged to join them.

"They spoke with the ox driver, who agreed that I was an unusual youth with much strength and a quick mind. I had always loved the servants better than my friends, and wept with outrage when they were whipped or mistreated. So the bandits trained me in secret, and around their campfires I learned of the abominations of the Mongols. As I grew into manhood, I learned that the princes of China had been stripped of all power, that all the poetry and painting and knowledge I possessed would be wiped out by these illiterate, flyblown barbarians who ran the show. I had developed a blazing anger by then, and a thirst for blood."

Wei Ku half smiled as he remembered. Pale golden sun bathed the room in warm light. "I planned to throw away my silk robes and join the bandits, but they persuaded me that I could accomplish more in two guises. As a bandit, I could strike directly at the Mongols. As a poet and blueblood, I could have access to the courts of the mighty."

He stood, lithe as a panther. "So I gained a reputation as a weak-kneed poet and storyteller, and Chang Hu himself gave me a letter introducing me to Kublai Khan. I made myself useful to the emperor by arranging entertainments—he is as simple as a child and loves to be amused—and I learned secrets."

"From Lady Feng?"

His eyes twinkled. "Lady Feng is a cobra, best kept in a basket. I saw at once that she craved power and would betray anyone for it. Once she knew that I had the Khan's ear, she wooed me"—he laughed at the memory—"and seduced me into a cabal with her against her husband and Prince Chang."

Shan T'u stood. "But why betray my father?" she asked emotionally. "If he was plotting *against* the Khan—"

Wei Ku shrugged. "It was expedient. His plot was foolish and doomed. It was the plotting of a warlord who did not see that his day was done, his power gone. The Sultan Akbar would have told the Khan of Chang's treachery had I not. By revealing the plot, I have gained great favor with the emperor and I will use this favor."

"How?"

"Ah," he smiled. "It is not for you to know my plans. I can lead Mongol hordes into ambushes, encourage doomed expeditions . . . all manner of mischief. I have gained vital confidence through this deceit."

"And Lady Feng has gained a step up to the throne."

"Pah," Wei Ku laughed. "What do I care for her ambitions? One sews intrigue with a sharp needle."

Shan T'u stepped toward him. "And a sharp sword."

"Exactly." His teeth gleamed as he smiled. "My red masks include many Mongol warriors who are sick of the Khan's tyrannical rule. They infiltrate the royal guard and commit sabotage. Slowly, we will cut the blood vessels leading to the emperor's heart."

Shan T'u raised her head and her eyes glistened. "And was I just a pawn in your scheme?"

"It had to be so, Shan T'u. I was only going to betray your father once you were delivered to the sultan. But you fell in love with De Rais. There was a chance that you would bolt from the caravan."

Her heart sprang up within her breast, as if from a terrible sleep. Every limb quaked as she realized the import of his words. Her fingers hovered near his sleeves and she could taste his nearness as she spoke in a terse whisper.

"Then . . . William did *not* meet you before he reached my father? He didn't plan the attack with you?"

Wei Ku's eyebrows knit, and then he threw back his head and laughed. His hands quietly closed around her soft arms. "You were listening too hard to what I said in the Great Hall. I knew not of William De Rais until I saw him at your father's palace."

"And he was *not* planning to kidnap me for ransom?"

Wei Ku's hands moved slowly to her shoulders. "*That* I cannot tell you. You must ask the knight himself."

The doubts rushed back like waves to the sea. She was suddenly more confused than ever, and Wei Ku's hands on her flesh disconcerted her more than she liked to admit.

"You were a fool, Wei Ku," she said throatily. "William begged me to run away with him and I refused. Did you know that?"

"I could not be certain. Love is a saboteur of duty."

"But were you not just a little jealous?"

He scowled and his hands dropped from her, leaving small tingling fires. "You see with sharp eyes, Princess. Perhaps I *was* jealous. I did not lie about my feelings for you."

"Then why did you paw me down at my father's river pavilion?"

"So you wouldn't question why I was there watching you." He smiled. "Also to touch you."

She turned away, arms folded across her chest. "That doesn't amuse me. My beloved is in chains because of your lies. If I must be given to the sultan, so be it, but why sentence William to torture and death for your jealousy? You hurt my heart beyond words."

"And *your* words hurt *me*," he whispered. He was behind her, his hands on her shoulders and his lean body ever so slightly pressing against her back. "I did not think I loved you so much, Shan T'u, not until the Yellow Beard took your heart. My love blinded my good sense. I risked my skin to see you. But I did not betray the knight out of jealousy. When he escaped with you, he threatened my plans. I *had* to let the Khan know where you were. I had to betray you before the emperor. De Rais would have been thrown to the dogs no matter what I said. At least now *you* are not tainted by your forbidden love for him."

She tilted up her head and breathed deeply, feeling her breasts push hard against the silk gown. Now his hands were around her waist, his cotton tunic touching the back of her caftan.

"Now . . ." His lips brushed her neck. "Now I put on my red mask and plunder once more. Now your father will be crushed by the Khan's armies."

Shan T'u gasped, jolted to her senses. She wrenched away from him and turned. "My father! I hadn't realized . . ."

"Yes, Princess. Not only Tuan Lei will be punished."

She moved to get past him, but he blocked her

path. "Let me go! I must warn him. I must tell him in time . . ."

"There *is* no time," he hissed. "Don't you see that? Your father must perish. Your knight must die. You must wed your sultan. Accept your fate."

Her fury had returned. "I'll die before I accept it!"

"Then you *will* die!" His face reddened and a storm arose in his eyes. "You are nothing. We are fighting for our history and for our lives. To overthrow the Khan, blood must be spilled, and hearts must be broken."

Shan T'u wept as he held her lightly. "But you had no right," she sobbed. "You are not a god to take my love from me."

"Daring words for a woman, Shan T'u."

"But not *your* woman, Wei Ku!"

Her words rang in the air, followed by silence. Wei Ku bowed his head for a moment, then released her. "True enough," he said. "But good or evil, the lots have been cast. Go to your sultan, Shan T'u. Accept your destiny."

He walked away from her, toward the window. "Wait," she said.

He turned, his eyebrows cocked.

"You are pleased with my destiny," she said bitterly. "You are not sad that William will die."

Wei Ku permitted a wan smile. "I won't deny that."

Shan T'u prayed fervently for strength. "May not *his* destiny be changed just a little?"

"Explain."

She swallowed hard. "You have influence with Kublai Khan. You have the power of life and death . . ."

"Not so much power as that, Princess."

"But nearly as much," she said impatiently. She calmed herself with effort, trying not to think of her father, who was beyond saving. "Spare William De Rais. He will not interfere with your rebellion. He will return to Arabia to swindle and get rich."

Wei Ku smiled broadly. "Shan T'u, you are hopelessly romantic. If he is spared, he will come charging through the grand palace looking for you."

"Not if he thinks that I have already been taken to India. And if he invades India, what concern is it of yours?"

Wei Ku nodded in appreciation of the point. "And why should I intervene on his behalf?"

She shut her eyes for an instant, then looked deeply into his eyes. "For my heart, Wei Ku."

His breath quickened. "How much do you promise?"

Please, she begged her tears, *don't shame me yet.* "You wished a bride. I will be your bride."

He moved a step toward her, his body like a drawn bow. "You swear this?"

She dropped her eyes, barely able to breathe. "Yes."

He exhaled lustily, trying to control himself. "Well, then." He strode to her, lifted her chin with his finger. His face was twisted with passion. "I must leave now, before the guards discover me. Meet me tonight by the golden pavilion near the grand palace. I will ask you then for proof of your vow. Do you understand?"

She nodded.

"Good. I will suggest to the Khan that the dukes of Burgundy not be angered by the torture of one of their own. And I will ask that the Sultan Akbar be sent a different woman and that you be allowed to wed me. I think he will say yes."

Shan T'u could hardly hear for the pounding of her heart. "Lady Feng will be infuriated."

He laughed softly. "Her bruised sensibilities are of no concern to me. Tonight, then, at the golden pavilion."

"Tonight."

He smiled. "This has indeed been a successful venture."

With two great bounds, Wei Ku scaled the wall of the room and leapt through the open window. She ran to the window and glimpsed him threading a path among the willow trees. Soon he was gone from sight. Shan T'u turned away from the window, her hand at her mouth, and sobbed in great, heaving gouts.

Chapter Sixteen

WHILE THE SUN THROBBED IN A BRAZEN SKY, TEN
retainers carried a litter into the stone courtyard of
the Khan's prison. Surrounding the courtyard were
low vermilion buildings ornamented in gold.

In the center of the courtyard, William De Rais lay
prone, stripped to his waist. Four half-naked Mongols
held him down on his stomach on the damp, hot
stones. He wore only white cotton trousers, which
were splashed with his blood.

A fifth Mongol brute wielded a bamboo stick,
flattened at the base and polished at the tip. As a
berobed officer shouted commands, the torturer
whipped De Rais with savage strokes. With each
stroke, De Rais's corded body quivered and a crimson
welt split his back. His head was twisted to the side,

his eyes half-shut. He uttered soft moans. The stick made a whistling sound as it descended, followed by a sharp slap.

The litter was borne into the courtyard and set down near the scene of torture. One of the retainers pulled open the tasseled curtain while two others waved peacock-feather fans. Out of the litter stepped Lady Feng in a richly embroidered silk gown of teal blue. Her hair was exquisitely coiffed and bejeweled. The fans swatted away horseflies as she walked with faltering little steps toward the Mongols.

The berobed officer turned to her with a scowl. "What are you doing here?" he demanded.

Lady Feng replied in Mongolian. "I asked His Majesty if I might observe the knight's punishment. He behaved lewdly to me at the house of Prince Chang."

The officer muttered under his breath. Lady Feng decorously averted her face to avoid his pungent aroma. "Okay," the officer said. "But don't get in the way."

Lady Feng smiled. "I simply wish to enjoy his suffering."

She waited as a chair was brought by two retainers. She was helped to sit down, and the fans provided shade. Lady Feng made a tent of her fingers and studied the bleeding body of the French knight. Her eyes ran slowly along his sinewed back, torn open by the blows of the bamboo stick. Raised welts crisscrossed his gleaming skin. Fresh blood oozed from new gashes. She watched as the torturer brought down the stick yet again and laid open a fresh cut over a swollen welt. How fascinating, Lady Feng thought, the way the tremors ran the lean, hard length of him.

She found herself breathing faster as she explored his leonine grace. Her cheeks flushed pink and her breasts rose and fell beneath her silk gown. Her fingers hovered near her throat, and a heated smile animated her perspiring face.

With great agony, De Rais opened his eyes and looked up. Slowly, he seemed to remember some dim, forgotten time. Inexorably, those eyes changed from shallow pits of despair to deepening wells of hatred. His barely perceptible breath quickened. His broad chest began to fill with air. His lips, cracked by thirst, struggled to speak.

"Good morning," Lady Feng said in Chinese. "Do you remember me, Burgundian? You saw me in the baths, in the palace of Chang. You thought me more of a woman than Shan T'u."

De Rais's eyes pleaded with the beautiful woman in silk. Lady Feng leaned slightly forward to better study the magnificent man. The torturer struck with his bamboo stick again, and De Rais drew his lips back to expose his teeth. Lady Feng's nostrils flared with desire.

"I see why Shan T'u became infatuated with you," she said. "You are very pretty to look at. Perhaps, if there's anything left of you when they finish, I might try you out. I can excite you beyond anything you've known." Lady Feng laughed, knowing that De Rais understood her words and the Mongol cretins did not.

But in her wicked taunting, Lady Feng failed to notice how cold and hard De Rais's eyes had turned. She did not realize that her words had penetrated the fog of pain that benumbed him. She was not aware that his strength slowly flowed back into his corded shoulders and thick arms, that the sting of his wounds began to infuriate him.

"Well, Burgundian," she said with a flick of her pink tongue across her red lips, "I'm afraid it's really too hot for me. As much as I'd enjoy watching you flayed raw, I must go back to my cool apartment at the palace. To sip iced wine and watch goldfish swim. How sad that you must stay here, in this—"

De Rais moved with blinding speed and brutal violence. He heaved his body backwards so unexpectedly that the four Mongols imprisoning his hands were flung away. De Rais rolled away from the Mongols, kicked to his feet, and moved toward Lady Feng. As the Mongols lunged for him, De Rais hurled aside the stunned retainers with their fans and yanked Lady Feng from her seat. She gasped as he viciously twisted her arm behind her back and snaked a brawny forearm around her throat. De Rais's muscles knotted under his glistening skin as he held Lady Feng motionless. Blood streamed in rivulets from his mauled back, dropping in red pools on the courtyard stones.

De Rais edged backwards toward one of the buildings. He growled, "I can snap her little white neck in a breath. I want my bride."

The berobed officer gripped his sword hilt with a hand across his body. "You can't get far."

"I'll get far enough, Tartar, with this saucy prisoner."

"No, Yellow Beard. The Khan doesn't care two pins about a Chinese woman."

"I think he cares about this one," De Rais bluffed. He shut his eyes for an instant as waves of dizziness swam through him. The Mongol officer leaned forward, his sharp eyes alert. De Rais forced his eyes open. "So you wait for me to swoon, eh? I've been hurt worse than this."

"Knight," the officer said, "we can talk about this."

"No talk!" De Rais said. "Bring me the princess."

De Rais edged backwards another step and nearly fainted. Lady Feng hissed, "You're hurting me."

"You lusted for my touch," De Rais snarled. "Enjoy it."

He pulled her more tightly against him and she shut her eyes in terror. But now there came the clatter of hoofbeats and De Rais turned his head. The horseman came rattling into the courtyard, hooves crashing on the stones. The rider was a Mongol baron of the highest degree, an officer of the highest degree. The baron reined to a halt and dismounted with a sharp, incredulous stare at the scene before him.

The berobed officer blurted, "He seized the lady!"

"I see," the baron said. "But there is no need for this. The prisoner is to be freed."

"Freed?"

De Rais did not loosen his stranglehold on Lady Feng, fearing a ruse. The baron said, "The knight is to be released and given a start of one day. If he returns to his own land, he is to be protected in his travels as any other wayfarer. If he tries to return to Kanbaliq, he is to be killed."

The berobed officer exhaled, clearly disgusted with the whims of his emperor. He waved a hand at the torturer and the Mongol guards. "So be it," he growled. He turned to De Rais, and his small black eyes held revulsion at what he saw. "Did you hear, Yellow Beard?"

De Rais shook off his light-headedness. "How can I know this is not a trick . . . ?"

"You don't know," the officer said. "If you want to hold that woman all day, then do so."

The officer barked a command to the other guards, and they walked wearily toward the buildings. Two more horsemen trotted into the courtyard, armed with bows and arrows. There was a brusque exchange between the horsemen and the baron, and De Rais knew that he was to be escorted to the palace gates.

Pain misted his mind. Taking a chance, he released Lady Feng, who clutched her throat and fell heavily to the stones. Her retainers scurried over, fanning her and poking at her. The horsemen dismounted and strode over to De Rais. His back was like a burning shield. He managed to whisper, "Where is my bride . . . ?"

One of the horsemen, a foul-smelling bear of a man, snickered and said, "Your bride isn't here. She has been taken to India."

De Rais bit back a wave of hopeless rage. Somewhere in the back of his tortured brain, his swindler's sense told him that this was not true. The Khan had asked the sultan to come to fetch *her*. He had to find Shan T'u and smuggle her out. But first he had to sleep . . .

"Come on," the horseman said. "You have to leave."

"Not yet . . ." De Rais mumbled between swollen lips. "Need to bathe . . . rest . . ."

The baron made a rude sound. "Go on, Yenchu, get him a bath and some perfume."

This brought hearty laughter, and De Rais felt himself dragged across the hot stones. As the sun struck his raw back, he screamed in agony.

* * *

Later that afternoon, Lady Feng was carried in her litter through the Khan's royal park, past glittering streams, wide meadows, and arcades of willows. The emperor stood in front of wooden cages housing gerfalcons and goshawks. He wore a billowing yellow robe, and in this verdant setting seemed a contented prince. Only the presence of mounted hunters with curled leopards slung over their saddles showed this to be the Khan's preserve.

Lady Feng was helped from her litter. She wore a fresh gown, and had been bathed and revived with food and drink after her ordeal in the courtyard. Still, her face was ashen and her white throat showed violet welts where De Rais had choked her. Her eyes flashed with black fire.

"Your Majesty," she said crisply, and kowtowed.

Khan turned lazily and regarded her with blinking eyes. His pink face glowed rose in the sunlight. The gaming birds set up a racket at her appearance.

"May I speak?" she asked.

"I granted you an audience," he said loftily. In a distant meadow, the Khan's white mares ran free, untouchable on penalty of death.

"Why have you released the knight?"

Khan looked sharply at her. "Are you questioning my decree, Lady Feng?"

"Forgive me, Your Majesty. I was nearly killed this morning."

"Yes, I know," Khan said, and tittered. *"You* wanted to watch him tortured."

"He was not supposed to seize me! How was that allowed?"

Khan responded with an aloof stare. His eyes darted, and trapped a little fallow deer hiding in a thicket. Khan turned to one of his hunters and said, "Let slip the leopard."

The hunter yanked on a leather leash, which held the cat in a pad on the horse's rump. The freed cat, with breathtaking speed, uncoiled and leaped from the horse. In a few silken bounds, it reached the thicket. The fallow deer pivoted and bounded away but the leopard brought it down and sank its fangs deep in the deer's flesh. The cat shook its prey and trotted back to the keeper, the deer limp and bloody in its jaws.

Khan knelt down, and as the keeper slipped the leash back on the cat, worked the deer loose. The leopard snarled. Khan held up the stricken deer by the hind legs. The animal's lifeblood streamed down its matted fur and covered the Khan's wrist. Its limbs still twitched and jerked with death spasms. Another keeper opened the door to the birds' pen and Khan tossed in the carcass. There was a rush of wings and a tumult of screeching as the hunting birds boiled over the prey.

Khan turned disdainfully back to Lady Feng and said, "He would not have seized you had you not been there."

Lady Feng swayed on her tiny slippered feet and said, "Nevertheless, Your Majesty, I protest the freeing of the knight. He is a dangerous enemy."

"He is a nuisance, nothing more. He wishes to make his fortune in Arabia."

"A lie! Who told you that?"

Khan scowled at her impertinence. "Why, your friend, Wei Ku."

"Wei Ku!" Lady Feng snarled, very much like the leopard had snarled when deprived of its kill. "Your

Majesty, Wei Ku is not a strong man. He is attracted to Shan T'u."

"I know," Khan said. "Wei Ku told me as much, and I gave the woman to him."

"You *what?*"

"Insolent, aren't you? Sultan Akbar has never seen the princess. I have already sent my warriors to find a Chinese woman of good birth. And Wei Ku has served me well." Khan giggled. "Did *you* want the knight, Lady Feng?"

A pink blush climbed to Lady Feng's ear tips. "You have made a grave error, Your Majesty."

Khan's face reddened. "You strain my patience!"

"The knight will seek his lady—"

"He believes her gone to India."

"He will find out the truth! He is most resourceful, Your Majesty, as you well know. He will seek Shan T'u. You must kill this princess and her knight."

There was silence following her presumptuous outburst. Flies droned in swarms about the half-eaten fallow deer. On the horse's crupper, the leopard licked its blood-flecked lips. Lady Feng had committed a deadly error in openly criticizing the Khan's decision. The emperor could not dream of listening to her arrogance now.

Khan called for his horse and said with supercilious finality, "You hate this princess deeply. But I will not decree an execution to suit your jealousies. I have done what I wished."

Lady Feng bowed and dropped her eyes. "Very well," she whispered. "You heed Wei Ku and not me because I am a woman. Then *I* must end the curse of Shan T'u myself."

"As you will," Khan said, as he was helped up into

the saddle. He steadied his kittenish horse. "Just stay away from the prison, will you?" He erupted into a braying laugh and snapped the reins. Lady Feng was left standing near the cage of hawks and falcons, who ruffled their wings and watched her with glittering eyes.

De Rais awoke to face a fearsome lion whose toothy snarl was frozen on his bronze face. The knight lay on his side on a lacquered bed. He remembered being stripped and bathed and having ointments rubbed on his back. He recalled being carried to this room in the apartments set aside for visiting ambassadors.

For a few moments, De Rais collected his thoughts. He knew that he had very little time to find Shan T'u. He knew that his strength was meager at best, but that might serve him. If the Tartars believed him sapped, they would not expect a counterattack. He tested his back by sitting up. Great gales of faintness swept over him and he had to bow his head and shut his eyes. His back felt stiff, almost as if a sheet of brass had been nailed to it.

Dim light filtered into the room, giving it a marigold glow. A table and chair furnished the room simply. De Rais cautiously swung his legs over the side of the bed and sat perfectly still. He wore only leather underpants, and his tapered, rawboned body gleamed in its near-nakedness. At the doorway of the room stood a Mongol guard, waiting for the knight to awaken and be kicked out. De Rais formed a plan in his mind and rehearsed it many times. It would need daring and luck, but those had always been his companions.

He stood upright and hissed through his teeth at the fresh bout of vertigo. He forced himself to stand without holding anything, until he was confident enough to take a few steps. At first he could only manage a shuffle, one foot at a time. His back shrieked with agony at each step. Sweat stood out on his forehead and streamed down his temples. Veins corded his neck. Soon, the pain became bearable as his steps became more certain. He circumnavigated the room many times, softly humming French tunes to take his mind off the pain.

At last, he felt ready to act. He couldn't afford to wait to be fetched. And once outside those walls, not his horse nor his sword nor all the love in his heart would get him back in.

De Rais prayed fervently and crossed himself. He moved with lithe steps to the doorway and stood for a moment, gathering every shred of strength he could find in his exhausted limbs. Then he drew a deep breath and cried out, "Help! The Yellow Beard has escaped!"

The guard came crashing into the room, drawing his sword. De Rais lunged from behind the doorway and flung his forearm around the guard's throat. Knowing that the Mongol would be powerful, De Rais wasted no time. He hugged the guard against his body and arched backwards, lifting the Mongol off his feet. At the same time, De Rais pressed his fist against the Tartar's skull while he strangled with his forearm. The Mongol struggled ferociously, but De Rais's strength was too great.

The Mongol gurgled horribly in his throat; his eyes bulged and his tongue flopped out of his mouth, swollen and gray. De Rais jerked his forearm back and he heard the Mongol's spine snap. The guard went limp in De Rais's arms.

De Rais stood over the fallen Mongol. He sucked agonized gulps of air into his inflamed lungs and felt his hard torso become sheathed in sweat. He knelt by the guard and stripped him of his raiment. He ignored the foul stench of the clothing and did not look at the shimmering sea of lice in the matted hair of the dead man's torso. Working with urgency, De Rais donned the costume and pulled the hat low over his forehead.

A few moments later, De Rais climbed the hillside planted with evergreens. The sun hung low in the west, painting a cloudy sky with iridescent hues of blue and scarlet. The dying light burnished the evergreens. The rich, loamy smell of pine stung his nostrils.

By the time he reached the green pavilion at the summit, De Rais was enervated. He rested for a few serene moments in a courtyard, listening to the murmur of a brook and the shrieks of exotic birds. No cry had been raised yet. He roused himself from the scene of limpid beauty, though his broad back flamed with a thousand fires and his limbs shook with fever. Infection could cripple him. He prayed for more time—and more strength.

He slipped inside the pavilion and hugged the wall. He heard feminine voices and flattened himself into the lengthening shadow of a trellis. Aya, the concubine who had watched over Shan T'u, walked past. De Rais waited until she passed him, then leaped from the shadows and dragged her back, his hand crushing her damp mouth.

She shuddered in his grip. "Not a word," De Rais

snarled in Mongolian, "or I'll snap your neck. Do you understand?"

She nodded.

"I want to know where the Princess Shan T'u is being held."

He slipped his hand from her mouth and she gulped air and panted with fright. "Who are you . . . ?"

"It doesn't matter. Answer me!"

Now, from the palace, came shouting "Quickly!" De Rais snapped.

Aya tried to still her heaving breasts. "She was here . . . but we were told that she was to be taken to the Golden Pavilion and left there, for service to the Khan . . ."

A chill raced up his spine. "Where is the Golden Pavilion?"

Aya pointed with a tremulous arm. "In the royal park, behind the palace. They took her minutes ago . . ."

He thought quickly. "Her riding garb. Do you still have it?"

"Yes."

"Have it brought here."

The shouting at the palace became more agitated. Bells were rung. Aya looked up with wide eyes. "There has been a murder at the palace . . ."

"There'll be another if you don't call your servants."

She nodded again, yielding a little in his grip. "You are the Yellow Beard."

"Then you know I'll kill you."

He could almost sense her shiver of enjoyment to be close to his naked skin. "The princess is most fortunate to be loved this way," she smiled. Her eyes gleamed. "I will have her clothes fetched. But you will both die before the night is over."

"Maybe we will, concubine. But we won't die alone."

He felt his heart thunder and his breath quicken as Aya clapped her hands twice and loudly summoned her servants.

The Golden Pavilion caught the last fire of the sun on each of its golden pillars. A golden dragon, claws outstretched, slithered around each of the pillars. The heads of the gilt monsters supported a roof of varnished bamboo cane. The fragile summer house was cunningly tied with silken cords, and dominated the vast park in this evening of frozen cerise splendor.

Shan T'u stood inside the pavilion in a gown of palest apricot silk meticulously embroidered with gold and silver thread. She wore a long stole against the evening wind and her hair was coiffed and pinned. Her brows were painted, her lips a persimmon color, her eyes luminous black pools. She seemed, in the violet dusk, a gently curving, gorgeously detailed porcelain figurine.

She looked out at the park, and at the grand palace in the distance. Her eyes filled with tears. By now, her beloved was gone. Whether he'd been just a roughneck and a swindler who'd used her, or whether he'd taken knightly vows at the sight of her, he had given her delight and fulfillment, and he would live in her heart forever. She sighed with grief. Now she would give her body to Wei Ku and content herself to be his wife.

She heard the crack of a twig and turned. Wei Ku stepped into the pavilion. He stood between two dragon pillars, and Shan T'u found her heart skipping. He wore a glittering brocaded robe of royal blue silk, and golden slippers. His hair was topknotted, and glistened with oils in the waning light. He smelled of spiced fragrances.

"Princess," he said. His voice was thick with passion.

She lowered her eyes.

"No," he protested. He strode to her and lifted her head. "Don't kowtow to me, Shan T'u. I want the impertinent princess who clawed me by the riverbank and presented her neck to my blade."

"Would you have slain me there?" she asked.

"Yes."

Her veins ran ice cold with mingled terror and fascination. "And yet you love me."

"You can't know how I've loved you, Shan T'u, from the first time I saw you. To slay you would have been to possess you, for your soul would have been kept from others."

She shivered in the wind. "You seemed such a weak and despicable man."

"It was difficult maintaining that guise. I had to remember to stoop, to whine, to cringe. But my efforts were rewarded."

Nervously, she placed her hands on his brocaded shoulders. He was hard and strong. "And now I see you like this."

"And are you more attracted?"

Her cheeks warmed. "Wei Ku, don't ask me to speak words of love."

He saw the tears spring to her eyes and he held her face in his cool hands. "I will not expect it, Shan T'u. Tonight I only want to claim your sweet body."

"Yes," she barely breathed. "I am yours."

His breath escaped in a wondering sibilance. "To hear those words . . . ! Ah, Shan T'u, the night is ours, the perfumed night, filled with birdsong and silver light."

She smiled painfully. "You are more poetic than William."

"Am I? Well, I'm more than a ruffian."

His head slanted and his lips pressed hers. His arms curved around her and slid to her tiny waist. He forced her lips apart and she cringed as his tongue tip slipped in. He took treasure from her mouth, stealing as surely as his red masks stole. He forced her head back and moved his mouth back and forth on hers as his tongue darted ever more quickly, a hummingbird greedy for each blossom.

Despairingly, she slipped her arms around his tapered shoulders and let her fingertips caress the beautifully spun silk. The breeze seemed to entwine her in a dark nightmare. Shan T'u's shame sent her visions of wizards and serpents and whirlpools.

Wei Ku penetrated deep into her eyes and touched amazed fingers to her cheek. "Let me see you . . . " he breathed.

Shaking, Shan T'u unsashed the silk gown and let it fall open. Wei Ku stood in stunned immobility, his eyes piercing, his mouth agape. Shan T'u averted her face as she felt the breeze caress her naked flesh.

"Mine . . ." Wei Ku choked. "Mine . . ."

His hands began at her quivering throat, and like twin fluttering doves, they flew slowly down her body, tracing each mound and curve and depression. He bent his head and tongued her nipples, making moist rings around them. She knew these sensations, but now they ignited no desire, only the sting of humiliation and the gorge of disgust.

His hands caressed her ribs and her hips and moved to her abdomen, and then down between her legs to her inner thighs, violating her most intimate flesh with questing fingertips. He panted with pleasure as she trembled. The silk gown floated around her.

"Come here," he husked.

With cold resignation, she stepped into his embrace and her skin recoiled at the scrape of brocade. He pulled her tightly to him and invaded her mouth with demanding kisses. She twisted her face to escape. "Please," she murmured. "It hurts . . ."

"I must have you," he groaned. His passion overcame his reason. His hands grew more violent, less patient. He prodded her now, tore aside the billowing silk, squeezed her breasts hard. His lips sought her throat.

She cried out in dismay. He stepped back, and his face had become a grotesque mask. He smiled a twisted smile and his eyes gleamed. He unclasped his robe with clumsy movements and stripped it off impatiently. His polished body shone in the last scarlet light. She grew maddened with fear as she saw his distended manhood poised, as his knife had been, to pierce her.

"No . . ." she mumbled as she backed off. "William . . ."

His face blackened with rage. "Don't call for him now," he said. "You are incredibly lovely, Shan T'u. So perfectly formed, so smooth."

The pavilion had become an arena for her degradation. She grasped the silken folds of her gown and clutched them futilely against her creamy nakedness. Wei Ku lurched toward her, drunk with his own desire. In moments, he would hurl her to the floor and stab deep inside her, enter where only William had been, take from her what only William had taken.

And she had promised to give this to him!

She wept as he approached her, knowing she could not run or resist. She barely heard the muffled thunder of hoofbeats. But Wei Ku heard, and looked up.

"Who rides . . . ?" he croaked.

Now Shan T'u heard the garbled cry of a Mongol officer. "Out of the pavilion! Out of the park! The Yellow Beard has escaped! Get out!"

Shan T'u's blood froze. Yellow Beard! William was supposed to be gone, riding toward Arabia. But he had not, he had not!

Wei Ku made a sound like the enraged spitting of a cobra. "I warned you, Shan T'u. I told you he wouldn't go."

"I didn't know," she swore.

"It doesn't matter now. I can't be found with you like this." He hastily refastened his robe. "We'll meet later tonight, Shan T'u. I will send for you."

She drew a deep breath and nodded. "Of course."

Wei Ku glanced around, trying to see where the idiot of a guard was riding. Then he gracefully fled from the pavilion and was swallowed in the darkness.

Shan T'u held her open gown in one tight fist in front of her naked breasts. Her litter was not due to return for hours, and if this Mongol was indeed drunk . . .

The horse reined up and she heard a man dismount.

Her terror-filled eyes searched the darkness and saw the robed warrior rush up the steps into the pavilion. Shan T'u backed against a pillar, feeling the stab of a gilded dragon claw in her back. She screamed.

"Shut up, you fool!" the man cried in Chinese. "Why don't you stay in one place so I can save you?"

Shan T'u stopped, staring. The Mongul swept off his hat and the yellow hair tumbled forth. He raised his head and she saw the wheaten beard, the crooked smile, the blue eyes.

"William!"

She lunged for him and he caught her up. She clung to his neck and her eager mouth devoured him. Her hands raced up and down his body, angered at the robe. Her heart pounded.

"No time," he whispered. "we must—" His eyes iced, seeing her. "What happened to you?"

"Happened? Nothing . . ."

He yanked the ends of the gown from her fist and saw them spread open. His eyes stared in shock at her nakedness. "Was it the Khan? They said he told you to come here, but I did not believe it so. Did that Mongol son of a whore touch you?"

She thought swiftly. If she said yes, he would go mad and try to kill the emperor. "No," she said. "It was two of the barons. They hoped to ravish me here."

"Which two?"

"I don't know, William. It was too dark to see. They fled when you rode up."

"What did they do to you, Shan T'u?"

She shook her head. "Nothing. They made me open my gown . . ."

"What then?"

"Nothing. I swear it, William. I was not touched."

Her hands sought his face, but found him cold. He took a deep breath. "We can't find them now. But I'll return to castrate them. If they violated you . . ."

"They did not," she swore, and now tears rolled down her cheeks. "I swear they did not. Please, William, take me away from here."

He nodded, collecting himself. "I have riding clothes for you. Put them on quickly. We'll try to trick our way through the gates."

"If they follow us . . ."

"Oh, be sure they'll follow us. But we'll ride for the river. Yes. I smell rain in the air. The river is swollen by typhoons. The Mongols cannot navigate, and I think we can outrun them and make the open sea."

"Do we have a chance, paladin?"

He gripped her shoulders, and his eyes were heavy with pain. "Shan T'u, I'm not going to let them torture me and make a whore of you without a fight."

She smiled up at him. "I'd rather die here with you than live a hundred years in service to the Khan."

"Well, we may both serve a hundred years if we don't hurry. Change your clothes."

He tossed the bundle of clothing to the floor in front of her. "William," she asked, "how did you find horses?"

"Here in the park," he grinned.

She gaped at him. "The emperor's white steeds! Only the descendants of Genghis Khan himself may drink of their milk or touch them."

"I don't want their milk, I want their legs. It was more difficult stealing rope to make bridles and reins than to steal the horses."

"The Khan will have you carved into ten thousand pieces if you are caught with his horses."

"And merely executed for killing his guard, no doubt. It matters little now, Shan T'u. I may as well be hung for a horse as for a princess. Hurry!"

Shan T'u smiled at his rough humor as she stripped off her gown and unpinned her hair. For a thrilling moment, she stood naked in the pavilion, only inches from him, but she dared not tarry. She swept up the riding garb as the blood danced in her body and her nightmare was sucked away by the strong, fresh wind.

Chapter Seventeen

ONCE SHAN T'U HAD PUT ON THE COARSE COTTON ROBE, the dark vest, the leather boots, and the headdress, she hurried from the pavilion. Masses of clouds sailed across the orchid sky. A distant roll of thunder promised a storm.

De Rais held two pure white mares by makeshift reins of rope. He turned over one horse to Shan T'u. "We'll try to trick them out of saddled horses and weapons as we pass through."

"What of your own horse, William?"

"I shall miss him. But he'll see plenty of action in the Khan's army. Shan T'u, we must go."

She looked at him with starry eyes. "I knew you would come for me, William."

"Well, we must thank whichever stars persuaded the emperor to free me."

Her eyes clouded at this, but she brushed aside her guilt. She threw her arms around him and kissed his mouth hard. "Paladin," she whispered.

"Princess," he replied, too choked with emotion to say more. He and Shan T'u swung up and onto the backs of their horses. "Stay behind me," he said. As he was about to ride off, he stopped and turned to her. "Shan T'u, if we are captured, kill me with my sword."

She nodded, her throat tight. "And you must then kill me with your dying strength."

His eyes were daggers of ice. "We will not provide entertainment for the Khan."

She smiled. "You have become Chinese, William, in many ways."

He grinned. "Come."

He kneed his horse and the proud animal plunged like white flame into the blackness. Shan T'u pressed her thighs tightly to her mount's unsaddled flanks as bells pealed in the palace. She kept her eyes on De Rais, trying not to think about her last moments with Wei Ku. She was with her lover once more, and with good fortune, she would find a swift death tonight.

At length, they approached the great white wall and headed for a gate. Shan T'u urged her horse alongside that of De Rais. "If they have discovered your escape and closed the gates . . . !"

"They know I've escaped, but I'm hoping that Aya will buy us some time."

"Aya?"

"Yes. I believe she will tell some lies for us to keep them searching the palace."

Shan T'u glanced sidelong at him. "So *that's* why the gates will be open."

He grinned into the night. "I told you, Shan T'u. I don't trust to destiny."

"What did you give Aya in return for her lies?" Shan T'u asked archly.

"Alas, not what I might have. But I was weak from my whipping—"

"They *did* torture you!"

He ignored the cry. "Aya was happy to abet our escape for the romance of it. However willingly she serves the Khan, a part of her soul is back in Tartary."

Shan T'u's heart swelled. "He was right. Everywhere there is rebellion."

"*Who* was right?"

She lowered her head against the wind. "Kung, the bandit chieftain."

"Oh. Well, *I* persuaded Aya that she was doing a great deed for all future generations of Tartar maids by giving us time."

"I can imagine, swindler. You always did spin a good tale."

"Ah, here is the gate. Now keep well back in the shadows. I hope to find you a weapon here, but I don't wish the guards to recognize these animals."

Obediently, Shan T'u slowed her horse to a trot. She pulled her headdress across her face as a veil. Dense clouds blotted out moon and stars. The guards at the gate moved out of the guttering torchlight.

"Who rides there?" a guard challenged.

"Nayan," De Rais growled. "I'm hurt. The Yellow Beard has escaped. He is armed."

A cry went up among the guards. "Should we report to the palace?"

"Yes," De Raid croaked. "I'll relieve you here, with this other guard."

The Mongol nodded swiftly. "It will be done."

De Rais waved an arm in salute. The guards rushed from the gate with a clank of swords against hips and mounted their horses. "Wait!" De Rais cried.

The captain of the guards turned his horse. "Yes, Nayan?"

"I need a bow and quiver of arrows. I was disarmed by the knight."

"Yes, of course. Chingis—arms for Nayan!"

One of the Mongols bustled to a horse and unloaded a quiver of arrows and a bow and brought them to De Rais, who kept his horse prancing busily in the darkness.

As the Mongols rode off, De Rais and Shan T'u galloped through the massive gate and cantered across the meadows. De Rais handed the bow and arrows to Shan T'u. Presently, they reached the second wall, and another gate. As they approached, De Rais cried out, "Help! The Yellow Beard is loose in the royal park!"

Once again, the guards swarmed to De Rais. He swayed convincingly and gasped, "I am Nayan. We pursued the Yellow Beard into the park, but he stole our horses. We had to mount the emperor's mares."

"Damnation!" a Mongol growled. "You can be skinned alive for that."

"Don't I know that? Quickly, into the park, and shoot on sight. And give me two horses. I'll relieve this post."

"But you're hurt . . ."

"Should I let a scratch stop me?"

The guard became contrite. "No, no, of course not. Nestardin! Two horses!"

A second guard brought two mounts, saddled and provisioned. De Rais said, "Thank you. Go now."

The Mongol hustled to his horse and ordered his contingent back toward the inner wall. The warriors thundered past De Rais and Shan T'u. The fugitives dismounted and climbed upon the Tartar war-horses. "Now," De Rais said, as he reined up his powerful mount, "the outer gate."

Shan T'u calmed her frisky horse and looked lovingly at him as the wind blew her hair across her face. "You are a master swindler, William."

"Thank you," he said with a doff of his hat. "That is more compliment than to be called a fair knight!"

He wheeled his horse and rode off, with Shan T'u following. Now she dared to hope, and her heart pounded like the hooves of the horses. This would be the most challenging ride of all—through the training fields of the Khan's *Kasitan*. For a moment, the moon slipped from ink black clouds and poured cold white light upon the fugitives. In the distance, they could see the barracks and storehouses, and the titanic main gate, which seemed to swarm with Mongol warriors.

Shan T'u cried into the wind, "William, there are hundreds of them!"

"Who believe that Yellow Beard hides in the grand palace seeking to slay the Khan—if Aya told her tales. Stay back, Shan T'u, and await my signal."

Shan T'u clenched her teeth. "We will never be allowed through that gate," she murmured grimly. "Never."

Shan T'u tugged back on the reins and let De Rais open a long distance between them. They hugged the stone outer wall, riding deep in its cold shadow. There were hordes of soldiers around the gate, some on foot and some mounted, and a thousand torches lit the night.

Abruptly, William drew his sword and raised it high over his head. "He has escaped!" he screamed. "He has escaped!"

At first, he could not be heard over the din of voices and neighing animals. But he urged his horse into a frenzied gallop and made the beast rear up, hooves flailing against the sky. The Mongol warriors turned. De Rais swung the sword in whistling arcs and shouted, "The Yellow Beard has vaulted the wall! He is in the city!"

A Mongol captain in full battle dress emerged on horseback from the mass of soldiers and cried out, "Who says so? *I'm* in charge of this war party."

William kept within the shadows. "Well, you'll be in charge of the eunuchs if you don't open the gate. The Khan is enraged."

"We heard Yellow Beard was in the palace—trapped there."

"Well, ask your emperor, man! The knight has already murdered one guard."

The Mongol sucked on his moustache and his eyes darted. "I need official word—"

"*I'm* the official word, you toad."

"Identify yourself. I can't see you in all this mess."

"I am Nestardin. I was guarding the inner gate when they told me."

The Mongol's eyes narrowed. He conferred with other mounted warriors, who all agreed that Nestardin *was* on guard at an inner gate. Shan T'u petted and whispered to her horse to keep it still.

The Mongol captain said, "All right, Nestardin. *You* go out there and look for him. *I'm* taking my men and storming the palace!"

There was much derisive laughter at this, and De Rais made a disgusted noise. "That's fine with me. I'll like being a baron."

This caused great brays of merriment among the soldiers. The captain called for the gate to be opened. De Rais paused, holding back his horse. The mighty bronze gate swung ponderously open, letting in a flood of torchlight from the city. De Rais waited until the gate was fully open. Then he said, "With luck, he has not gotten far."

"He is in the palace, I tell you," the captain insisted.

"If you say so," De Rais smiled. He signaled with his sword and kicked his horse into a run. Shan T'u sucked in a deep, deep breath and pressed the flanks of her animal. Keeping her head down, she galloped through the open gate and down the broad boulevard of the city. As she passed through, she thought she heard the Mongol captain cry out, "Hey! Who in hell is *that*?" but she did not slow down to hear more.

An hour later, they galloped through the empty, moon-swept countryside. Toward the horizon, towering thunderheads piled high. De Rais reined up his horse and bent over in the saddle, gasping. Shan T'u pulled up beside him. Perspiration drenched her skin beneath the cotton robe. Her heart slammed against the walls of her rib cage. Yet a profound exhilaration buoyed her.

"William!" she cried. "We did it! We escaped from the grand palace of Kublai Khan!"

276

He nodded, sucking in great draughts of air. "Yes. So far."

She looked about her, eyes ashine in the night. Only her cameo face showed in the frame of the headdress. "Are we truly safe?"

"*Safe*?" He grunted and jutted his chin. "I'd guess that the Khan's battalions are less than a half hour behind us, perhaps much less."

Her eyes shadowed. "Yes, of course they'll follow."

"With elephants, if I know the Khan. He will be *very* insulted."

Shan T'u laughed, a little maddened with excitement. "I am still amazed at our escape."

He smiled. "To swindle, Shan T'u, you must be swift, like a magician, and you must know your victim."

"But to fool all those warriors—"

"Pah! Fooling them was easy—it was doing it quickly enough to give them no time for second thoughts. *There* lay my wit. The Mongol army is fearsome—as an *army*. But the individual Mongol soldier is an ignoramus. These Tartars are filthy louts. Their *organization* makes them unconquerable, not their intelligence. Not one of these dolts can think in a tight spot or make decisions. Without ten thousand of his brethren riding alongside, the Tartar is hopeless."

"You may not be a poet," Shan T'u said, "but you have a pretty way with words."

His brows knit. "I don't ken *that* remark, but let it go. At any rate, all I did was flaunt my authority. The Mongol is trained to obey."

"And you fooled them all."

"Long enough to ride through the gates. But they will be organized once more, and dangerous."

The wind was strong and stank of river. "How long, do you think?"

"How long?" His brow creased with sudden worry. He slid from his saddle and knelt on one knee. He bent his head and touched his ear to the earth. He looked up. "Damnation."

"William . . . ?"

"They caught on pretty quickly for louts. I can hear the hoofbeats."

"Then they're right behind us!"

"Let's make for the river, Shan T'u."

"Will there be a boat?"

He nodded. "I kept my ears open while they tortured me. I learned that wherever a river must be crossed by the Khan's minions, the peasants must keep boats waiting."

"Then there will be boats for *them*."

"For some of them. But they cannot navigate well." He glanced at the heaving sky. "And a good blow is afoot."

Shan T'u pursed her delicate lips. "Lead, paladin."

The two lone figures, on horses of wind, pounded through the stormy night as the clouds piled high and thunder shook the ground. Shan T'u dared not look back. They passed small villages and terraced farms, clattered across bridges, and splashed through muddy streams. She did not hear the war cries of the Mongols behind them but she could sense their closeness in her very nerves. Once within range of the Mongol arrows, she and De Rais were as good as dead. And suddenly, Shan T'u did not want to die.

Her stamina was giving out. Her lungs were afire, and her bones howled in pain. She glanced at William;

how much pain must *he* be suffering? she thought woefully. She made a determined face. If her knight could ride on with his bleeding wounds, she could follow.

And then, suddenly, she saw the river. The clouds loomed over the water like immense ebony mountains, but where the clouds broke, luminous moonlight silvered the water. De Rais guided his horse at full gallop along the riverbank and she pursued. Far ahead, the river curved majestically and Shan T'u could see dark mountains in the distance. Her heart lifted. She could almost smell the sea, and freedom.

The river flowed beside them, infinite and swift. But where were the boats? Her heart sank as she fought for each breath. The Mongols had to be closing fast, and there was nowhere to run. She leaned low over her horse's neck and half lifted out of the saddle as she urged the animal to gallop faster and faster. She could feel the powerful equine muscles moving beneath the lathered skin.

There! Did her eyes trick her? Were those not torches? Imperceptibly, De Rais quickened the pace. Shan T'u gave herself over to the sensations of riding, to the shock of hoof striking earth, to the wind biting her raw skin, to the keening in her ears, to the sky racing overhead.

The torches were close now, and she saw the sails of junks and the great paddle-wheeled warships reserved for the soldiers of the Khan. They rocked ponderously, these hulking vessels, their pennants snapping in the wind. As she rode up to the dock, Shan T'u shivered with excitement at the proximity of these intimidating ships. Each of the vessels had four enormous sidewheels, and the cabins were emblazoned with golden demon heads. The ships were moored side to side in an implacable flotilla.

De Rais reined up his horse as an ancient man in a worn tunic hobbled up the embankment toward him. Another man by the dock had already donned a straw raincloak. The wind sang in their ears now. Shan T'u felt drops of cold rain torn from the clouds.

De Rais dismounted and held the reins of his horse. He turned to look back where they had ridden, and his face turned ashen.

"What is it, William?"

He pointed grimly. "Look there."

Shan T'u twisted in the saddle and felt her heart fall. The massed riders were far in the distance, barely around the bend in the river, but their thunder shook the earth. She looked back at De Rais, stricken. "Can we fight?"

He shook his head. "There will be no less than two hundred of them."

Shan T'u tasted a thick, leaden despair in her throat, but she dismounted, her legs quivering. The old boatman kowtowed ludicrously to De Rais. "Is there a war?"

"Yes," De Rais said tersely. "I'm the advance guard. I must have my own boat. Those warriors will take the others."

The boatman's watery eyes gaped. "But you can't sail a warship yourself . . ."

"I don't want a warship," De Rais snapped. "I want a junk."

Shan T'u was jolted. "A *junk*? But they will sail the warships."

"I know," De Rais said. "I want a sail. What about it, old man? Do I get a junk or do I run this through your guts?" He drew his sword and stuck its blade into the boatman's concave chest.

The boatman wheezed with terror and clasped his gnarled hands together as tears sprang to his crusted eyes. "Please, take any boat . . . the Khan is great . . ."

"The Khan is a baboon's mother," De Rais growled. "Come on, Princess. We haven't much time."

Shan T'u barely glanced at the frightened and baffled old boatman as she followed De Rais down the grassy embankment. The water lay still and scummy, pelted by rain. The man in the straw raincloak had disappeared. De Rais walked out on the dock, which was built of timbers lashed together.

"*William!*" Shan T'u cried. "Here they come!"

She could now clearly see the first wave of horsemen. They came like warriors of hell, thirty abreast, riding in perfect unison. A thousand hooves struck the yielding earth as one, throwing up curtains of dirt and grass. The ground shook and the cannonade boomed like a tidal wave. The boatman fell to the ground, prostrate. De Rais didn't look back; with wet, slippery hands he fumbled with the rope tying a worn junk to its mooring.

"Get in," he ordered Shan T'u.

"*William!*"

He looked up. The Mongol warriors were upon them, blotting out land and sky. Without a word, a hundred bows were raised, a hundred arrows loaded.

Shan T'u flung herself at De Rais and clutched him desperately, with her bow in one hand, the arrows across her back. She scented his beard and sweat. "I love you, William . . ."

"*Get into the boat*," he hissed.

"We cannot . . ."

The first shower of arrows rained down and De Rais moved like lightning. He grasped Shan T'u's robe and threw her down on the dock, dropping beside her. Arrows sizzled through the rainy air, hissing into the water, thunking into the boat and the dock.

"We must swim for it," he whispered.

"William . . ."

"You must."

Shan T'u could no longer feel any part of her body; terror rooted her to the dock and she lay paralyzed with her soft cheek on the slimy wood. She managed to raise her head a little, and with blurred vision she saw the bows raised again.

But now she must have been hit, for what she saw made no sense. Three of the Mongol warriors in the front rank dropped their bows and keeled over on their horses, with arrows quivering in their backs. She saw the other warriors turn in great confusion.

"What in hell . . . ?" William cried.

Shan T'u fought to clear her mind. The dock pressed hard into her breasts. The rain slashed her. She smelled the heat of the lightning, heard the boom of the thunder and the neighing and stamping of two hundred horses. "I don't understand . . ."

"Nor I," De Rais muttered. "But I won't question it."

Shan T'u allowed De Rais to yank her to her feet. She stood for a dangerous moment on the windswept dock. "Someone is attacking them," she declared. "Someone we can't see."

"We'll thank him later," De Rais snapped. He

stood now in the junk, unfurling the deep red sail, which caught the gale's blast and billowed out. The boat rocked treacherously. De Rais stuck out his hand and Shan T'u grasped it as she stepped gingerly into the boat. Her feet slipped on the scum that coated the floor, but De Rais grabbed her shoulders.

"Sit down and hold fast to the gunwales," he commanded. "We're going to pitch. And keep that bow ready."

Shan T'u nodded, licking rain from her lips. De Rais grabbed the tiller and perched on the stern, steering the junk creakily out to the middle of the river, where the wind whipped the water into white-caps. Shan T'u looked back at the shore. The Mongols were reloading their bows and aiming at the junk. The arrows flew in a storm, but the junk was too far out and too quick a target. Shan T'u shut her eyes and listened to the deadly shafts whistle by.

The river boiled around them as the rain hissed. There was no longer a sky, only a heaving black volcano luridly lit by lightning. The junk rolled per-ilously as waves smashed across its prow. The peeling wooden hull glistened and the sail beat a drumlike tattoo. De Rais held onto the tiller with both hands, blinking away rain.

Shan T'u's heart hammered as she strove valiantly to keep her soaked hands on the sides of the boat. The storm shrieked in its full fury now. The wind howled down and dredged up the river. Again and again, titanic black walls of water fell onto the junk, splinter-ing the wood, lifting the craft out of the river and dropping it back again.

Shan T'u peered with crazed eyes through a curtain

of rain. She could barely see De Rais through the sheets of water. She looked harder . . .

Shan T'u screamed in horror!

Impossible! Another figure—rising up from the floor of the boat—a phantom clad in peasant tunic and trousers and hat—a phantom who swung a sword over his head—

"William! In front of you!"

The phantom brought down the sword. De Rais released the tiller and rolled to one side in time to dodge the thrust. The sword buried itself in the stern with a heavy thud. De Rais groped for his own sword.

The phantom wrenched his blade from the wood and held it with both hands. He brought it down like an executioner's axe. De Rais lunged between the phantom's legs and toppled him. The phantom sprawled, still holding his sword. De Rais pulled himself to his feet, rocking. He drew his sword from its sheath as the phantom rose up again.

Shan T'u sat without breath. It was Wei Ku! And De Rais was weakened from loss of blood and his punishing ride. She shivered with dread as the two men parried blows. Their blades rang and sparked in the downpour.

But De Rais was tiring, his torture and exhaustion too much for even his gallant body. He swayed, and his sword hand dropped. Wei Ku seemed to wait. De Rais regripped the hilt of his sword with both arms. He lifted the blade as his lips drew back over his teeth. As rain shone on his skeletal face, he viciously struck at Wei Ku with an uppercut. Wei Ku side-stepped. The force of the mighty blow spun De Rais and he lost his footing. He went to his knees. Vanquished, he clung to the side of the boat, his valiant head drooping.

Wei Ku raised his sword with ease and the blade caught the blue blaze of the lightning. Shan T'u moved without knowing her motions. In seconds, she had slipped an arrow from her quiver and pulled back the bowstring. "*Wei Ku!*" she screamed.

The bandit glanced at her and saw the steel tip aimed at his throat. He paused, his sword still lifted high over his head. "Don't interfere," he shouted.

"You will not kill him," Shan T'u sobbed.

"*You* won't kill *me*."

"I've killed before," she said.

"After what we have shared?"

"Don't force me, Wei Ku."

Weakly, De Rais managed to turn, his sword still in his hand. He leaned heavily against the side of the junk and stared at the macabre scene. The storm began to abate.

"I don't understand . . ." De Rais murmured.

"He is the bandit chieftain," Shan T'u said. "He must have hidden in this boat."

"But you called him Wei Ku."

The bandit lowered his sword and yanked away his soaked mask. De Rais's eyes widened. "That is who I am, knight," he spat. "Do I surprise you?"

"At this moment, *everything* surprises me. Why do you go to all this trouble?"

"Trouble?" Wei Ku laughed bitterly. "Your princess means a great deal to me."

"Yes, I know."

"You know nothing. You can outwit a few moronic

Tartars, but a Chinese scholar is more than a match for you. Would you have lived if I hadn't asked the Khan for your life?"

"*You . . . ?*"

"Shan T'u, did you tell him nothing?"

Shan T'u kept her arrow trained on Wei Ku, but she trembled with shame and fear. She bit down on her lip as her tears flowed, warm where the rain was cold.

Wei Ku curled his lips into a triumphant smile. "*I* had the torture stopped. Your princess assured me that you would flee to Arabia to make your fortune. But like a love-struck calf, you looked for her. And found her at a most inopportune moment."

De Rais raised his head and his glazed eyes raked Shan T'u. "What is he talking about?"

"Quiet," Wei Ku ordered coldly. "And still, I watched over your miserable life. Directly I overheard your plans, I left the palace and rode here to the river to await you. And I made certain that my red masks were among the Mongol war party."

"Red masks?" Shan T'u said.

Wei Ku laughed into the rain as he gripped the mast with one hand. "I told you, Shan T'u, my men have infiltrated the Khan's hordes. It only needed a few of them to spread confusion at the palace and abet your escape. It only needed a few others to kill their comrades at the riverbank to give you time. I *wished* your escape so that I might at last kill this meddlesome knight myself."

"Why?" De Rais demanded. "Do you think she would go with you?"

Shan T'u bowed her head. Wei Ku saw it, and his

286

smile became more wicked. "I *know* she will go with me," he said. "She promised herself to me, knight, in exchange for your worthless life."

De Rais stared at Shan T'u. "Is this true?"

"Yes," Shan T'u breathed. "They would have killed you, William. I could not let you die."

De Rais glared at Wei Ku. "She would have promised anything to save me, you fool."

"No," Wei Ku whispered. "*You* are the fool. She met me at the Golden Pavilion to redeem her pledge. When you rode up, we were close to fulfillment. Do you not remember how you found her, knight? Do you not—"

De Rais roared to his feet, so explosively that Wei Ku was defenseless. The poet raised his sword, but De Rais swung first and with a fearsome clang lifted the blade from Wei Ku's hands. The sword flew across the junk and clattered to its floor. Wei Ku's hand snaked to his boot, but De Rais savagely thrust upward with his knee and caught Wei Ku hard between his legs. Wei Ku screamed in agony and doubled over. De Rais grabbed him by his tunic and hurled him against the mast with such force that the sail shuddered. Wei Ku slumped down to an ungraceful sitting posture, moaning softly.

De Rais whipped the knife from Wei Ku's boot and gripped it in his left hand. With his right hand, he thrust the tip of his sword under Wei Ku's chin. The poet's eyes fluttered open.

"This is what it's like to have a blade at your throat," De Rais snarled. "In a moment, you will feel the blade sever your heart."

Wei Ku panted for breath. Rain pattered on his

face. "You may slay me now," he gasped. "You have won. But you will not change the truth. She was about to redeem her promise."

"For your lies," De Rais said, "you will suffer longer."

"No," Shan T'u whispered. She had set aside the bow and sat miserably on the drenched seat, her hands folded in her lap.

De Rais looked at her with deep dread. "Shan T'u?"

She felt a great weight on her chest, as if she'd been locked in a yoke for public humiliation. "He tells the truth, William. I went to the pavilion to give myself to him. I was . . . as you found me because we had begun to . . ."

"To make love," Wei Ku said.

Shan T'u's eyes dropped, burning. "To indulge his lust—not to make love. He had not taken me yet, but he would have done so."

De Rais's deep chest heaved beneath his robe and his rugged face twisted. "And did you enjoy it, Shan T'u?"

"Don't torment me." Her hands covered her face. "How can you ask such a thing? I was frightened and in despair. Did it matter if I was bedded by the sultan or Wei Ku? At least this way your life was spared."

"Did you like his hands on you?" De Rais spat. "Did you beg him to split you?"

"*Stop!*" Overcome with tempestuous emotion, she swept up the bow and aimed a deadly shaft at De Rais. "Does it matter which one I kill?" she sobbed. "Which of you hurts me more? What do you want of me, William? I would have given my life for you. But my life would not buy your freedom. The price was my flesh. Why did I not slay myself? You taught me always to hope—to cling to even a shamed life. I hoped that you might return."

In anguish, she threw aside the weapon and turned away, weeping helplessly. Faint morning light touched the heavy sky.

Wei Ku looked up at De Rais. "Will you kill me now? At least act like a knight, De Rais. Don't make me suffer."

"Why not?" De Rais whispered numbly.

Wei Ku laughed weakly. "Yes, I *am* guilty of hurting you. If I can never possess Shan T'u, at least I had that pleasure."

"You *can* have her, for all I care."

Wei Ku shook his head. "No, Burgundian, you are still stupid. She does not love me, and will never love me. I thought, I hoped, for a moment . . . but I deceived myself. She despised my touch. This big-footed imp of a princess wants her hot-blooded scoundrel. Kill me, De Rais. My work will go on."

De Rais stood immobile for a long moment as the dawn bathed him in silver-gray light. He was haggard, his eyes extinguished. At last he regarded the sword in his hand and offered it to Wei Ku, along with the knife. "Shan T'u," he said, "aim your arrow at his throat."

Shan T'u froze within, but with numb hands, she obeyed. De Rais said, "Wei Ku, the storm is over. If you are not in the river by the count of three, Shan T'u will fire an arrow through your neck."

Wei Ku sat upright. "A risk, knight. What if she *does* love me?"

"Then she will put the arrow through *my* neck. I live by taking risks."

"So I've noticed," Wei Ku said with grudging admiration. He stood painfully and faced De Rais. "It should not end this way. It is a humiliation to accept my life from you with no repayment."

"Then keep the news to yourself," De Rais snapped.

"And my true identity?"

De Rais waved a weary hand. "Safe. Now go, in the name of all the devils."

Wei Ku turned to Shan T'u. "We will met again, Princess."

Shan T'u averted her luminous eyes, her heart filled with despair. "Good fortune, Wei Ku," she whispered.

Wei Ku put one boot on the gunwale and his eyes searched the sky. He sniffed the rainy river wind. "A long swim," he mused. "I may not survive." He looked at the others and smiled. "But you will go mad with wondering." And then, in a breath, he was gone.

De Rais moved to the prow of the boat and retrieved the bandit's sword. He studied it, then stiffened. His fingers moved along its soaked blade. "Hell and damnation," he breathed. "This is the sword I took in the mountains."

Shan T'u looked up at him with wet eyes. "Perhaps it is a sign, William."

He turned his eyes to her, but those eyes held no passion. "There are no signs, Shan T'u. This sword brought him no victory." He paused. "And none for me. We have many days to sail and many days to ride."

"Where are we going?"

"To your father's province. Where I will leave you to whatever fate you may find." With that, he returned to the tiller. Shan T'u bowed her head and wept in black despair.

Chapter Eighteen

TWO DAYS LATER, DE RAIS DEVELOPED A SEVERE FEVER from infections of his wounds. For three days he lay in the bottom of the junk, delirious, while Shan T'u sailed the boat and fought off hunger and thirst.

She put in at a seaside village and they were taken into the humble home of a fisherman, a one-room abode with a tile roof and a dirt floor. A local doctor applied seaweed dressings to De Rais's wounds. Shan T'u gagged when she first saw the pulsing network of festering welts and cuts that lacerated his skin. Who this yellow-haired man was, and how he had come to be tortured, was a subject of great interest in the village.

For six days and nights, De Rais hovered near death as he screamed piteously and shook with palsy. Shan T'u kept a vigil near him, consumed by guilt and sorrow. She sponged his sweat-soaked torso, heartsick at the gleaming nakedness that seemed about to die. She wept for him at night, and burned incense in the local Buddhist shrine. The fisherman and his family prayed to their ancestors at their altar, and Shan T'u was deeply moved.

On the morning of the seventh day, De Rais opened his eyes. He was drenched with sweat and his ribs stuck out. The bones of his skull protruded and his eyes had sunk deep into their sockets. But he was able to sip tea, and after two more days he was able to sit upright and eat fish. His hair and beard were shaggy, his lips cracked. But this cadaverous stranger was alive, and Shan T'u stood looking out to sea, exultant.

As the days flowed by, De Rais regained his strength. The wounds on his back healed, forming scars that would forever bespeak his torment at the hands of the Mongols. During the weeks that he and Shan T'u lived in the fishing village, they wore the dyed cotton garments of peasants. De Rais sailed out with the men and dragged the nets. Shan T'u cooked with the women, wove and dyed cloth. She and De Rais rarely spoke to each other as De Rais wrestled with his jealous heart. Sometimes Shan T'u watched him as he slept, and she touched her loving fingers to his roughened skin.

At last, De Rais was strong enough to continue the journey. The villagers washed and dried the Mongol garments, still baffled as to how this patrician Chinese woman and this odd foreign man could be Tartars. De Rais and Shan T'u took back the costumes, but stowed them in the junk. They elected instead to remain dressed in the tunics, trousers, and coned hats of simple peasants, De Rais in an outfit of brick red, and Shan T'u in white. But De Rais did take back and carry his sword, which had been reverently cleaned and polished.

They returned to the junk, which the villagers had repaired, refitting the sail as well. The villagers crowded the broken-down wharf and hung in crowds from a bridge to wave farewell. The visit of the strangers would provide stories for many winter evenings.

De Rais and Shan T'u sailed for two more weeks, then put in at a large waterfront city where De Rais outgambled some teamsters and sedan-chair bearers for two horses. He and Shan T'u rode the rest of the way, stopping each night to make camp. They both hunted for game, and cooked it by firelight. Still, De Rais was taciturn and aloof, and Shan T'u bent her head in anger and grief.

Two months after escaping from the grand palace of Kublai Khan at Kanbaliq, the knight and the princess rode over the gentle green hills into the province of Prince Chang Hu.

The army of Kublai Khan had reached the province many days earlier. They had marched directly from Kanbaliq. The general in charge of the expedition rode in an elaborate wooden howdah borne on the backs of four elephants. The beasts were fitted with heavy leather armor, decorated with cloth of gold and silver harnesses. Khan's banners streamed from the turrets.

Behind the elephants rode six battalions of mounted warriors armed with bows. Behind the cavalry marched two hundred infantrymen carrying lances and swords. More horses followed, carrying musicians with cymbals and drums. This fearsome attack force, its silver and gold blazing in the sun, rolled like summer thunder over hills, mountains, and plains, through villages and cities and farms.

The army first assaulted the palace of Prince Tuan Lei and overran it in a morning, murdering five hundred soldiers, burning the pavilions and sacking the gold and porcelain, and putting Tuan Lei to death. Surviving soldiers galloped to the palace of Chang Hu and hysterically told their tale of horror, warning of the approach of the Khan's hordes.

Prince Chang stood silently upon hearing the news. He suspected who had betrayed him but it didn't matter. He was a warlord and he would meet his death with dignity. He gave permission to his retainers and servants to flee to the hills. He ordered his knights to don their armor. He rode his own black stallion up and down the pathways of his estate, making sure all the walls were fortified with crossbowmen and catapults. On the eve of the battle, he gave a feast for his soldiers. He ordered musicians to play and dancers to twirl. He sat on his throne and looked with bleak resignation at the festivities.

Before dawn, Prince Chang mounted up again, this time in full armor, and as the rays of the sun struck the battlements, his armor's gold ornaments blazed with points of light. He looked out into the valley and saw the hordes of Kublai Khan. As Prince Chang watched, the Khan's musicians sounded their drums and cymbals and the Mongol warriors sang a rhythmic, bloodthirsty chant of war.

At the throbbing height of the song, the general signaled his attack. The right and left wings rode out to flank the palace. Prince Chang's gate opened and his soldiers rode forth in a dusty thunder of hoofbeats. The earth shook beneath the pounding, and the blue morning air became black with arrows. The whistle of bowstrings was like a gale, and in the red smoke of battle, men and horses tumbled and sprawled. Soon, the valley rang with screams and the clash of weapons. Soldiers met on foot, whirling maces and lunging with swords and lances. By midafternoon, the earth was strewn with corpses, and still the deadly conflict raged. The Prince's forces were heavily outnumbered, but his men fought with courage and refused to retreat.

The inevitable was only delayed. By dusk, the Tartar hordes had surrounded the palace. The elephants bearing the howdah lumbered forward and the crossbowmen fired volleys into the hearts of defending soldiers. Catapults in the palace hurled stones and exploding grenades, but the Tartars broke through the gate and swiftly slaughtered the soldiers who manned these weapons. The Mongols engaged the surviving soldiers hand to hand throughout the palace grounds. The invaders overran the gardens and courtyards and pathways. They plundered and vandalized the chambers and banquet halls. They ripped silk hangings with their swords. They smashed porcelain vases and shredded painted scrolls. They uprooted gardens, and they cruelly murdered any servant or soldier they encountered. Master Po was decapitated with one stroke of a Mongol sword as he sat at his table in his garden.

Finally, the Tartars ignited all of the buildings with torches. The night lit up in blazing fury as pavilions blackened and crumbled, trees and shrubs were consumed, and gilt and paint bubbled and crisped. It was then that Prince Chang Hu rode slowly through his melting gate, his bulky form silhouetted against the towering flames. He presented himself before the Mongol general. The general recited to Prince Chang the orders of the Khan of Khans that the traitorous nobleman be put to death. Prince Chang replied that he considered the emperor a filthy, ignorant swine.

The general paid no heed to the epithets. Two large carpets were brought and Chang Hu was bound hand and foot and laid out on one of the carpets. The other was laid over him and pointed stakes were pounded through the edges of the carpets to trap the prince between them. The largest of the elephants was brought and the beast was whipped until it reared up and brought its treelike limbs down upon the carpets. There was the snap of bones and a long scream of unutterable agony. The elephant was made to crush the prince's body thoroughly before being led away. Thus Prince Chang Hu, though Chinese and a traitor, was accorded the honor by Kublai Khan of being punished without the sun or air witnessing the shedding of his blood, an honor usually reserved for those of the imperial family.

* * *

Shan T'u and De Rais rode tiredly over the last of the sloping hills, hooves rustling in the drought-dried grass. Shan T'u's heart beat quickly as she anticipated the sight of her father's palace. In her deepest soul, she knew that the Khan's armies must have been there. Still, at this last moment, she prayed that it was not so.

No survivor of Chang's court would have recognized his princess. She wore the black hat and white cotton tunic and trousers of a Chinese peasant woman, with the boots of a Tartar's wife. Her fine-spun face was suntanned and windburned. A quiver of arrows was slung across her now-strong back and her bow was lashed to the saddle of her horse. Her dainty body, beneath the simple clothes, was leaner and more supple. She rode like a Tartar, tirelessly and fiercely.

De Rais, too, had been ravaged and changed. His cheekbones protruded and his startling blue eyes gleamed from deep wells. Pain had etched its memory into his handsomeness. His blond hair and beard, washed in clear streams, had turned nearly white from the sun. The brick red fisherman's costume hung loosely on his rawboned frame, but underneath, the play of sinew and muscle was still beautiful.

Finally, the two weary riders topped the hill and looked down into the valley. As soon as he saw the hideous scene De Rais tried to reach Shan T'u and cover her eyes, but she had already looked.

Most of the hundreds of corpses of men and animals were decayed. Grinning skulls and bleached skeletons had been picked clean by vultures and jackals. The shattered bones poked out of dried leather armor, still glinting with gold and silver ornaments. Flocks of carrion-eating birds still feasted on partially rotted horses, half bones and half flesh. The dead littered the hillsides like blackened tree limbs torn by a hurricane. Here and there were severed limbs or heads. Boiling clouds of flies covered some of the corpses, and when the sunlight struck a certain way, the maggots snaking in swarms in and out of orifices caught fire and blazed white. The loathsome stench of decomposing cadavers revolted and overpowered the riders, though fortunately, much of it was borne away by a hot west wind.

Shan T'u raised her offended eyes and saw the still-smoking husk of the palace. Most of the outer walls still stood, though blackened by fire. Within the walls there was only devastation and waste. She saw great mountains of hot ash, pyres of debris, thousands of flecks of gold and jade and marble where floors or basins or carvings survived. There was no trace of garden or bridge or pool. The vast hunting gardens were now a black, ruined prairie, like some panoramic hellish desert. Seared trees still lined the path to the riverbank, and miraculously, the riverside pavilion where Shan T'u had watched the naked knight at his bath still stood. Only that pavilion gave a clue that this havoc had once been a royal estate.

Shan T'u looked in terrifying silence at the rising spires of smoke. Her eyes brimmed with tears, and emotion heaved within her, sending molten showers of grief to each limb. She mourned for her childhood, which had been raped and slaughtered; for her maidenhood, which was lost forever; and for her innocence, which had been corrupted in blood.

De Rais walked his horse beside hers. "I pity you," he said.

"Liar."

He sighed. "Shan T'u, whatever has become of my feelings for you, I still have heart to grieve for your loss."

"You cannot know my loss."

Abruptly, Shan T'u snapped the reins and kneed her horse into a gallop. At frenzied speed, she careened down the sloping hillside. She guided the skittish horse past dead bodies that shimmered with insects, past fallen animals, past abandoned armor, past lances and swords that rusted in the sun, past snapped bows, past chain mail and saddles. The earth was pitted and blackened.

She slowed her horse when she reached the destroyed palace. She stopped here and looked desolately at the twisted remains of the mighty gate. She remembered her wedding caravan, rolling through this gate with banners flying. She remembered her father bidding her goodbye, knowing then that he had used her to betray the Khan and had ordered the murder of De Rais. She remembered Lady Feng lolling beneath her parasol. She remembered Wei Ku, too ashamed to see her off. It was no accident that she sat astride a horse now and gazed with despondency on her gutted home. All of the plots and counterplots had brought the Mongol hordes down upon this palace, and for all her secret arts, she could not prevent it. She had been a chess piece to be sacrificed.

Shan T'u sensed the presence of another. She glanced up to see De Rais. He looked with impenetrable eyes at the blackened wall, and his weathered face showed a voiceless devastation that moved her. The ears of his horse twitched away flies and a dry hot wind blew around them.

"The gate is open . . ." he suggested.

She shook her head. "No. It is no longer my home."

He nodded. "I understand."

She looked at him with feral eyes. "Do you? And have you seen *this* sort of thing before?"

"Aye."

"Have you ever destroyed a castle? Burned a man's home? Destroyed beauty—"

"Yes, I've stormed castles!" His voice cracked with emotion, and for the first time since their escape, his eyes poured directly into hers. The summer sky was in those eyes now, and his hair blew like cotton. "I've set the torch to tapestries and drapes. I've slashed paintings and overturned ladies' bureaus. A knight does cruel things on a crusade. Battle takes the soul out of a man and leaves the beast."

"Like the red masks?"

"Aye, Shan T'u. Like the Tartars as well. Like your bastard of a father. This is what happens between men."

Now her tears fell freely. "But not always, William," she wept. "There is honor between men, and beauty. Scholars paint and write. Farmers plow. There is government and law, music and science. Oh, William, my land has seen centuries of beauty and enlightenment. The Mongol has brought on this butchery!"

"No!" De Rais cried in anguish. "Was your government corrupt? Did your scholars compete and despise? Did some wear silk and some wear cotton? The Mongol is like the vulture, Shan T'u. He feeds on the dying."

Shan T'u turned away, her face etched in afternoon light. "Yes," she whispered. "Yes, they were all corrupt. My father. Lady Feng. All of them."

"And you?"

She turned sharply to him.

"Are *you* corrupt, Shan T'u?"

"I do not take your meaning."

He urged his horse closer to hers. "Is there purity in Cathay still, Princess? Is there goodness?"

"There may be," she choked. "And in France?"

He smiled, the first smile that had touched his full lips since his fever had broken. "Aye, there is goodness in France. But like an ignorant lout playing with rare glass, I did not see the precious thing for what it was and I let it break."

"It is still in you!"

"Is it?" His voice broke. "My jealousy ate my innards. I sat in holy judgment of you, I who deflowered a hundred country virgins and left them bloody and weeping. I could not bear to think that this poet had aroused you."

Shan T'u's head spun. "Only his words aroused me. I dreamed of a bold warrior, but part of me was still a spoiled princess who was ashamed of your rough ways and sought polish. Wei Ku was a scholar, do you see? *And* a dashing bandit! Oh yes, I grew excited at his patriotic fire, at his brilliance. . . ."

"Did you love him, Shan T'u?"

Her face paled and her eyes sparkled. "*Love* him?" Oh, you stupid stupid man. I have never loved any man but you. He was romantic and brave and well-spoken. I admired him. I even liked him in a way, but *love* him? Oh, never."

De Rais grinned doltishly. "Then I deserve a flogging for doubting you. If you require polish, then I must study my books and lute." She smiled at that. "But best to be my own poor self, maddened with love for you, and pray each holy evening that you are lunatic enough to love *me*."

"Oh, William," she cried gladly. "What has softened your heart?"

He gestured toward the burned palace. "This. Another empty shell that once housed the mastery and stupidity of men. I nursed my childish jealousy the way men nurse jealousies for land and position. And *this* is the result! I see it in the corrupt bishops of the Church, in the feuding barons, in the knights who rape in the name of chivalry. Was *I* like that with you? Greedy, grasping, selfish? I sought wealth, and found treasure. And I nearly flung it away. Shan T'u, if you take me back, I shall never again let jealousy cloud the skies of my love."

Her heart overflowed like the river in spring. "William . . . oh my love . . ."

She walked her horse alongside his so that her arms could fly around his neck. His lips tasted of scorching sun. Her moist tongue lashed his mouth. She grasped handfuls of his hair and pressed her palms to his roughened neck. His shoulder muscles corded as he hugged her and his calloused hands slid lovingly over her body.

"How very disgusting," came the hated voice.

Shan T'u sat bolt upright in the saddle. Her eyes

widened in shock and rage. Lady Feng sat astride a milk white mare. She wore a brilliant red silk gown, and her hair was perfectly coiffed. Flanking her were twenty mounted bowmen, their arrows aimed fatefully.

"Do you recognize them?" Lady Feng asked harshly. "They hardly recognized *you* in that appalling peasant costume. They were your father's soldiers. They accompanied your wedding caravan. Until you and your scheming knight led them into ambush and slaughter."

"That's a lie!" Shan T'u cried.

"Convince *them*," Lady Feng smiled. "I persuaded the Khan to let me return here to deal with you. He graciously provided a cart and an escort. My Mongol guardsmen rounded up these soldiers and brought them to me. They are now in my command. I shall find them places at the Khan's court—where the rest of your father's soldiers are now."

"Cowards!" Shan T'u spat.

Lady Feng laughed. "Please, no further heroics. It is certainly miraculous that you survived your escape and your journey, but the game is quite, quite over."

"Why kill us?" De Rais asked. His hand lingered at the hilt of his sword.

"Why, to be *rid* of you," Lady Feng said wearily. "Really, you tire me. These lands will now be mine to administer. Well, I did promise Wei Ku a share, but I don't think he will have the guts to collect, do you?" She laughed evilly. "Such weak and stupid men. You are an exception, knight. Even though you were quite rude to me, you are really quite delicious. I regret that I will not taste your body, but your death is far more expedient."

Shan T'u's cheeks burned. "You would shoot us down right here?"

"Where better?" Lady Feng said. "There are already so many bodies about. Once you and your meddlesome knight are dead, there is nobody to stand in my way. I will rule the southern lands on behalf of the Khan and raise tribute for him."

"And for yourself," Shan T'u said acidly.

"Oh, a commission here and there," Lady Feng smiled. "But I have higher ambitions."

"Empress to the Khan," Shan T'u said coldly.

Lady Feng smiled a crimson smile. "It *would* make me very powerful. And I am so much quicker of wit than the Tartar, don't you think?"

Shan T'u fought her bounding pulse. She was outraged and frustrated. "Well, get on with it," she snapped. "Kill me swiftly so I may be spared the sight of you."

Lady Feng laughed richly. "A fitting last whine for an impudent little princess. Now—there is one last responsibility before I kill you, Chin Li!"

The commander of the soldiers dug beneath his tunic and brought out a small scroll. He urged his horse forward and held out the scroll to Shan T'u.

"Take it," Lady Feng said. "It was given to Chin Li by your beloved Master Po when your wedding caravan left. It was to be given to you if Master Po perished."

Shan T'u's eyes brimmed. "You are certain . . . ?"

Lady Feng smirked. "His head was found, half-eaten by worms. When Chin showed me the scroll, I bade him keep it should we encounter you. I feel honor–bound to let you read his last pitiful words before you join him."

Shan T'u snatched the precious scroll from Chin Li and locked eyes with him for an instant. She saw no compassion or respect in them for his princess. The soldiers had been betrayed, and they were all too human. Seeing their prince dead and their palace destroyed, they had joined the winning side. William knew his warriors.

Shan T'u opened the scroll with shaking fingers. The characters were in classical Chinese, beyond the reading abilities of the soldiers. Shan T'u read the message and her heart thundered beneath her white tunic.

Princess, he had written. *I must be brief for your caravan is about to depart. I wrestled with my own judgment, wondering whether to let you know the truth. I decided to entrust my message to this warrior, who will know of my death when it comes.*

When you were born, princess, I went on a journey of retreat. A few days after I left, a bearded astrologer tottered into the palace and astonished your father by revealing his innermost secrets. Having gained Chang Hu's trust, the astrologer made a dire prediction about the baby princess.

Yes, Shan T'u, I was the astrologer. I wished your feet to be unbound. I intended from the first to train you. I wish you to know this so that in all adversity you will remember that destiny and fate are in your own hands. Never fear to create your destiny.

Oh, and lest you wonder, I knew not that a French knight would ride into your life. But I welcome this trick of fate. He seems himself a maker of destinies, and perhaps he will help you to find your own heart.

Shan T'u rolled up the scroll and thrust it beneath

her tunic. Shaken and grieving, she blinked away tears. "It all came to be as he wished," she murmured. "He was wiser than I ever dreamed."

"Enough reverie!" Lady Feng snarled. "Was your message worth the waiting for, Shan T'u?"

"Yes," she said proudly.

"Good. Bowmen, watch the Yellow Beard. I wish to kill the princess myself. The knight may watch."

De Rais tensed in the saddle, his fingers at his sword hilt. "You will die first," he warned.

Lady Feng chuckled. "Killed by a pincushion?"

The soldiers trained their arrows on De Rais. Lady Feng said to two of her bowmen, "Take her from her horse and bind her." She unsheathed her glittering dagger.

Shan T'u's blood roared in her ears. Her eyes swept the scene desperately. The gate! If she could make it through the gate, she could load her bow. She had to try! No longer was she the confused child—princess who bowed to her fate.

As the bowmen approached her, Shan T'u slapped the reins and shouted to her horse. The beast surged forward. Shan T'u heard the snap and whine of a bowstring and the thud of an arrow slamming through the muscled chest of her mount! The animal screamed in pain as the arrow sought a path toward its heart. Shan T'u tried to control the rearing horse, but its hooves tripped in the mutilated earth and she writhed to throw herself clear as she and the horse crashed to the ground.

Stunned, Shan T'u tried to rise then saw that her booted foot was trapped beneath the horse's body. She pulled desperately at her foot and ducked her head to avoid the animal's flailing hooves. As she struggled, a shadow passed over her.

"Idiot," Lady Feng said, "I wouldn't allow them to shoot you. I insist on the pleasure of the kill. Now your horse has proved cooperative. I have no need to bind you."

Shan T'u was lying on her quiver of arrows. Her foot throbbed with pain as she looked up at Lady Feng's serpentine body in flagrant red silk . . .

Red silk . . . !

Shan T'u's skin turned to ice. The red serpent! And the prediction—that she would be unable to run because her feet were bound! Master Po had fabricated the prophecy but he had been cruelly, ironically right. Her feet *were* bound, by the bulk of the fallen horse, and the red snake stood over her, deadly and inescapable.

Lady Feng advanced, brandishing the dagger. "And now . . ."

Shan T'u battled the agony in her leg. With one hand, she clawed at an arrow in the quiver, extracting it inch by inch.

"Pray, Shan T'u," Lady Feng whispered.

Lady Feng raised the dagger high. Shan T'u bowed her head as if to receive the blow. She clutched the shaft of the arrow like the hilt of a knife. She tightened her grip.

"Die!" Lady Feng snarled.

She lunged at Shan T'u, but her lily feet slowed her charge. Shan T'u raised the arrow and stabbed upward with every ounce of her strength. She felt the steel tip puncture the silk and stab deep into yielding flesh. Lady Feng reared backward, gagging and clawing. Her dagger clattered to the ground. Her eyes rolled back; the arrow remained buried in her breast.

Shan T'u arched her body to avoid Lady Feng as she toppled and fell. Her lithe, silk–clad corpse sprawled only a few feet away and Shan T'u looked with horror at her cold, staring eyes. The beautiful lady was finally ugly, in death.

Shan T'u quickly looked up at De Rais, and the soldiers. The tableau remained as before, but now the faces of the soldiers showed uncertainty. De Rais took the tone of a commander. "Listen! The lady is dead. She was your entry to the court of Khan. What will you gain by killing us now?"

"You betrayed us," Chin Li said tersely. "You and the princess."

"A lie!" De Rais snapped. "Your own prince betrayed you by plotting against the Khan. But what does that matter now? Your palace lies in ruins, and you have no prince. Leave us in peace."

"Why should we?" Chin Li sneered.

"Because," Shan T'u cried, "if not, some of you will die!" The soldiers looked, as did De Rais. Shan T'u had managed to retrieve her fallen bow and had awkwardly loaded an arrow. She lay half twisted on her side, aiming her shaft at Chin Li's throat. De Rais took advantage of the diversion to draw his sword. "You know how swiftly I can move. Two of you will die at least. Who will pay you for risking your necks?"

The summer heat shimmered in the field of rotting death. A bank of majestic clouds floated, like warships, past the sun. Chin Li's face darkened, and then he barked a command to his men. With a snap of reins and a jingle of armor, the soldiers wheeled their horses and galloped off, across the hillside. With a swelling heart, Shan T'u watched them depart, and gratefully dropped the bow and arrow.

De Rais sheathed his sword and dismounted, hurrying to Shan T'u. "Magnificent!" he cried. "What bluffing!"

"Never mind your swindler's talk," she said. "Can you get the horse off my leg?"

He grinned. "I would not have watched you die. Had you not spurred your horse, I would have ridden through the arrows to you."

"Then why did you not do so when my horse fell?"

"I saw that you could defend yourself," he quipped. De Rais tugged hard on the reins and the horse shook its great head. With another tug, the animal rolled off Shan T'u's leg and shakily got to its feet. De Rais examined the arrow in its bleeding chest. "I can remove this," he mused, "with a fire, and some water."

Shan T'u rubbed her numb leg, close to tears. "Would you consider helping me up, too?"

He offered his hand and pulled her to her feet. "Once you killed that spider of a woman," he said, "I knew I could talk the soldiers out of killing us."

She smiled. "With my help."

"I can accomplish little without your help," he said tenderly. "Are there more foes to face this afternoon?"

Shan T'u looked down at the corpse of Lady Feng with a great shudder. "No," she said softly. "All the prophecies have been fulfilled. All the destinies have come to pass." Suddenly, she looked at him with frightened eyes. "All but one, William."

"Oh?" he asked innocently.

"*Our* destiny."

"Ah, yes, that needs some thinking," he said. Then he grinned and opened his arms. With a huge, joyful cry, she buried herself in those arms, shutting out the stink of the dead, the ghastly sight on the hillsides, and the nightmares she'd been through. She snuggled tearfully in the folds of his tunic.

"William," she wept, "will you stay with me?"

"Can I not?" he whispered. He gently took off her hat and ran his strong fingers through her thick, black hair. She looked up at his brown face with its veined ruggedness. "My princess is no barbarian," he said. "*I* am the barbarian. Your heart is as pure and beautiful as that of any lady in Christendom. No—you exceed those ladies in every way. My love will not falter again."

"Nor mine," she murmured into his broad chest. "I will strive always to be good enough for thee, Roland."

He laughed pleasantly. "I am no Roland. We are not legends. We are flesh and bone. We have seen horrors to chill the soul, and we have put one foot into the next world. I want only to drink the honey of your mouth and warm my scarred old hide near the fire of your body, whether we lie in king's chamber or forest floor."

She hugged him jubilantly, her heart beating against him. "Where shall we go, William?"

His eyes sought the pure, promising sky. "I will not return to Burgundy yet. This land calls to me with the cry of the oppressed. No race that has invented and written and painted such wonders should perish under the whip of a Tartar dog. We will find a home here, Shan T'u, and I will lend my sword to harass the Khan. Besides, the bastard still has my best horse."

Tenderly, Shan T'u rocked in his arms. "I will fight beside you, William, and bear your children and live with you in the green hills or in a fine house, whatever fate may grant. And if you should long to return to France, I will return as your wife and face any outcry. I am a princess no longer. I am your lady now."

He held her at arm's length and looked with burning love at her tattered cotton garments and sunburnt face and flowing hair. "Dear God," he breathed, "you are every inch a princess."

With agony, she looked at the bloody hillside, so incongruously serene in the summer sunlight. "Take me from here."

"Of course."

"To someplace wild," she murmured, as she remembered words she had uttered a lifetime ago. "Where the mountains are deep, where the waterfalls crash in the mist, where the moon is white jade and a dark warrior unclasps the jewels from my body."

He smiled. "And where you may find a garden, with rock and water, to rest and contemplate."

"My garden is where you are William. In a rock there is hermitage. And you are, my rock."

Her hair blew in the the wind and her heart sang. She stood proudly, a princess in peasant white, a proud and lissome figure on the grim hillside, as De Rais fetched their horses. She joined him and took his hand tenderly. As he held the reins of both animals, they walked together, away from the corpses, away from the desolate palace, away from death and treachery. With faces into the wind, they walked across the swaying green grass of the hillside, under a blue sky, toward the waiting forest.

Tapestry

HISTORICAL ROMANCES

Breathtaking New Tales

of love and adventure set against history's most exciting time and places. Featuring two novels by the finest authors in the field of romantic fiction—<u>every month</u>.

Next Month From Tapestry Romances

DESTINY'S EMBRACE
by Sheryl Flournoy
FIELDS OF PROMISE
by Janet Joyce

POCKET ℙ BOOKS

_____ DEFIANT LOVE
Maura Seger
45963/$2.50

_____ MARIELLE
Ena Halliday
45962/$2.50

_____ FLAMES OF PASSION
Sheryl Flournoy
46195/$2.50

_____ THE BLACK EARL
Sharon Stephens
46194/$2.50

_____ HIGH
COUNTRY PRIDE
Lynn Erickson
46137/$2.50

_____ LIBERTINE LADY
Janet Joyce
46292/$2.50

_____ REBELLIOUS LOVE
Maura Seger
46379/$2.50

_____ EMBRACE THE STORM
Lynda Trent
46957/$2.50

_____ SWEETBRIAR
Jude Deveraux
45035/$2.50

_____ EMBRACE THE WIND
Lynda Trent
49305/$2.50

_____ DELPHINE
Ena Halliday
46166/$2.75

_____ FORBIDDEN LOVE
Maura Seger
46970/$2.75

_____ SNOW PRINCESS
Victoria Foote
49333/$2.75

_____ FLETCHER'S WOMAN
Linda Lael Miller
47936/$2.75

Tapestry

_____ GENTLE FURY
Monica Barrie
49426/$2.95

_____ FLAME ON THE SUN
Maura Seger
49395/$2.95

_____ TAME THE WILD
HEART
Serita Stevens
49398 $2.95

_____ ENGLISH ROSE
Jacqueline Marten
49655 $2.95

_____ SNOW FLOWER
Cynthia Sinclair
49513/$2.95

_____ WILLOW WIND
Lynda Trent
47574 $2.95

_____ DESIRE AND DESTINY
Linda Lael Miller
49866/$2.95

_____ ARDENT VOWS
Helen Tucker
49780/$2.95

_____ ALLIANCE
OF LOVE
Catherine Lyndell
49514/$2.95

_____ JADE MOON
Erica Mitchell
49894/$2.95

Pocket Books, Department TAP
1230 Avenue of the Americas, New York, New York 10020

Please send me the books I have checked above. I am enclosing
$_____ (please add 75¢ to cover postage and handling. NYS and NYC
residents please add appropriate sales tax. Send check or money order—no
cash, stamps, or CODs please. Allow six weeks for delivery). For purchases over
$10.00, you may use VISA: card number, expiration date and customer signature
must be included.

Name _____

Address _____

City _____ State/Zip _____

801

☐ Check here to receive your free
Pocket Books order form

Home delivery from Pocket Books

Here's your opportunity to have fabulous bestsellers delivered right to you. Our free catalog is filled to the brim with the newest titles plus the finest in mysteries, science fiction, westerns, cookbooks, romances, biographies, health, psychology, humor—every subject under the sun. Order this today and a world of pleasure will arrive at your door.

POCKET BOOKS, Department ORD
1230 Avenue of the Americas, New York, N.Y. 10020

Please send me a free Pocket Books catalog for home delivery

NAME _____

ADDRESS _____

CITY _____ STATE/ZIP _____

If you have friends who would like to order books at home, we'll send them a catalog too—

NAME _____

ADDRESS _____

CITY _____ STATE/ZIP _____

NAME _____

ADDRESS _____

CITY _____ STATE/ZIP _____